AN AFRICAN ADVENTURE

MEMOIRS OF A MISSIONARY COUPLE

BY

RALPH AND JEANETTE REAVES

PublishAmerica
Baltimore

First printing

ISBN: 1-4137-2607-0
PUBLISHED BY PUBLISHAMERICA, LLLP
www.publishamerica.com
Baltimore

Printed in the United States of America

Jordan,

Thank you for sharing
our adventure through
our book.

Ralph &
Jeanette Reaves

DEDICATION

This book is dedicated to the children of Good Shepherd's Fold Children's Village, Buundo, Uganda.

To our many friends who were victims of the genocide in Rwanda, both living and dead.

To all missionaries, wherever you may be.
May God bless you, and all that you do.

PREFACE

I think I'm finally beginning to understand Uganda English. I was sitting on the front steps this morning before school, drinking a cup of coffee and watching the children play, when Secunde, one of the twelve year old boys, came toward me crying.

"What's the matter now?" I asked.

"I beat my leg with a stone!" he wailed.

I studied on this for a minute and then asked, "You beat your leg with a stone? Now why would you beat your leg with a stone?"

"But for me, I was playing football," he said through gasps and hiccups. "I was passing from heah, while Ruben was disturbing me, and Kajuna abused me for Ruben. Then, when I kicked at the football, the stone beat my leg."

I looked down at a bloody big toe, and it all became clear. He was playing soccer with Kajuna, another of the twelve year olds.

CHAPTER 1
THE BEGINNING

Where do you begin to tell the story of the greatest adventure of your life?

I suppose you begin at the beginning and that would be the day I accepted Jesus as my personal savior. That was the summer I turned nineteen.

I was working as a cowboy on a cattle ranch near Scotland neck, North Carolina. I wasn't a bad kid. I was hardly ever in trouble. I was just what we called an outlaw. Not to be confused with the outlaws of the old west who were murderers and robbers; in our jargon an outlaw was simply someone a little rough around the edges. We called a bad horse or bull an outlaw, as in, "Hey, I hear you drew ol' ring-eye for Saturday. I hear he's a real outlaw."

In my case, it was someone who chewed tobacco once in a while, had a bad trash mouth and got into an occasional fight. I had a really bad temper which I didn't even try to control. I was as prone to pick up a fence post and knock some sense into a recalcitrant cow or horse as look at it twice.

I remember one day I was riding into the yard and one of the field hands on the farm end of the operation sprayed my horse with a garden hose, causing her to shy and dump me in the mud. I got up, brushed myself off, walked over where he was washing a truck and without any warning, hit him right on the ear with my fist. Now, have you ever been hit a solid blow right against the ear? It hurts like crazy! He grabbed his ear and started wailing, but he must have seen me hit a cow between the eyes with a gap gate lever a couple of days before because he and the other two helping him wandered off grumbling. They didn't mess with me or my horse after that.

Then one Sunday morning, after chores, I was in the bunk house, alone, watching a TV evangelist. Of course I was watching because of the healing and the theatrics, but for whatever reason, when the invitation was given to pray the sinner's prayer, I felt the conviction of the Holy Spirit to kneel in front of the TV to pray and right there on my knees, all alone, I asked Jesus to forgive me and be my savior and the Lord of my life.

My upbringing had not been without religious instruction. I had been brought up in church and Sunday school and I had been taught to put my trust in God. I knew the Bible stories about David and Goliath, Sampson and Delilah and Daniel in the lion's den, and I knew about God and Jesus. I had head knowledge but I didn't have heart knowledge.

I had heard of John 3:16: "For God so loved the world that He gave His only begotten Son that whosoever believes in Him shall not perish but have everlasting life." What I didn't realize was that the "world" meant me. God so loved Ralph Reaves that He gave His only begotten Son. I had never applied the verse to myself. I didn't know I needed to. I wasn't all that bad, and I'd never really considered myself to be a sinner.

My life didn't change radically. Oh, I threw away my pouch of Red Man and I tried to be a little gentler with the stock. I even went to the guy I'd hit on the ear and made amends and we became pretty good friends, but I still had a struggle with my language.

I have had to ask His forgiveness time and time again over the years but like the true friend He is, He is always faithful to forgive me. He's been my closest companion since that first day I met Him; sometimes my only companion. We've had many good times, He and I, and although I know I grieve Him constantly, we have a relationship like no other I can describe.

Like me, Jeanette grew up in a God-fearing home, the

granddaughter of a Baptist preacher. She attended church and went to summer church camp in the Sacramento Mountains near El Paso where she grew up, but it wasn't until we were married that she heard the plan of salvation presented in such a way that she knew in her heart that "there is no other name given unto man by which you must be saved." That name, of course, is Jesus. It was at that particular service that she heard the Holy Spirit calling her to accept Jesus as her savior. Later, however, she was to hear an entirely different call.

"Ralph, I believe God is calling me to be a missionary in Africa."

I must have looked at her like I'd been struck dumb and, in fact, no sensible words would come to me. Then finally I said something like, "Well, honey, you know I will support you in any way that I can but try to understand. He may have called you to be a missionary in Africa, but He hasn't called me." Her heart must have sunk to her heels for the second time since she had first heard the call. I mean, how could she even consider being a missionary in Africa if I hadn't been called as well?

The first time her heart sank was when she went to our pastor as a young married woman and new Christian and told him of her feeling. He had patted her hand and said, "Dear, your mission field is your husband and babies. Go home and care for them." So she came home and she took care of me and raised her children. She buried her call to Africa deep inside and never mentioned it to me, but she never forgot it. Now, when the kids were finally grown and she told me about the call she had heard, so many years ago, I responded that I had not heard any call.

Actually as I look back on it, it wasn't that God had not called me. The phone was ringing: I just wasn't picking up the receiver.

CHAPTER 2
THE ADVENTURE BEGINS

These were Jeanette's words to me as we sat on the runway at JFK International Airport waiting for our 747 to take off for Athens, Greece. A few years before, we had taken a tour with Dehoney Travel to the Holy Land, so when we got a letter inviting us to join them on a safari and mission tour in Kenya, we jumped at the chance. Even if I wasn't answering the phone as far as being a missionary was concerned, I was all too ready to go on safari. Since we were traveling on an airline pass, our plan was to make our own way from Albuquerque, New Mexico to Nairobi and join up with the rest of the group at the hotel.

To say that I fell in love with Nairobi at first glance would be an understatement, and my recommendation to anyone making their first trip to East Africa is to begin it in Nairobi. It is a beautiful, cosmopolitan city with modern, well kept buildings and nice clean hotels and restaurants. In other words it is a great way to slip into African culture gently and easily. Don't misunderstand me. Nairobi has its slums and shanty towns, but so does Albuquerque.

We met the rest of our group that afternoon and spent the next day in Nairobi, resting up from our long flight and walking around the streets, visiting shops, museums and the African Cultural Center. As I walked, I fell more deeply in love with Nairobi and Africa (or what I perceived Africa to be at that time), and I could tell that Jeanette felt the same wa. The old longing to be a missionary in Africa was still burning strong.

SUNDAY MORNING

The whole group has been invited to attend church services at Parklands Baptist Church, a beautiful little white church with blue trim and a bright blue front door. It could be any number of small Baptist churches anywhere across America. We are excited since this is our first opportunity to visit an African church and although there are more white missionaries in attendance than Africans, we are graced by a dynamic young African preacher and an African choir. It is very gratifying to know that this is what my tithe money is producing, and I have to say right here that I am not disappointed in any of the mission work we have seen so far.

MONDAY MORNING (EARLY)

We straggle out of the hotel, sleepy eyed, dragging our luggage behind us. We will need to take everything we brought because we will be spending the next two weeks on the road. We start out through the African countryside and the famous flame trees of Thika, and Jeanette's words become real: "The adventure begins."

I guess you could say our African adventure really begins at the Outspan Hotel at Nyeri. It is a very pleasant resort at the base of the Aberdare Mountains. At one time, back in the late 1800's, it was a British outpost where travelers would stop for the night and outspan their oxen from their yokes.

Being at an altitude of around seven thousand feet, it is quite chilly. The fire in the fireplace and a hot pot of coffee in our room is a welcome sight.

Here we are treated to a fabulous safari buffet and a Kikuyu tribal dance, complete with spears, traditional costumes and white body paint. At one point during the demonstration, several of the 'warriors' converged upon Jeanette, surrounding her with pointed spears. She happily played along with them, pretending to be the damsel in distress.

Tomorrow we will visit Lord Baden-Powell's grave, the Nyeri Baptist high school and then head up into the Aberdare Mountains to Tree Tops Lodge.

TUESDAY

Now Tree Tops Lodge is probably the most unique hotel I've ever stayed at in my life. It is exactly what it sounds like, a tree house, a big one for sure, but a tree house all the same.

We are met here at the entrance to the grounds, some two hundred yards from the actual hotel, by our guide and host. His appearance is both comical and reassuring. He is a square built Englishman with a nose that has been battered a few times and a petulant lower lip that seems to say, "Go ahead, batter my nose again if you dare." He is dressed in traditional safari garb with the many-pocketed khaki shorts, a bushket with just as many pockets and a slouch hat, pinned up on one side. He is also carrying the biggest double barrel rifle I've ever seen.

Before we begin our march from the front gate over to the hotel, he lectures us on how we need to stay together and move from one 'bull pen' to the next, "just in case we're attacked by rogue elephants, cape buffalo" or, I think to myself, *the pesky baboons that are following at a safe distance.* Laughing, he says we don't need to worry about the dozens of little wart hogs that are scurrying around. "Those are my special pets." His main concern seems to be the baboons. "They will run up, snatch a lady's handbag, your camera or the hat off of your head if they can get by with it," he says. "I can't shoot the bloody rascals. Too dangerous to my visitors." And his lower lip sticks out even farther than before. "My askaris will take care of them if they get too bold." I look around and see several young African boys with clubs skirting the group and sure enough, a large male baboon makes a feint at a lady who has stopped to adjust her shoulder bag, then barks a yelping cry as two of the young guards take out after him, swinging their clubs. I get cold shivers as I look at the sharp canines he is baring at the askaris and I tell Jeanette, "If one tries to steal your camera, let him have it."

Our room is tiny, just large enough for two twin beds formed like an L with the only storage space under the beds. To change clothes, one of us has to put our suitcase on the bed and stand in the small space between the beds while the other one waits on his or her bed for their turn. The bath is down the narrow hall. We have a little window that overlooks the back and the path from the front gate to the hotel. It doesn't matter though; as soon as it gets dark we will go down to the observation lounge where the whole front is windows and looks out over the lighted water hole. We are hoping to see some animals as they come in for a midnight drink. So far, since being in Africa, we've only seen a couple of giraffe and ostrich in the game park just outside of Nairobi and, of course, the wart hogs and baboons.

We've been sitting in the observation lounge for several hours now. In fact it's nearly daylight and so far we have been rewarded with one Cape buffalo, which was magnificent, a couple of bushbucks and quite a few wart hogs. A few minutes ago, a woman, not in our group, spotted something out beyond the floodlights, crouched in the grass. We can't make out what it is. There's a lot of speculation as to what it might be. Some think it's just a wart hog bedded down for the night, others are convinced it's some kind of cat waiting to spring on an unsuspecting antelope as it comes up to drink. We've come up with a pair of binoculars but it's still too dark to make it out. Whatever it is, it's patient. It hasn't moved a muscle in hours.

The sun is beginning to come up over the mountains now and everything is turning grey. No spectacular sunrise, just turning from black to grey and things are beginning to take shape. Nothing has come to the water hole for hours. We all think it's because they know that there's danger out there. I have the binoculars and have been watching our mysterious guest in the grass when all of a sudden it emerges from the shadows of night and I can see clearly what it is, and I start to laugh. Everybody is anxious to know what it is but I give it a dramatic pause while I study the object and then say, "It's a burned out stump."

"No way," says the lady who first spotted it. "I saw it move several times."

I shake my head and say, "No, ma'm, it's a blackened stump."
The woman is adamant. "Young man, I saw it come out of the
forest."

About this time our host has come in from a good night's sleep.
He's seen it all before, you see. I hand him the binoculars and ask him
what he sees. He doesn't even take a good look. "Oh, that's where the
original lodge used to be. It burned down several years ago."

By now it's quite light and you can see with the naked eye that it
is, in fact, a burned stump. The lady who "saw it come out of the
forest" is nowhere to be seen.

It's full light now so we go out onto the balcony for breakfast and
the askaris are busy keeping the baboons at bay. They are intent on
stealing some unwary soul's sweet roll. We enjoy a cup of coffee and
roll, and talk about the night's entertainment, then decide to go to the
room for a nap. As we are going down the stairs, we run head long
into a baboon coming up at full speed with a club-wielding askari
right behind him. Jeanette lets out a blood-curdling scream and drops
to the deck; the baboon lets out a blood-curdling scream, leaps over
the rail, and goes straight down the side of the building. Jeanette is so
startled, she's in hysterics; laughing and crying so hard the tears are
running down her cheeks. "The last time I saw you laugh and cry so
hard at the same time was watching Sally Field in *Steel Magnolias*,"
I say shakily.

WEDNESDAY

We load into the vans again and strike out straight north with
beautiful Mt. Kenya on our right. We go through the little town of
Nanyuki where we stop for lunch and visit the open market which is
very interesting. There is everything for sale here you can imagine,
from little pyramids of tomatoes and onions to goat carcasses and
live chickens.

Wayne Dehoney has been to Kenya many times, and it's obvious
he loves Africa and its people. I have learned by now that white
people can't go into a town like Nanyuki without drawing attention,

and it seems to be the African way to surround you to stare at you without any discomfort whatsoever - discomfort to them, that is. As Americans, it gives us a very uneasy feeling. Wayne has gathered a few youngsters around him, and he is talking to them. I can't hear what he's saying but suddenly, he reaches into his pocket and pulls out a rubber snake. You never heard such squealing or saw such scattering in your life. Soon, however, there's a large group of people, some adults, creeping forward to see the snake. Wayne laughs with them when they discover that it's rubber, then reaches back into his pocket and starts handing out religious tracts. I can see that Wayne has been at this game a long time.

Even though it's probably only a hundred kilometers or so up to Samburu National Park, it seems to be a long trip. I guess it's because there's not much to see on this stretch of road, and we're still tired from our night vigil waiting for a stump to spring on some unsuspecting antelope.

The country has become more desert here, hot and dry, whereas the Aberdares were high and cool. I like this country. It reminds me of south central Texas with its thorn trees which resemble mesquite trees. The only game we've seen are gerenuks standing on their hind legs under the thorn trees, stretching their long necks into the higher branches to reach the tender leaves. We have seen several herds of long-horned Ankole cattle and a few flocks of goats trying to graze, but the land is poor and badly overgrazed.

When we enter the gates of the park the land takes on a completely different aspect. Here the people are not allowed to graze their flocks and herds, and the grass is long and plentiful.

We travel inside the park for a couple of miles and then come to the Ewaso Ngiro River. As we are about to cross the bridge over the river, I look out and see what appears to be logs lying lengthways in the current. Some of them are quite large. Then on closer inspection, I realize they are crocodiles, hundreds of them. My blood races; wild Africa at last. The area around the river is a riverine swamp-like area or, as we would call it in New Mexico, a bosque.

On the other side of the bridge we spot a pair of waterbucks standing belly deep in the water, grazing the bottom.

Jeanette's and my cottage is a little A frame with chicken wire on the front and back. It's comfortable, with a double bed under a mosquito net. The sidewalk out front is covered with chirping little birds of all kinds which thrills Jeanette no end. She is a bird lover. I'm more into the monkeys playing around in the trees and on the chicken wire. I believe they're vervets, but I'm not sure. The crocodiles are right out our front door and just down a very small embankment. I can actually walk to the edge of the embankment to within maybe thirty feet of the river. There are no barriers except the steep bank. I'm sure a determined crocodile could climb it if he wanted to, but they seem content to lie in the river facing the slow current. They seem to be drowsing, but every now and then one will lunge and snap at his neighbor. They are fascinating, and I could watch them all evening, but it's now time to head down to the dining room for supper.

When we get to the dining room, they are not quite ready for us so we decide to take a walk down closer to the river. The walkway takes us down the embankment right to the river's edge. Here they do have a waist-high fence to keep the diners from becoming dinner because here, the only thing that separates you from the crocs is the fence. The cooks have thrown what looks like a cow's hindquarter with the meat stripped off to the crocs. One giant grabs it in his jaws, flips it up and swallows it down. I step him off and he's 28 feet long and about 6 feet wide. I've heard stories that they have actually found whole gazelles and parts of canoes inside of them.

After a great supper, we go to an observation deck and watch the forest on the other side of the river where an askari has hung a goat carcass as bait for a leopard. We wait for a couple of hours and sure enough our guide points quietly at the base of the tree. At first I can't see it, but then I do see it as it stealthily and very quietly leaps into the tree, pulls the goat loose and steals away into the forest. We're very lucky, our guide tells us. Leopards are so shy that sometimes you miss them altogether. I'm elated. This was no burnt out stump. It was a real live, wild leopard, and I saw it.

THURSDAY (BEFORE DAYLIGHT)

We're up and out in the safari van. It's a regular Volkswagen van, but the top can be unlatched and pushed up so that we can stand with our head and shoulders above the roof. This gives us an excellent vantage point for viewing game. We see several more waterbucks crossing the river, and they raise their heads to watch us pass by.

Our tour takes us to Buffalo Springs; lots of game here. There is a rather large herd of reticulated zebras drinking and, like wild horses anywhere, they bolt and run off a hundred yards, then turn to look at us. The gerenuks are plentiful, and there are even a few giraffes and mixed herds of antelope.

After lunch, we don't cross the river. We turn and skirt the river in the opposite direction. I notice that some of the trees here along the bosque are pushed down like a bulldozer has been working, and the trees that are still standing have some of their branches torn out. "Elephants," the driver says; "they will destroy this area and then move on to another one. They literally eat themselves out of house and home."

He pulls into a thicket that hasn't been demolished too badly and turns off the engine. He has heard something the rest of us missed. Soon enough it's evident what he heard because within minutes we are surrounded by elephants. They come up to within a few feet of the van, going about their daily task of tearing the forest down to get their lunch. One big matriarch with huge tusks walks sedately up to a big thorn tree, puts her two tusks on either side of the trunk and pushes it down as easily as I could push over a hat rack. The smaller elephants come over to it and start eating the branches that are now accessible to them. She goes off now to rip the branches out of other trees for herself. Did I say the crocs were fascinating? The elephants are a show. I love them!

While we're sitting here, there have been two babies playing around under the bellies of the others. All of a sudden, one of them looks up at the van and braces like he hadn't seen us before this. He scurries under his mother, or an aunt, and then tentatively steps out. He stands there for a minute - gathering up his courage, I guess - then

19

with ears spread wide and tiny trunk raised, feints an attack at us. He backs up and does it a few more times, and by now every one in the van is cracking up. Jeanette is delighted and says, "He's so cute! 'I'm tough. You'd better watch out.'"

This little piece of drama is only the prelude to the big act, however. In just a few minutes a fairly good-sized male comes charging into the clearing, trumpeting, and we are terrified. If he decides to attack us, van or no van, we're in trouble. He could push this van over as easily as the matriarch did the thorn tree. Luckily, he could care less about us; he's challenging another male. They close and trunk-to-trunk, they begin a pushing match. It seems serious to me because they are tearing up dirt and shoving each other around like a couple of sumo wrestlers. One pushes the other perilously close to the van, and we collectively hold our breath. The driver says they're just playing. Still, if they push each other into us, we're going over.

FRIDAY
Again we have spent the morning, since daybreak, driving around looking for game; or I should say looking at game and looking for lions. We are told that there is at least one pride of lions in this area, but so far they have eluded us. This afternoon, we'll go to a Samburu village and then head back south.

Well, that was interesting. The Samburu put on a show for us the way the Kikuyu did, only they are totally different. I'm told that the Samburu are related to the Masai. They wear red, wrap around sarongs and coat their hair with red ocher which makes it like orange rope. The men wear their hair long, and the women, short. Part of the dance they do is to bend their knees, keeping their upper bodies rigid and leap high into the air. Some of them look like they're clearing the ground by three feet or better. Then the young men slap the ladies across the face with their long plaited hair. This is supposed to show her that he's sweet on her.

Their beehive houses are very small, maybe ten feet long by six feet wide and only about four feet high. The door is a small opening that they have to crawl through, and there are no windows. I guess that's all the room they need to sleep; that seems to be the only thing they do inside. The women cook in outdoor kitchens, and the men spend their waking hours with their herds or out hunting. They are impressive people, though. They are tall and carry themselves like the warriors they are.

Our return trip has taken us back down the road to Nanyuki, and somewhere between Nanyuki and Nyeri we turn off toward Mt. Kenya and start climbing into the foothills to the Mt. Kenya Safari Club. This is some beautiful country, and the resort is fabulous. We are told that this resort and the adjoining animal sanctuary and hospital were started by William Holden and Stephanie Powers to take in and care for orphaned animals; babies whose mothers have been the victims of poaching, mostly, but sometimes injured animals are brought in, as well.

The resort is not your normal safari camp. It is very expensive. Our room is -what's a good word - expansive, grandiose? Anyway, it's big and roomy and has a shower like something you might find in a Roman villa. You walk down a flight of three marble stairs to enter it and once in it, there are no less than three showerheads on three different walls all pointing at one focal point. Me!!!!

There is a small nine-hole golf course on the grounds, so after my shower, I decide to play a round. Jeanette doesn't play and none of the others want to go, so I go out by myself. It's a unique course. The fairways are pretty rough, and the rough is African bush. The greens are covered with the coarse African bermuda. Now there's a contradiction in terms. Either it's African or it's Bermudan. How can it be both? Oh well, whatever it is, it doesn't make for easy putting. As I tee off on the third hole, my ball slices and goes into a small water hazard. It looks like it just went in at the edge so I decide to retrieve the ball and take a drop, but as I approach the shore, a small crocodile rises up hisses at me and plunges into the water. I'll just let that ball go.

When I come back from playing golf, Jeanette is in the bathroom getting ready for supper, so I decide to take a swim in our own private swimming pool right outside our room. I do this because, like the man said, it was there. I don't swim long, though, because we're more than five thousand feet high and as it was at the Outspan, the air is cool even though it's early afternoon. I plunge in, swim the length of the pool once and climb out blue. I rush down the steps into our shower, which is still steamy from Jeanette's shower, and stand there in bliss as hot water pummels me from three different directions.

As you may have noticed, I refer to my evening meal as supper. That's the Texas way; but I've got to tell you, this is far more than supper. This is fine dining at its best: soup, salad, fruit and cheese, and the main course is an eland filet mignon graced with the long tender African green beans. It just doesn't get any better than this. If you've never eaten eland filet, you haven't eaten. An eland is a *huge* antelope with spirally twisted horns. We saw one on the horizon one day, and it looked like a house moving toward us.

After dinner, we stagger back to our room and fall into bed.

SATURDAY

Breakfast is as grand as supper was last night. We have our choice of eggs: boiled, fried or scrambled. There is fresh milk and juice, coffee, and tea for those who prefer it, several different kinds of yogurt, and smoked salmon with trays of cheeses; for those with large appetites, there are breakfast steaks.

Because this beautiful place is so expensive, last night is the only night we'll spend here. That's okay; any longer, and I could get used to that shower. But I'm ready to see more of the real Africa now. I had mentioned to Wayne up at Samburu, that if we turned around and left right then, I would be satisfied and feel like I'd gotten my money's worth. He had said, "You ain't seen nothin' yet."

Today will be the longest of the road trips yet, over two hundred miles as the crow flies and probably closer to three hundred road miles. It is a journey that will take us over the Aberdares, down the rim of the Great Rift Valley, past the Mau Escarpment where the Mau-Mau rebellion took root, past Nyahururu Falls, then to Lake Nakuru and on to Lake Naivasha. From there, we will turn to a southwesterly direction and travel to the Tanzania border and the Masai-Mara.

Lake Nakuru, the lake of a million flamingos. Actually, over 1.4 million flamingos have been recorded here. Today, I'm sure the number reaches close to a million. The entire shore of the lake, all the way around, is pink. As we drive along the shore road, the flamingos rise ahead of the van, sail effortlessly out over the lake and close in again behind us. It is a beautiful spectacle. We are told to keep our eyes peeled because if we are going to see a black rhino on this safari, this will be the area to see it. We really don't spend enough time here to see much of anything, though, and before we know it, we're back out on the highway heading down the road to Lake Naivasha.

Now Lake Naivasha is a true lake. Lake Nakuru is just a shallow, brackish pond in comparison. Here we take a pirogue out onto the lake and see cormorants, kites and even some pelicans, but the big thrill is when a colony of hippos surface not too far from our boat. I'm elated and urge our boatman to motor over closer to them so I can get some good pictures. He looks at me like I'm nuts and shakes his head. Nothing I can do or say will entice him to move closer and, in fact, when a big one surfaces just 20 yards from us, he starts the motor and speeds away. How naive I am, but at this time I don't know that the hippo is responsible for more human deaths than any of the other big five animals of Africa. Number two is the Cape buffalo. Lions and elephants are way down the line.

One of the reasons the hippo is so dangerous is that they're vulnerable on land, and if a person gets between them and the water, they will run you down to reach the safety of the water. The other reason is that in the water they are at home and as graceful as ballerinas, and they're very territorial. They will attack a boat and chomp it in half with those massive jaws of theirs if you chance to invade their territory. Again, we don't spend much time here, just enough to explore the lake in the pirogue and have a cup of coffee at the lodge. I'd like to come back here some time. It looks like a nice place to spend a couple of days.

If we continued on this highway for about 50 more miles, it would take us back to Nairobi on the opposite side of town from where we left. In other words, we've made a large circle with side trips on the north and south ends of the circle; but we don't continue. We turn off on the southern-side trip and head down a dirt road. This is one of the few places where I've actually seen a wire fence, and the driver says it's a private ranch. It gives me a real feeling of nostalgia. If it weren't for the gerenuks, giraffes and Tommies (Thompson gazelles), it could be Texas.

As we travel further south, the land becomes more of a treeless, rolling plain. Oh, there are still a few scattered thorn trees, but the dry scrabble landscape has given way to long yellow grass. It still looks like Texas, but now it looks more like the Panhandle of Texas.

It must be close to suppertime now, and we've arrived at the entrance to Keekerok Game Preserve at the northern end of the Serengeti Plain. I can't believe my eyes! There are wildebeest shoulder to shoulder as far as the eye can see, and that's considerable out here. Wayne wasn't joking; I truly hadn't seen anything yet. Not only are there literally millions of wildebeest, there are mixed herds of Grants gazelles, Thompson gazelle, hartebeest, topi, impala, zebra and, of course, the carnivores who skirt the herds like a bunch of sheep dogs. Separated into smaller groups of their own are families of giraffe, peaking out over the flat tops of thorn trees. It is awesome and I am overwhelmed with the feeling that, *I am really in Africa seeing this.*

When Wayne comes out from checking us in at the lodge, he says to Jeanette and me with a grim face, "I've got some good news and some bad news for you. The bad news is they've overbooked, and the cottage you were to have isn't available. The good news is they're going to put you up in President Moi's bungalow."

"President Moi's bungalow!! You mean the President Moi who is president of Kenya?"

He says, "That's right. Last month Pope John Paul was staying there, but right now it's vacant, so they're going to put you up there."

We drive about two hundred yards up away from the main lodge to a nice little bungalow made of grey and pink river sandstone with cedar wood trim. In front, there is a nice well-trimmed green lawn and a couple of round cement tables in the yard. Our driver says, "Whenever you are ready, call up to the main lodge and someone will pick you up to bring you to dinner."

As I am freshening up, I hear a noise right outside our bedroom window, so I go over to open the blinds and check it out. Right there in our yard, scratching their hides against the cement tables is a small herd of zebra. They're not ten feet from the window. What a thrill to stand so close and watch these beautiful creatures crop the grass in our front yard. Jeanette suggests that we sneak out onto the front porch so we can take their picture, and we actually did get a few good ones.

"Do you want to call for a ride or just walk down to the lodge?" I ask Jeanette. "It's not that far."

"We can walk," she answers.

It's beginning to get dusk now, so we get our flashlights and start out. Now, in the tropics, night doesn't come in stages. You may have a beautiful sunset for a couple of minutes, but in those two minutes all the red, yellow and gold gives way to complete darkness. At least, that's the way it is this night. So by the time we get out of the ring of light created by the street lamp just outside our door, we have to turn on our flashlights to find our way. I say, find our way; actually, we can see the main lodge just down the path in all its lighted glory. It's just a matter of needing the flashlights to see the path.

As we walk along, we begin to hear coughing and grunting all around us, so I turn my light out into the darkness, and it returns to me a thousand shining eyes. I don't think either of us is particularly afraid, just a little nervous trying to figure out what animal is behind those eyes. We are both exhilarated to be in the midst of wild Africa; however, we quicken our pace.

When we get to the lodge, the maitre d' asks, "How did you get down here?"

"We didn't want to bother anybody to pick us up in a van, so we walked," I reply. "It's really not that far." I thought he was going to have a stroke right there.

"Please, don't ever walk out there again," he says, "especially in the dark."

I promise that we won't, and we join the rest of the group for a wonderful supper.

While Jeanette and I are waiting for our supper to be served, I notice a movement on top of the wall back by the kitchen, so I start watching the spot carefully. I guess I should explain that the wall only goes to within about a foot of the roof there, leaving a space between the two; for ventilation, I guess. As I watch, I see a little nose poke out from the shadows and a set of huge shining eyes, and then a spotted, furry little animal stealthily moving along the wall. I call the waiter over and point to it.

"What is that?" I ask.

He runs over and chases it away, then comes back, apologizing like crazy. "That was a genet," he explains. "They are always trying to steal food from the kitchen."

No wonder I love Africa so much. Not only does it look like Texas, even the little genet looks remarkably like a Texas ringtail. I have to laugh; as soon as the waiter turns his back, the little nose and luminous eyes reappear.

SUNDAY MORNING

Everything in me tells me just to walk down to the lodge for breakfast. I mean it is a beautiful clear morning. The birds are singing and the front yard is not filled with animals, but dutifully I call up to the lodge and in just a few minutes, a driver shows up to haul us the two hundred yards. I feel silly but don't say anything. After all, I did promise. I'll follow their silly rules, but I'm shaking my head. What's a couple of zebras or a wildebeest going to do to us?

We haven't gone one hundred feet from the front door when I shrink back into my seat and feel the heat rise up into my neck and ears. Right in the path there is a big spot of dried blood, the green contents of a stomach, and four black hooves. "Is that what I think it is?" I ask the driver. "Oh yes!" he smiles. "The lions made a kill there last night." I look over at Jeanette, but she is looking sheepishly out the window.

What a day!! During our drive this morning, we come up on a small pride of lions. Actually, I don't really know if it qualifies as a pride since there were no males in the group. This is just an old female with a couple of cubs lying on a big flat rock. We pull up to within about twenty feet of them and park so we can watch them. They don't even acknowledge our presence. They're mostly doing what lions do best, taking naps. The cubs are playing a little, but half-heartedly. We have been watching them for about a half hour, I guess, when the old girl sits up and begins looking intently out into the tall grass right past our shoulders. We can't tell what has caught her attention, but whatever it is has done so completely. Then we notice that the cubs are acting agitated and begin prowling around the edge of the rock and looking out to where their mother is looking. We wait and watch for what seems a pretty long while, then the mother rises, walks to the rim of the rock and grunts. Actually, it starts as a low cough in her chest and then erupts into a series of loud roars; in a few minutes, from somewhere out in the waist-deep grass there is an answering roar. We have been watching with the top open, and now our driver tells us to be prepared to shut it quickly if we need to. It seems that just a day ago, a lioness had become agitated and leaped up and tried to reach in through the top at the people inside. I loosen the locks that hold it in place but continue to stand with my head and shoulders out. In just a few minutes, we see another lioness, a young one, coming through the grass. When she reaches the place where the others are, the old lady grabs her around the neck with her paws and begins licking her face all over. You never saw such a happy family reunion in your life. They are all greeting the new arrival with hugs and kisses, rolling in the grass and playing like a basket full of kittens. We stay in this place for an hour or more when the driver decides to show us a place closer to the Mara River, so we start driving again. We don't drive more than half a mile before we come upon another pride, and this really is a pride. There are three big black-maned males in this group. Again, they are sprawled about a wash in various positions and stages of sleep. We watch them for a few minutes before continuing toward the river.

As we top a rise, out below us is a wide valley dotted with little groves of trees and a huge herd of Cape buffalo. We stop some distance away and I do a quick count, estimating a little over three hundred. Someone in the van questions, "How can you do that with them milling around like that?"

"Oh, it's an old cowboy trick," I say. "You just count their feet and divide by four." Actually, it's a lot less complicated than that. When you've tried to count cattle going into a packer's truck as much as I have, it's not that hard to estimate the size of a herd. You can pretty well look at a herd standing in a field and guess, pretty accurately, how many there are. Just like in the airline business, I got to where I could look at a lobby full of people and determine, within a few, how many were there.

We watch them from the hillside for only a couple of minutes and then proceed on down and drive right through the middle of them. Like a herd of cows, they run to the side as we pass, then close in around us. We have seen only one herd of elephants but they appear to be heading to the river with a purpose, so we don't try to get in the middle of them as we did at Samburu. We just watch them from a distance.

Soon we arrive at the Mara River, and the driver points to the other side. "That's Tanzania over there," he says. We get out of the van here and walk to the high bank overlooking the river.

"Stay out of the paths leading to and from the river," he cautions. "You don't want to get between a hippo and the water." Down in the water there are several hippos playing in the mud, but unlike Lake Naivasha, the water isn't deep enough for them to really submerge and swim. What astounds me are the crocodiles lying side by side with the hippos.

"Don't the crocs bother the hippos?" I ask.

"Oh no, they have a very symbiotic relationship," the driver says. "Sometimes a hungry croc will take a baby hippo, but for the most part they live in peace."

It's early afternoon now, and we are driving back over the hill where we first spotted the buffalo herd. The driver points out through the windshield. "Look, there's a herd of eland." He seems as excited as we are to see them. "You don't get to see them very often," he explains. "They are very shy of humans."

The cows disappear over the hill soon after we spot them but the bull, when he reaches the top of the hill, turns and watches us approach for a second. He is magnificent. He is bigger than a Brahma bull. He must stand well over six feet at the shoulder. He shakes his head at us, flinging slobbers as he does, then turns and chases after his cows. Nobody even speaks. It is that cool.

It's late afternoon now and we are so tired, we just watch the moving mass of wildebeest silently. I had to laugh earlier in the day. Floyd, one of our group who is a very sedate, quiet gentleman has sat in the shotgun seat since we started. He has watched everything without any outward show of excitement; even the bull elephant fight up at Samburu. Well, this morning as we were starting out on our drive, with the herds filling the horizon on all sides, he shook his head and said matter-of-factly, "Man, look at all them wild beasts."

If we are so tired we're in a trance, our driver is not, and as we approach a mixed herd of topi, gazelle and zebras, he pulls over and turns off the motor. We all come alive and start looking around. "What is it?" He points to a patch of tall yellow grass and there, crouched low, is a lioness. "And there." He points to the other side of the herd and there is another one low in the grass. "They're shopping for their supper," he says. We sit there and watch for an hour as the lions inch closer to the herd. But they are not just inching toward the herd. I don't know how they have communicated to each other, but they have picked out one topi in the herd and are intent on his every move. As he moves around inside the herd, they creep toward him. We have watched for well over an hour now and it is getting pretty dark, so our driver starts up the engine to leave. Several animals in the herd stop their grazing to watch us pull away, but the two lionesses never take their eyes off their prey. It's too dark now for us to see the kill, if and when the hunters decide to make their move, but it has been exciting to watch the stalking just the same.

MONDAY

We left Keekorok this morning right after breakfast and drove up through the Masai Mara triangle to the Mara Serena Lodge, seeing game all the way of course.

This is a very unique lodge and I can see why Wayne wanted us to see it, even though we're not going to be able to spend the night here. It is built on the saddle of a very high hill, or as they say in Africa, a kopje. Just looking out over the spreading plains, rolling hills and scattered woodlands, I would say it's probably around 2000 feet above the valley floor. It's built in the design of a Masai manyatta or village with individual domed huts scattered around a small swimming pool in the shape of a water hole and wandering down the hillside. It looks like it would be a great place to stay for a couple of days. I'm sorry we can't.

From the veranda where the pool is, you can look out and watch the myriad herds of African wildlife as they migrate from the south. This is almost the northern extent of their journey.

A little while ago, I saw a large herd of elephants moving across the plain going toward the Mara River and, of course, the herds of wildebeest, zebra and various kinds of antelope which have become so commonplace we hardly get excited about them anymore.

I'm lying here next to the pool taking in some sun. We just had a fabulous lunch buffet, and I swam for a little while. Now I'm sitting here watching a delightful little creature and trying to avoid watching another. The one is a hyrax, and the other is a striking blond who has decided to go for a swim wearing nothing but the very skimpy bottom of a bikini.

The hyrax came out of a crack in the rock wall around the pool and very tentatively came over to me to see what I might give him from my desert. I've been hand feeding him some of the cake I brought out by placing it on the wall a couple of feet from me and letting him come snatch it and scurry back into his rock hiding place. They tell me that the hyrax is the closest living relative to the elephant. I guess they know what they're talking about, but he looks more like a groundhog than an elephant to me.

30

TUESDAY

We're at Brakenhurst Baptist Assembly now. It's a beautiful place and is the African equivalent of Glorieta in New Mexico or Ridgecrest in North Carolina. The director has just taken us out and showed us a wonderful Shorthorn bull he bought to breed to his Ankole-Watuse cattle and his field of hybrid corn or, as they call it here, maize. Having grown up on a ranch, these things are of great interest to me and I turn to Jeanette and say, "You know, if I could be involved in a project like this, I wouldn't mind being a missionary over here." She just nods her head and doesn't say anything. I guess I've kicked against the goads too long now, and she knows me too well.

Earlier today, we spent a delightful hour or so at a tea plantation in the Ngong hills where Karin Blix "had her farm in Africa" and wrote *Out of Africa*. I can see why she loved it so much. It is beautiful country.

We went for a walk in the forest near the plantation and saw a group of Colobus monkeys scampering through the tops of the trees. They are beautiful animals, black with white backs and long, bushy white tails. They look like tree climbing skunks, only larger than most skunks. I'm amazed at how they leap through the branches ahead of us.

WEDNESDAY (ABOUT MIDNIGHT)

We're now sitting in the departure lounge at Jomo Kenyatta Airport waiting for our flight back to the States. We're tired, but thoroughly content. It has been a great trip, and both of us are in love with Kenya.

We spent the morning visiting some more of the Baptist mission work around Nairobi and meeting some of the missionaries. One of the places we went to was Shauri Moya Baptist church where the missionary there has a school for the local children and a sewing school for young women. Shauri Moya is in a very poor part of town, and right across the street from the church is Nairobi's largest slum section. This is a perfect spot for this kind of ministry because the people here have no means to better themselves without it. Like so many spoiled Americans, I'm appalled at the poverty and apathy of the people here. Maybe it's not apathy so much as that they have just given up on life. Their homes are sometimes no more than a cardboard packing crate, situated around a city dump. There are no latrines, and their water supply is a cold water tap out in the middle of the compound. There are literally thousands living here. I look at the impossible task of reaching out and helping these people. If I had a moment of weakness about being a missionary when I was out at Brackenhurst, going over a picture postcard farm operation, I have returned to reality and know I'm not cut out to do what these brave, selfless missionaries do.

We joined some of these brave, selfless people for dinner tonight at a very fine Chinese restaurant and, even though they're heroes in my book, they're just down to earth, ordinary people who like to laugh at jokes, have fun and have a great meal at a fine restaurant occasionally.

CHAPTER 3
JEANETTE'S UGANDA CRUSADE

From practically the very day of my accepting Jesus Christ as my personal Lord and Savior I had a love for the African people and a deep desire to go to Africa as a missionary. From whence came this love I do not know; only that God bound my heart to them. I even went to my pastor at that time and told him how I felt God's leading me to go. Even though what he told me made practical sense, I remember being disappointed at his response. He said, "Your mission right now is being a mother to your new baby and a wife to your husband."

Through the 27 years of going about the business of raising a family and being very active in church in a number of areas, missions always being at the very center of my involvement, my longing to go to Africa never ceased. I'll never forget the day we received a brochure from Dehoney Travel describing an upcoming safari to Kenya, Africa. I was so excited; I showed the brochure to Ralph and said, "What do you think?" Amazingly, he said "Yeah. Let's look into it." Thus began the realization of my dream.

We went on safari in Africa! And it was a wonderful experience, even one in which we visited several missionaries at their work, but it only increased my hunger to go and actually be with and work with the people.

God is so faithful. He knew my desire because not long after we returned from safari, I learned that International Crusades was putting together the first-ever evangelistic crusade to Uganda, Africa the very next year, 1987. I immediately asked Ralph what he thought about going on the crusade, and he had many reasons (or excuses) for not going. Not willing to give up so easily, I asked him if he would mind if I went without him. Being the giving husband he had always been, he gave me his permission and blessing.

I excitedly began preparations by building a base of prayer support by some powerful and faithful prayer warriors in our church. I worked on my personal testimony, which would be printed by IC into the Luganda language. In order to save on some of the trip expense, I decided to fly space available on a TWA pass all the way to Nairobi rather than travel with the rest of the crusade team on confirmed seating. I knew this could be risky because I was going to have to be in Nairobi in time to meet up with the rest of the team before they left for Jinja, Uganda; but I also trusted in the prayers going up on my behalf being heard and answered by my Father.

And then, I received a call from IC that women would not be allowed to go on the crusade because they were afraid it would be too dangerous and too difficult. Idi Amin had just been ousted from the country and effects of the war were still being felt. It was also the premier crusade in Africa, a "trailblazer," with many unknowns. Needless to say, I was sorely disappointed, but my prayer partners continued praying with me. Only a day or two before time for departure I received another call with the good news that the "no women" decision had been reversed. What glad tidings to my ears! I was on my way at long last to a destiny long in coming.

SO BEGINS THE JOURNEY

Ralph decided to travel with me as far as London, where I would catch my flight to Nairobi. It was good having him along that far; good companionship, someone with whom to see London, someone to carry the bags, someone who knows the ropes of the trade to get me through all the check-ins. What a handy guy!

When we arrived at Heathrow airport for check-in, the gate area was so full of people going to Nairobi that the agent just shook his head when we told him I was flying on a space available pass. He said, "I'll put you on the list, but I don't see any way you'll make this flight." Ralph immediately began to worry and fret because he knew I had to make this flight. Now, I'm the fretter and worrier in our family, not Ralph! But I wasn't worrying! I was inexplicably calm. You see, I knew my prayer warrior was on her knees right at this particular time because I had told her that making this flight out of London was crucial. God certainly knew it, and it was in His hands.

Standing behind the crowd, but within range of the boarding agent's voice, we watched as the full fare passengers boarded, then as the full fare stand-by's were boarded. We listened with bated breath as the agent began calling names from the space available list. One person after another stepped forward as they heard their name. By now, Ralph was at the agent's elbow looking at the list and shaking his head. Coming back to me, he said, "That's it. You won't make it. They have three seats left, and there are three names ahead of yours."

"It's going to be alright," surprising myself with the words. Two more passengers boarded as the agent called the last name, "Barton Pierce."

No stirring in the few remaining people standing by. "Mr. Pierce." Heads turning, looking, hoping. "Mr. Pierce." Silence for a few long moments. "Jeanette Reaves." Isn't God good?! A quick smile, tears, hugs, and I was on my way!

As I was walking the long walk from the airplane in Nairobi to the luggage area, I was wondering to myself, "What do I do now?" I knew the rest of the team was arriving in this same airport the next morning, but what should I do in the meantime? Where should I go? As I looked upon the sea of faces watching for loved ones or tourists, I saw a sign with my name on it held up by a pleasant looking gentleman. "I'm Jeanette," I said as I approached him. "Hi, I'm Jim Richardson. Webb Carroll asked me to meet you." Another prayer answered! Jim was a Southern Baptist missionary serving in Nairobi with his wife, Marcia. We loaded my luggage into his car, and off we went through the streets of Nairobi to his house. Marcia graciously showed me one of the children's rooms where I would stay the night, and upon her suggestion I laid down for a short nap before an afternoon shopping trip with her.

The next morning Webb Carroll, a legend in Uganda because of his many years serving and loving the people even at risk of his own life during the Amin genocide, picked me up at the Richardson's to go with him to the airport to meet and join the rest of the team. What a spiritual giant this man was. He impacted my life in an enormous way, and it was because of him Ralph and I would later return to Uganda as co-directors of an orphanage. But I'm getting ahead of the story.

After the arrival of the rest of the team (about 27 of us altogether) around 9:00 in the morning, we all boarded the bus, which would take us to Uganda. Webb wanted to take us through one of the game parks on the outskirts of Nairobi before we hit the highway for Jinja, so it was late afternoon before we actually started the long trip to our final destination. We were on the road to the Kenya/Uganda border but still just barely outside of Nairobi, when suddenly the bus just quit. The driver managed to pull it over to the side of the road, and there we sat.

Now Webb was in his private vehicle leading the way, but it wasn't too long before he realized we weren't behind him. As soon as he did, he came back, discovered we were broke down and said he would have to drive back into Nairobi to see about getting another bus.

Of course, by now, there were many curious black faces staring into every window of the bus at the mzungu. Many of us began to pray that God would work something out so that we could be on our way. Some began to break into their snacks and pass them around, as we hadn't had anything to eat since breakfast. And then the most wondrous thing began to happen around me as I just sat, watched, and was so amazed and impressed. Some of the team left the bus and went out into the crowd of curious people to share their testimonies and tell the people about Jesus. I do not know how many understood the spoken words, or if many could even read the written words which were lovingly put into their hands, but I know the Spirit of the Lord was present. Eternity will tell how many came to know Jesus that night on the shoulder of the road on the outskirts of Nairobi, Kenya.

Late in the evening, Webb finally arrived back at the bus with fried chicken for everyone, followed by Jim Richardson and his van. No bus. So we all crowded tightly into the two vehicles with only our hand-carry bags to get us through the night. All the luggage and trunks with all the crusade materials and tents had been sent ahead to Uganda on a big truck. We arrived back into Nairobi where we had begun the day many hours before, checked into a hotel, divided up into rooms, and crashed.

By the time we awoke and dressed the next morning, a new bus had arrived to continue the journey. And so we did. Around noon we stopped in Kericho for some lunch and a stretch, then hurriedly piled back onto the bus. We caught our first glimpse of Lake Victoria at Kisumu, but striving to make up valuable time we did not stop. After all, we would be seeing much of the lake, as Jinja is right on it.

Finally, at Kakamega we stopped for the night, our second night in Kenya. After supper, several of the team members were recruited to collate and staple together much of the materials we would be using in the crusade. It was a great time to really get to know everyone and certainly made a mountain of paperwork go faster once we got a system going.

In the morning we headed for the Kenya/Uganda border at Tororo. When we arrived, it was quite a lengthy process as everyone's passports and visas had to be checked, as well as the great amount of luggage and supplies. But, finally, we were actually in Uganda. At one point in the very long, tiresome day, Webb stopped the caravan in order to show us all a site I will never forget. We walked over to a spot near the road we were on marked by white stones and sun-bleached white bones and skulls with shreds of material among it all. He proceeded to tell us of the terrible day some of Idi Amin's soldiers stopped a bus full of school boys going home and executed every one of them right there on the spot, then just left the bodies as they fell. This would be one of many tales of horror we would hear from Webb and others we would be meeting who had actually lived the nightmare.

Very soberly we all climbed back into our vehicles to continue the journey to Jinja. The drive was one of the roughest I have experienced because the used-to-be paved road was now pocked with great rough areas of hard-packed and deeply rutted earth in between small jagged patches of broken pavement. Webb wheeled and careened ever closer to our destination, jarring the very teeth in our heads. Late into the night we finally entered Jinja and arrived at the Global Outreach house. It took some moments for each of us to get the kinks out of our legs and backs, but how very grateful we were for finally reaching our destination, and reaching it safely. Most of the team members would sleep right there until the next morning when they would be transported to the various villages where they would work and live for the next week. Their accommodations would be the tents which one of the trucks had been hauling. I must admit I was pleasantly surprised and grateful to be one of six who would be staying at the guest house right there in Jinja. Ben and Betty Hurst were the fine and gracious hosts welcoming us and showing us to our rooms. I had a small room to myself, and it felt so good to get into the narrow bed and stretch out. I remember having no light in the room, so I was able to make good use of the little homemade flashlight my brother had made for me to take on the trip.

Early the next morning, after a light breakfast and filling our canteens with filtered water, six of us piled into the four-wheel drive vehicle which would deliver us to our respective places of service, three each going to two different villages. When our ride wheeled us up to the front of the little square mud church of Waikisi, we were rushed by dozens of boys and girls of every age, shape and size, anxious to see and greet the long-awaited three mzungus. The little girls kneeled on the ground before us as a welcome, and it bothered me very much. I was not royalty, no one worthy enough to be greeted in such a manner. I and my team members, Ken and Betty Terry, a married couple from Logan, New Mexico, realized this was their way of showing respect. We returned their gracious greetings with good old west U.S.A. smiles and handshakes. I must admit, as I looked at all the faces, bright smiles and tattered clothing, I began to fear and thought to myself *what am I doing here? Oh, God, help me!* Well, believe me, I prayed for His help many times in the week to come. I was overwhelmed with a sense of inadequacy so often as I saw the many needs of the people.

Bill Ratliff told us he would pick us up on the highway around 5:30, then off he went.

Eventually Pastor John worked his way through the crowd to introduce himself and two of the deacons in the church who would be walking through the bush with us to the different homes of people the church was trying to reach for Christ. Mostly, the people had been contacted before our arrival and had given their consent for our visit. Many had even invited friends and family to be there to meet with us.

After a morning of street witnessing in the village, we headed back to the church for lunch. All of us on the teams had been told to carry our own food and water, as it was recommended we not eat anything the villagers might offer us. Well, when we walked into the church we noticed a long table and chairs had been set up, and the pastor led us to sit. He told us his wife was preparing lunch for us and would be bringing it soon. Betty, Ken and I looked at each other with a startled question on our faces, but we took our assigned seats at the front of the church. On the table were tin plates and cups. While we waited for the food to arrive, we prayed together for God's protection as we ate and drank village food and for His guidance and blessings upon us, the church workers and those to whom we would be witnessing through the week.

Soon the pastor's wife arrived with an older child to help carry the baskets containing our lunch. We did not know at the time just how far this woman had walked to provide for us, and we were humbled when we did find out. Immediately upon her arrival, the pastor brought us a steaming teakettle and began to pour us tea. But it didn't look like tea. It was white and very sweet. They serve their tea the English way with milk and sugar. Brother John then ladled chicken stew into our bowls, after which he sat down to watch us eat. He did not join us in eating, even though we urged him to do so. This was a meal for their special guests only. It was very tasty, and we were actually rather relieved to not just be eating our cheese and crackers we had brought with us. By the end of the week we will have shared many a meal "out in the bush," and God saw fit to keep us well. Our concerns centered on the lack of sanitation as water right out of the Nile River was used for washing dishes and bodies, many times with no soap. We also had heard about a disease called AIDS which was beginning to run rampant in Uganda and was of great concern among the people.

After lunch, we began what was to be our daily morning and afternoon routine, spreading out into the bush around Waikisi to visit in the homes and share our testimonies. We did this with the printed copies and a very unique record and record player, all in the language of the villagers. The record player was a three-piece cardboard, one piece holding the record turned by hand using a pencil, the other two designed to fold over the record with a needle. The uniqueness of the record player and the sound coming from it always drew people walking by. Of course, the blond white lady playing the record certainly drew attention, also. Our interpreter would help the people read the testimony of the one whose turn it was to share, after which they would listen to the recording. Then was a question and answer time, followed by the sinner's prayer for those accepting Jesus as their Savior.

Pastor John made sure we were back at the highway by the designated time for our ride back into Jinja. After a long while of waiting, and as the sun got lower and lower on the horizon, we began anxiously watching the horizon for a vehicle. Soon, and very suddenly, it was dark. When the sound of drums from the direction of the village began to reach our ears, Pastor John said, "We must not stay here any longer. Follow me closely; I will take you to my house." So we crossed the highway and began our descent down an indiscernible path through very heavy growth to we knew not where. We had only one flashlight among us, and it was very difficult to see anything. I began to remember the advice to watch for snakes as we went about in the bush because most of them were poisonous, like puff adders and cobras. After a while we came to a small dwelling into which the pastor led us. The room which we entered was nearly as dark as the jungle path we had just walked, lit only by a small candle in the floor around which sat the pastor's wife and three of their children. I was impressed with how quickly she jumped up and shooed the children out of the room. Quickly we were shown a bench at a small table right beside the door we had just entered, and the candle was placed upon the table. Pastor John brought in one more chair for us, and left the room. Our unspoken questions and concerns began to tumble from our mouths into the stillness and blackness of the room with no soothing answers to quiet those concerns.

"How is Brother Bill going to find us now?

Even if he knows where we are, there's no way he can get here in a car. Where will we sleep?" was our thought as we tried to see beyond the candle glow into the darkness around us.

"Where's the toilet?" two very concerned women were thinking, knowing whatever facilities there were would be outside in the bush somewhere.

"May I fix you something to eat?" suddenly a voice outside of our little huddle asked. The pastor's wife was graciously offering to go to the outside kitchen and prepare some supper for us. None of us were really interested in eating, but she insisted.

Silence engulfed us again then. I remember wrapping my skirt tightly about my legs so that it wouldn't drag on the ground, allowing something unknown to crawl up onto me. I began to feel dizzy and weak and wondered where or when this was going to end. Then Ken took out his little Bible and began to read the Psalms aloud to us.

I do not know how long we sat there listening to the reading and silently praying to ourselves. It seemed like a very long time to me as I began to feel sick. Suddenly, the room lit up. It took us a moment and the honk of a horn to realize we had been rescued! Soon Bros. Bill and Webb poked their heads into the entry, and we quickly gathered ourselves and our belongings to rush as quickly as possible to the open doors of our waiting carriage.

Just as Webb started the engine to back out of the opening he had found, the pastor's wife came running out with her hands full of egg cakes for us. Ken thankfully accepted them and began to pass them around to everyone. By that time, I knew there was no way I could put anything in my stomach and expect to keep it down, so I passed on the food. I just wanted to get where I could lie down and curl up.

I awoke the next morning, not only weary but with a terrible head cold. The coordinator for our team told me it would be best for me to stay in that day to try to gain my strength and doctor the cold in order to get through the rest of the week. I watched with sadness and disappointment as the other five members loaded into the four-wheel drive for the trip to the villages. However, later I was thankful for Bro. Ratliff's wisdom in making me stay behind because the extra rest throughout the day surely helped me. Later in the afternoon Betty invited me to go errand running with her, so I was able to get my first view of Jinja in the daylight and meet some of the locals.

When I told Betty that my church had donated money for Bibles, she took me right to the place where I could purchase them. One task completed! We arrived back at the guesthouse with just enough time to prepare supper for those who would be returning soon from the bush. It was great sitting around the table listening to their experiences of the day, and I was anxiously looking forward to the next day when I would join them and gather some more of my own experiences. I was soon to discover that I would reap numerous blessings with those experiences, blessings beyond words which have stayed with me through all the years since my first crusade to Africa.

I will not even attempt to systematically relate each day's occurrences, but only highlights, those things which have been embedded in my memory for all time. The one prominent thing happening over and over throughout the week – well, it was not a thing at all, it was He, the Holy Spirit, working through me and through each of us on the team. Again and again, I had the realization that I was being used by the Holy Spirit in a way I never had experienced before. When witnessing to a Muslim woman, she confronted me with many questions about my beliefs. I was astounded at how I was able to turn to just the right scripture in my Bible to answer each of her questions. In the end, she actually prayed the sinner's prayer, asking Jesus to be her Savior.

I must say here that each day was saturated with prayer. There were people in my home church praying every day, our teams began each day praying, the pastor and people of the churches where we were working were praying, and as I or Ken or Betty were doing the talking, the other two were in prayer. What an amazing and wonderful time it was; and is this not the way our Lord would have us do each day of our lives, whether it be in the bush of Africa, or in the mainstream of our daily lives at home? I can imagine what an incredible difference Christians could make in our world if each of our days was saturated with prayer.

Some days in the heat of the afternoons after lunch, we would stay at the church for preaching and Bible study. The men actually met in one place, and the women and children stayed in another.

While the children colored Bible pictures as the story was being told, the women would gather for "woman talk." On one such afternoon, my conversation became centered with one troubled young woman. She obviously was very unhappy because her husband was cruel to her, and she had very little self-worth. I'm certainly no marriage counselor, but I showed her in scripture how very special and loved she is to God. After much discussion, reading and prayer with her, she asked Jesus to save her and be with her. Before she left the church that day, I asked her, "Fatima, do you know Jesus?" She nodded very shyly. "How do you know?" Her eyes were glowing as she said with her closed hand over her heart, "He is here."

Many pictures come so vividly into my mind as I think back, bringing with them the sounds, smells and feelings of Africa. I almost have to cover my nose as I think about the little typical mud hut, dark and sweltering inside as several of us packed into it to share with a family. I remember women in their bright gomas sitting under banana trees weaving sleeping mats for their families. I feel humble when I remember the young man who sought us out to come to his home to pray for his sick grandmother. We went and we placed our hands upon her and prayed; she and her family were so grateful. We saw no miraculous healing that day, but we saw a family's faith in God's power to heal. I'm sure in God's sweet heaven we will see her and know. I can still hear children singing for us in their little one room school with no desks or supplies, only the dirt floor with a few benches and a committed teacher with a blackboard. I felt very privileged when on a particular visit with a family; a young woman looked at me and asked if I would bless her newborn baby girl. It was such a warm, God-filled moment to hold this precious child and pray His blessings upon her and her parents.

One morning we set up a clothing distribution line in the church for the people of the village. Webb had several shipping containers full of donated clothing from people in the U.S. I'll never forget one little guy who had picked out a hooded sweatshirt for himself and promptly putting it on in spite of the intense heat of the day, then running briskly toward his home with shirts for all his siblings who could not come to the church.

One special visit several of us made one afternoon was to an orphanage in downtown Jinja. It was certainly nothing of what an American would visualize an orphanage to be. I remember the children, the outdoor kitchen and toilet, and a few rooms with very little furnishing. I fell in love with one little fellow and would have brought him home in a minute if I could have. The children did a few dances and sang for us. Little did I know at that moment in time, in that very small building filled with needy children that I would return to Jinja in ten years to work in an orphanage. Little did I know that I would be going to college upon my return home to study nursing, and that I would not have a degree but just enough training and knowledge to enable me to be the "medical" person at that orphanage. God truly works in mysterious ways.

The week was coming to an end. On our final day in the village, the pastor and his wife invited us to their home for lunch. We returned to that place which had struck such fear and uncertainty within each of us that night our ride failed to show up. It was good to be there, to see it in daylight, and be totally comfortable with it. It was good to go out behind the house to visit the family and to watch them bathe the youngest in a tub with the laundry detergent I had given to the pastor's wife. By then, we didn't even have any qualms about freely eating the delicious fish stew that she had prepared for us.

After lunch, we began the hike down to the Nile where Pastor John would baptize all those who had made saving decisions in the Lord Jesus Christ during our week there. People began pouring out of the bush by various trails to join the joyful event, and as I walked with them I had visions of how it must have been when Jesus walked by and the crowds rushed out to follow him. I cannot remember how many were baptized that day, but I remember the smiles and tears as each, one by one, climbed up out of the river onto the steep bank. It truly was a time of rejoicing as everyone headed back up the hill to Waikisi church for one last get together and praise service before our ride collected us. The church presented us with small gifts; out of their poverty, they gave what they had. I have a visual reminder of them every time I open my Bible because the page edges are stained with one of those gifts, three fresh chicken eggs.

By the time we picked up another team on the way back to Jinja, we were packed like sardines in the Land Rover. One of the women was holding a live chicken, that team's gift from their church. I was holding the eggs in a small woven basket with my Bible during the bumpy ride back into town, and did not know until our arrival at the guesthouse that one of the eggs had broken and soaked the pages of my Bible with its sticky contents. As soon as I got to my room I spent an hour or so flipping the pages while blowing so they would dry without sticking to one another. This particular Bible is so precious to me because of the memories packed into its pages, memories from all of the crusades which were to follow this first one to Uganda.

The next day, Saturday, was the day all the teams from out in the bush would be arriving back in Jinja, and a late afternoon picnic at Bujigali Falls of the Nile had been planned. It was quite an eye opener to see the folks arriving, quite disheveled and very weary looking. While we in the guesthouse had thought bathing in a small closet by turning on a hose with cold water was bad, these people had not been able to bathe more than a spit-wash from a basin. While each of us had a room with a bed at night, they had a cot in a shared tent, which was never private as there were always curious eyes looking in at the muzungus. While we were baptizing in the beautiful Nile river (albeit there were crocodile watchers at the time), they were baptizing in mud holes filled with leaches. Actually, I remember feeling ashamed that we had had it so easy while our brothers and sisters had been physically sacrificing every day. But none of them were complaining, just telling it as it had been. Quite a few of them couldn't wait to jump into the river there at the beautiful seven falls and commence washing bodies, hair and clothes all at the same time. It was a great time of fellowshipping, sharing and rejoicing as we ate all the delicious food Nancy had prepared. She had even made and decorated a beautiful sheet cake welcoming everyone back.

Sunday, our final day, the day we would be heading back to

Nairobi for a late night flight. But first there was an early morning worship service and sharing of testimonies as representatives from all the churches where we had worked and all of the International Crusade coordinators and team members gathered. Again, I cannot remember the exact number of converts from the week's efforts, but I do remember it was over 800. What a moment of exultation, clapping and tears when Bro. Ratliff gave us the final count of those we would one day greet again in heaven at the feet of Jesus. What an awesome job and responsibility we were leaving the local pastors and members. Theirs was the privilege of discipling all of those new babes in Christ and to draw them into the fellowship of believers. We had no worries, for we had just spent a good week witnessing the enthusiasm, commitment and love of these people for their own. We also were confident that God would complete the work He had begun, through us, in the lives of so many.

I left Uganda with a strong desire not to leave. There was so much to be done; this was where I wanted to be. But somehow I knew this was not the right time. Somehow I knew I would be back.

CHAPTER 4
JERICHO WEEK

AUGUST, 1992, GLORIETA, NEW MEXICO

I have been running from God so long now, I don't know how to stop. I know He's calling me to Africa to be a missionary. I've known it since Jeanette went to Uganda without me. I think that's when I finally answered the wake up call. I am reminded of His words in Genesis 6:3, "My Spirit shall not strive with man forever, for he is indeed flesh." I wonder how many excuses He will permit me before He says, "If you're not willing to go, I'll send her alone."

I love Glorieta. I've always loved the mountains around Santa Fe and enjoyed the assemblies here. I didn't see any harm in coming up here for Jericho week, a time when foreign missionaries are commissioned to overseas appointments. I have an affinity for missionaries. I've visited them on their home ground. I've been giving to the cooperative program for years to support them. I thought it would be fun; maybe I could even take some hikes up into the mountains.

Now I'm standing here gripping the pew in front of me until my knuckles are white. Tonight is the final evening. The commissions have been made, and the new missionaries have been recognized. Now the pastor has called for anyone who would like to rededicate their lives to come forward. We're singing "Jesus is Tenderly Calling," all except me. My jaws are clenched tight. I know it's time. "My Spirit will not strive with you forever. Jesus is tenderly calling."

The blood has gone out of my head and I feel faint. Slowly I release my death grip on the pew-back and my left foot moves a little, then I'm moving down the aisle, hurrying to take the pastor's hand and tell him of my decision to become an African missionary if God will still have me. I'm not aware that Jeanette has followed me until I feel her slip her hand in mine. I look over at her, and her eyes are dewy, but her smile is warm. I feel like a thousand pound weight has been lifted from my shoulders. I feel like shouting hallelujah, but I just bow my head as the pastor prays with us. Okay God, I've made the commitment, now the ball's in your court.

CHAPTER 5
RWANDA CRUSADE

Since I have never been particularly good about witnessing, and have actually avoided visiting church members in their homes, it was with much trepidation that I finally agreed to go on an evangelistic crusade in Rwanda. Oh, I've stood up in front of the church to lead in prayer, make announcements and welcome guests. I've even given my personal testimony a time or two, but nothing I've ever done would prepare me for the experience that was ahead of me.

Even though we had made the decision to go several months in advance, somehow it hadn't become a reality until a day or two before we were to leave. To begin with, we really didn't have the money for a trip like this. Naturally, I took this as a sign from God that we weren't supposed to go after all; even though Jeanette kept reminding me, "If it's the Lord's will for us to go, He will provide the money." Two days before our departure, we received an unexpected check in the mail that would exactly cover our expenses.

Then to make matters worse, International Crusades called the day before our departure to tell us that rebel forces had crossed the border from Uganda into Rwanda, and there was fighting in the northern provinces. Now I was sure that we weren't supposed to go. IC assured us, however, that there was no danger. We would be working with a church near Butari in the south. The fighting was contained in the border regions in the north.

We departed Albuquerque at 9:30 AM on Thursday, February 11, 1993 and arrived at the Kigali Baptist mission around 9:30 AM on Saturday, February 13. Needless to say we were walking zombies. We met the local pastors, other team members and interpreters, and were given our assignments. We learned that we would be working with five churches around the Kigali area, and our interpreter would be Emanuel Rubaduca, a young African from Burundi. I would come to learn that not only was Emanuel the best interpreter in the crusade, he was an able evangelist as well.

As we were getting settled in at the mission guest house, Fredrick Murindahabi, the African pastor at First Baptist Church of Kigali, came by to tell me he would like for me to bring the message at the Sunday morning service----tomorrow! I guess I hadn't really considered what I'd come halfway around the world to Africa to do, but I certainly hadn't figured on preaching the Sunday morning service at the largest Baptist church in Rwanda. I began to protest, and tried to make the excuse that I was no preacher, and that I could never deliver a sermon. I didn't even know how to prepare one. Jim Flinchum, one of our veteran team members, laughed, and said, "You might as well give in. He's not going to take no for an answer. Not only that, but you're going to have to preach before this is over, so you'd just as well get started tomorrow."

That night, as I lay in bed, too exhausted to sleep, I thought about the task ahead, and I panicked. I truly panicked. I prayed, "God, what am I doing here? How can I do this? I'm no preacher and I don't even like church visiting." If there had been any way to go back out to the airport and catch a flight out of there, I would have; but of course, Sabena Airlines only operated on Mondays and Saturdays, so I was stuck, at least until Monday night. Then God spoke to my heart and said, "Fear not, for I am with you." I was too tired to try to work up a sermon for the next morning, even if I'd known how. So there I lay, unable to sleep, and too tired to think. Sometime around midnight I finally fell asleep, and around 4:00 AM good old jet lag kicked in, my eyes popped open, and my body was telling me it was day and time to get started. I got up, made myself a cup of coffee, sat down with my Bible, a book on how to write a sermon by J.B.Fowler, a spiral notebook, and started to write. Lo and behold, in about two hours, I had a fairly decent outline on love and obedience from the book of Philemon.

To say that I mounted the rostrum that morning with fear and trembling wouldn't be doing my emotions justice. I stood behind the podium with my knees shaking and began to read my outline word for word. Almost immediately, I discovered that Emanuel was taking my "read" outline, and was turning it into a well delivered message. When the service was over, Frederick came to me, and complemented me on a great message. I think it was about then that I realized that for the next ten days, Emanuel was to be my best friend and ally.

Later, Jeanette asked me, "What was the rush?"

"What do you mean?" I asked.

"Well, your message was good, but it only took you five minutes, with interpretation."

"That's okay," I shrugged, "most preachers preach way too long anyhow." It may have only taken me five minutes, but it felt like an hour.

Because it was Sunday, we were given the rest of the afternoon to rest and look around Kigali. We were invited to eat Sunday dinner with Marvin and Anice Ogle, a volunteer missionary couple from Tennessee, and Emanuel and his wife, Angela. We spent a very enjoyable afternoon getting to know these four wonderful people and learning more about the mission work in Rwanda. That evening, Jeanette and I ate our supper of canned tuna and crackers, a meal we would eat more than once this trip, and again, at about 6:30 PM, our bodies lied to us and told us it was late at night and time to go to bed.

MONDAY, FEBRUARY 15

I wake up around four again this morning, sponge myself off with the hand sprayer, and go outside with my cup of coffee to watch the sun come up. Celestine, one of the men I met yesterday, is here. He is the night guard at the mission compound. He speaks very little English and, of course, I've only picked up a couple of words in

Kinyarwanda, pronounced, "Kinguanda." He is holding a dog-eared Kinguanda Bible, which he reads under the street light during the night. I nod and say "mwaramutze" (good morning). He smiles at my attempt to speak his language, shakes my hand and returns, "mwaramutze." I offer him a cup of coffee by holding up my cup and pointing to it. He shakes his head no. We stand quietly as the sun breaks over the next mountain top, and watch the mist rise off of the river below us. It's a good time, and we enjoy each other's company in silence.

Marvin has volunteered to drive us to Jari in the mission truck. Jari is a small village over on the next mountain to the north. "Isn't that where the fighting is, in the north?" I ask.

"Yes, but farther north." Marvin assures us. "Up around Ruhengeri."

Celestine has hitched a ride with us, since his home is near Jari. Marvin tells us he usually walks the hour and a half hike each way to come to work in the evening, and then go back home in the morning.

We snake around the twisty streets of Kigali to get down to the river. If we could have gone straight down the mountain from the compound, it would have been about a half a mile, but that is only a foot path, so we take the scenic route through downtown, which takes us about three miles out of the way. When we get to the river, we are stopped at a roadblock.

"Nothing to worry about," Marvin tells us. "They're just taking precautions because of all the refugees. They don't want rebels infiltrating the city with them."

Sure enough, there are dozens of vehicles crammed with people coming into the city, plus hundreds on foot, carrying all that they own, either on their heads or in push-carts, fleeing the north. The guard gives Emanuel and Celestine a hard look, but waves us through. The fact that there are three white people in the truck, and that we are heading north out of the city, instead of into the city from the north, seems to satisfy them. The thought occurs to me that tonight we have to come back this way, but I keep it to myself.

As we go up the highway toward Ruhengeri, both sides of the

road are jammed with people. Most are refugees, but some are people from around Jari coming down to market. Again I notice that they carry everything from big bunches of bananas to five gallon jerry cans on their heads, and the women usually have an infant strapped to their backs as well. I see a man on a bicycle with a huge load of something on his head, seemingly unaware of his burden. Well, at least he's coming down the mountain. Maybe going back, he'll only have to carry a pocket full of Rwandan francs.

We travel on the paved road for about twenty minutes, and then turn off onto a dirt track. It doesn't seem much better than the footpath from the compound to the river, but the little four-wheel drive truck digs in, and up the mountain we go, dodging pedestrians with their head loads, and a herd of the African long-horned cattle being driven along the trail. I have to laugh because the herdsman is about seven years old, maybe less. It's hard to tell about ages, especially with the children. They are all so under nourished they look smaller than American children that same age.

He runs up to a cow with especially long, thick horns, and gives her a whack on the backside with a stick to get her out of the way of the truck. She turns, gives him a soulful look, and then plods on, grabbing a mouthful of weeds from the side of the path.

We switch back and forth on this serpentine trail for about another thirty minutes, finally reaching the top, and there at the top of this mountain, on one side of this dirt road, are about a dozen mud huts, some with thatch roofs, and some with tin. This is Jari. At the end of the road is a somewhat larger tin-roofed, mud house with a small wooden cross over the door. This is Jari Baptist church. Out front, waiting for us to arrive, are about a dozen people with Innocent, the young pastor. He is probably thirty, but again it's hard to tell. All of the church people are young, at least the ones who are helping with this crusade. Innocent is small, and his face has a striking resemblance to a mountain gorilla. He gives us a warm, but shy, smile and welcomes us. He has things well organized, and we spend only a short time discussing the visitation strategy before off we go down the other side of the mountain on a footpath that leads through well-kept farm plots called urugos. Each farm is small compared to American standards. Most are around five acres with a small bare yard, surrounded by a high brush fence. The houses are all mud wattle with thatch roofs, and if they're painted at all, they are painted with a mixture of water and cow dung. I understand this is to make a kind of cement, as well as a decorative covering.

The farms are planted for maximum productivity with banana and avocado trees. Under the trees they plant their corn and pole beans, and under that, they plant yams and manioc. No space of arable ground goes to waste, and, remember, this is on the side of a steep mountain. Coming from the dry southwest myself, I am amazed that they don't have any wells, not for the fields or for their homes. They depend on rainfall, and if it doesn't rain, they haul water from the river which is sometimes four or five miles down the mountain.

When I stood in the mission garden this morning and looked out over the valley with the rising mist, I thought it was beautiful, but now I'm almost overcome by the beauty of the mountains as they roll away in wave after high green wave with the neat little urugos tucked in their protective little terraces; and two mountains over, a rain storm is forming up. I reach out to take Jeanette's hand. She just looks at me and nods. I guess we've lived together so long we communicate without words now.

The visitation is good, though heart wrenching. We visit eight or ten urugos and cover around five miles, I guess. At least it feels like that far.

At one place we visit, the family chief is a little old man who is crippled. His right leg is deformed and withered. He has pulled himself around using his arms and knees for so many years, he has developed a large cartilage on his right knee, which he uses as a foot. It's hard for me to see some of the hardships here and know how to deal with them.

His urugo is typically African with the traditional round mud hut, a single door, and thatched roof. He calls all of his children in out of the field to listen to our testimonies. We have to set up in the yard. His house is way too small to accommodate all of us.

I haven't said anything about our testimonies yet. IC has had our personal testimonies printed up in Kinyarwanda, and on the inside are the questions: Do you believe in God? Do you believe that Jesus Christ is the son of God? Do you believe that you are a sinner? Do you believe that Jesus Christ died for your sins? Do you want Jesus Christ to save you from your sins? Each question is referenced to scripture, and then there are the four steps to accepting Jesus as your savior, the sinner's prayer, and a place for them to record their decision, all in Kinyarwanda, of course.

As the children straggle in from the field, and they range in age from five or six to young adult, they greet us with either "mraho" or "mwidiway," which are just different ways of saying hello. They extend their forearms to us. Since they have been working in the fields, it's impolite to offer their dirty hands. We grasp the forearm in a sort of handshake, and Emanuel introduces us. If our hands were dirty as well, we would just touch forearms.

We start off by playing the record we have brought. The record player is an ingenious device which is nothing more than a piece of folded cardboard with a metal pin as the needle to play a phonograph record, turned manually with a ballpoint pen. We have several records, each with a different message in Kinyarwanda, and the family sits spellbound as they listen. Emanuel reads one of the testimonies, and asks if they would like to have Jesus as their personal savior. They all answer yes, but they have many questions and concerns. The old chief says that, as a child, he was baptized into the Catholic faith. He wants to know if he has to become a Baptist to be saved. We assure him that it's not our intention to convert him to the Baptist faith. Our only goal is to introduce him to a personal friend, and tell him of the wonderful gift of forgiveness this friend has to offer. He says he knows about Jesus from Catholic primary school, but admits that he has never accepted Him as his personal savior. I think how alike we are. I knew about Jesus, and yet I didn't know Him. Emanuel leads the family through the sinner's prayer, pausing to make sure that every one in the family understands what they are praying. I watch him as he patiently leads them through it, and I think, *Lord, is this a young black African, or is it an angel you have sent to help us?* Of course, he is just a black African, but he is one who has a love for his people, and his desire is to lead Africa to a saving knowledge of Jesus Christ. Each member of the family asks Jesus to come into their hearts, to be Lord of their lives, and when it's all done, I notice a light in the eyes of the old chief that wasn't there earlier, and I know it's been a successful visit.

Later on, one of the last places we visit before going back to the church is a very pleasant farm, well tended, with a square, tin roofed house. I can tell at a glance that this family takes a great deal of pride in their home. Unlike most of the places we have visited, this house is painted and consists of more than one room. It has a small grass lawn in front, and in the middle of the lawn they have planted some kind of spreading tree which has been trained on trellises to cover a shady bower where we can sit as we visit. As before, the whole family, including the very small children, is out in the field working, and as we pass, they stop to look at us. After all, a group of people traveling through the countryside with two white people, is an occasion to stop work and look.

I wave and shout, "Mraho." A little puzzled, they wave back and say "mraho."

Emanuel explains briefly to them what we are doing, and they invite us up to the house. This is hospitality at its best, for this family to stop work in the field to listen to what we have to say.

The family consists of a young couple with two small children. The little girl, about two, steals Jeanette's heart with her big brown eyes, but mostly because her name is Jeanette, pronounced the French way, emphasizing the last "e." This young man reads the testimony for himself and already has questions, even before we have a chance to start. He is eager to learn about this personal relationship with the Son of God. As we talk, another young man stops by to visit the family, and he sits down under the bower to listen as well. Before we can play the record, the father asks if he can pray the prayer, and accept Jesus as his savior. We go ahead and play the record because it is on the basics of salvation and answers questions before they are asked. Then Emanuel leads them through the prayer, and all accept Jesus, even the young man who has stopped to visit. We discover that he is a policeman at Jari and a friend of the young family. As we get ready to leave, the whole family walks to the edge of the urugo to say goodbye. Then the young man says, "If we had a Bible, I could read it to my family and teach them about God." As it happens, our church had donated well over two hundred dollars for us to buy Kinyarwanda Bibles to distribute among the people, so we assure him that Innocent will bring his family a Bible.

I am starving to death! It's been a *long* time since breakfast, and that was only a can of mixed fruit and a piece of toast. Not only that, but last night's supper was a can of tuna and some homemade crackers that Anice gave us. As hungry as I am, however, I have mixed feelings about eating. We've been cautioned to eat only what we can cook or peel. We've been told that the churches will provide for our lunch every day, but we've brought a couple of cans of tuna, just in case.

When we get back to the church, our lunch is spread out on one of the benches. There are four or five large metal serving platters, and each one contains the same thing. First, there is a huge mound of rice, and around the rice are some white sweet potatoes. On top of that they've dumped a pot of red beans, and on top of that there is a mixture of cabbage, tomatoes, and a green vegetable similar to collards. It looks like something to be thrown to the hogs, but it smells good, and we are hungry, so we dive in like the rest, they with their hands, and we with the forks they have provided for us. They have tried so hard to be considerate of our needs and want to accommodate us however possible.

After lunch, Innocent tells us there are two or three more places he wants to visit; so, again, we head off through the mountains, finding little urugo terraces carved out of the side of the mountain. It is now the heat of the day, so most of the workers have left the fields.

As we walk down the path, a little boy joins us, kicking a soccer ball he has made out of banana leaves tied up with long strands of grass. He is very good and can maneuver the homemade ball with his feet like a professional. I start trying to kick it away from him, and a soccer match ensues right there on the trail. He is good, but I'm not, and in just a couple of minutes, I inadvertently kick his ball off the trail, and down the steep side of the mountain. Undaunted, he bounds down the mountainside like a little goat, and before I know it, he's coming back up through the lush growth, kicking his ball and grinning.

We make our final visits, and they are productive ones. The last one is at the house of a handsome young man. He is a Christian and a member of the church, but is using his house to gather some of his neighbors to hear the testimonies and records.

We are supposed to be back at the church at four to begin the afternoon preaching service, but we are operating on African time. You get there when you get there. It's almost five when we finish up our visiting.

I can hear the racket coming from the church long before it comes into sight. It is the sound of African drums and chanting. It is a wild sound, a primitive sound, a frightening sound, but somehow hauntingly beautiful.

When we enter, the people are up in the aisles dancing, waving their arms, and singing this wild, primitive, beautiful song. I look over at Emanuel for assurance, but he has joined in the revelry. I look to Jeanette, and she seems as frightened as me. I keep hearing the word Imana, and I know this is Kinyarwanda for God, so I'm certain it's not a pagan ritual they do just before they cook you. Besides, they can't be that hungry. We had a very large lunch. The singing goes on for at least a half hour before Innocent steps forward and yells, "hadaduya." Since their "l" and "r" is pronounced pretty much the same, and sound like "d", this is what passes in Kinyarwanda for hallelujah. After three or four "hadaduyas" the singing stops, and he introduces Jeanette and me.

This time, I have prepared a six page sermon on God's plan of salvation, and I'm a little less nervous than yesterday. Still, I pretty much read my notes, and again, Emanuel skillfully turns it into a sermon as he does the interpretation. This time, including the interpreting, it takes a whole fifteen minutes. I'm elated. Several people come forward at the invitation to make decisions, and the member whose house we used to make the last visit, comes forward to give a testimony. He tells us how, before he accepted Christ as his savior, he drank heavily and would pick fights with everyone. He would hide in the jungle at night with his panga (machete) and attack people as they passed by on the trail. He literally beams as he tells us how his life has changed, how he is now a deacon in the church and a respected member of the community, and all because Innocent told him that God loves him and wants him to be free from sin. As I listen, I'm astounded at how cruel and wild Africa still is. I think of the news accounts of people being hacked to pieces with pangas in South Africa, and right before me is a young man who has been guilty of just that. I shake off a shudder and thank God that He can change even a man like this.

It's been a long day, and we've walked many miles through rugged mountains, so I'm glad when Marvin arrives with the truck to take us back to the mission. I'm looking forward to my can of tuna and tiny African banana supper and bed.

When we reach the river, the refugee traffic has picked up. The security at the roadblock seems tighter, but we are passed right on through. Celestine has come back with us. He spent the day visiting with us. Now he is returning to the compound to stand guard all night.

We say goodbye to Emanuel and make arrangements to meet him here tomorrow morning at seven. Marvin is going to take us out in the truck again. This time we are going to Shyrongi. It's like a mission church to Jari. It's under Innocent's direction, but the congregation is led by Jean Claude, a tall skinny kid who looks to be in his teens, but is probably in his mid-twenties.

TUESDAY, FEBRUARY 16

Four AM. I'm up and ready to go again. I've waited until this morning to work on my sermon. I seem to be able to think better if I do it when I first get up. Normally, I'm a night person and think better at night, but here, with the jet lag, night is day and day is night. At least, that's what my body thinks.

My theme for today's sermon is, "Our constant God." I've used several scripture passages, including Malachi 3:6 and Hebrews 13:8. This one is eight pages, so I should be able to go for at least twenty minutes today.

I take my coffee outside and stand with Celestine while Jeanette is getting ready. It's the same as yesterday: "mwaramutze," his gentle smile, almost shy, "mwaramutze," and then we stand in silence as the sun breaks over the mountain, and the mist rises off the river. He is wearing the same worn pants and torn green windbreaker that he's been wearing since Saturday, when we first met. I decide on the spot to give him a pair of my Levis and a shirt that is too small for me. He is so grateful, I want to give him my whole wardrobe.

I point toward Jari, and ask, "Shyrongi?" He shakes his head, and points to the mountain behind, the one further north.

He hitches a ride again, and goes with us to Shyrongi. When we cross the river, we stay on the paved road, and go on the west side of the Jari mountain. When we arrive, I am surprised. Shyrongi Baptist church is a very nice red brick building. Marvin tells us that since it's located in a strategic area, between two main towns, and on a paved highway, it was built by the Southern Baptist Convention of Maryland, in partnership with the Eglis Bautist du Rwanda. It seems that many Baptist state conventions have partnerships with foreign countries, and people from those states volunteer to come and help the local people build churches.

As we get ready to start out on our visits, an army truck filled with troops speeds by. I notice that the driver and one other are white, so I ask Emanuel about this.

"Oh, yes," he says, "the French have sent troops to help the Rwanda troops against the rebels. The rebels have taken Ruhengeri. Things are very bad up there."

"And how far is Ruhengeri?" I ask him to remind me.

"Oh, about seventy kilometers," he says.

Somehow, the knowledge that the French army has been called in because armed rebels have taken a major town only fifty miles away doesn't give me much comfort. I feel a little better when we start walking back along the highway, but that is short lived when another truck load of troops passes us.

We only walk about a mile, maybe less, along the highway, and then turn down the west side of the mountain. We can actually see the mountains up by Ruhengeri from here. It's so beautiful it's hard to believe that people are killing each other there, but we do believe it because now we can occasionally hear the thump of artillery in the distance.

We've been on this trail now for an hour, and still haven't come to our scheduled visit. I think Jean Claude is taking us to Zaire. He must sense what I'm thinking, and calls back, "Not much farther now."

Yeah, right.

The trail is narrow, and cuts across the side of the mountain, rising steeply on our left and dropping off just as steep on our right. We have to go single file because of the thick jungle on both sides, and wouldn't you know it; we meet a man driving his cattle on the same trail. You remember, the ones with horns the size of elephant tusks.

We startle them as much as they startle us, but there's no place for either of us to go; somehow, though, we squeeze past them without anybody getting kicked or gored. Good thing they're as tame as pets, because we have to rub up against them in order to pass.

Actually, it's kind of funny, and I get a charge out of it. I'm an old cowboy anyhow, you know.

Sure enough, Jean Claude is right, and we reach our destination in about another twenty minutes. Over at Jari, where we visited yesterday, the urugos were in pretty close proximity, and on leveled out plateaus. Here, the mountain is too steep and the forest too thick. We haven't even passed a farm in miles. Up ahead, the land levels off just a bit, and in a clearing, there is a small urugo. It's isolated! When we arrive in the brush-enclosed yard, there is no one around; so Jean Claude leaves us there, and goes off down the side of the mountain to a small banana grove to see if he can find the residents.

We wait for about five, maybe ten, minutes, before he returns with two women. The women's hands and feet are caked with mud from the field, so they extend their forearms to us. We're beginning to learn something about their etiquette, so we touch their arm with ours, and say "mwiriway." One of the women is younger than the other, and from the conversation I perceive that she is the daughter-in-law. I can't understand from what Emanuel is saying whether her husband has gone into town for the day, or just gone, and these two women live here alone. At any rate, these two women are all that is here in this lonely place so far from anything. The young one is very attractive; in fact, I've found that the Rwandans are a handsome people. She has a smooth complexion and delicate features. When she first sees us, her face registers surprise as she stares at Jeanette, who is very fair and blond, with something akin to awe. The thought occurs to me, we are the first white people this woman has ever seen. Jeanette shares her testimony with them, and really carries this whole visit since the only men present are the ones on the team. Through Emanuel she witnesses to them, and they pray to accept Jesus as their savior. As is their custom, they walk with us to the edge of the clearing, which is straight up the mountainside. No path or trail, just straight up the mountain, and when we reach the place where they leave us, even the Africans are panting.

We go a few miles on up the mountain, and come to another isolated urugo. Again, there are no men present, but this time, there are several small children playing in the yard. When one little boy sees us, he starts running away from us, crying and waving his hand at us, as if to shoo away something evil. I get the distinct impression that the people on this side of the mountain don't get many visitors, white or black. The women welcome us in, though, and we witness to them. Then, all of them make the decision to accept Jesus as their savior.

As we are leaving, one of the older women runs up the path after us, calling, "Madamu, madamu!" It's obvious she's pleading with Jeanette for something because she is holding her hand out in a begging gesture. Jeanette is concerned that something is wrong, but

I say, "No, she just wants a handout." Jeanette is adamant, however, and calls Emanuel back, as he has already gone on up the trail. When he returns, the woman tells him what she wants in that pleading, wavering, almost panicky voice. "She wants you to give her a Bible," he says. We promise her that we will send one back with Jean Claude, and we continue up the mountain. I can barely see the trail for the tears welling up in my eyes, and I drop back so no one will see me cry. Their spiritual need is so great. I think of Jesus' words, "The harvest is truly plentiful, but the workers are few."

We go straight up the mountain from here for about three or four more miles, and panting and rubbing cramped leg muscles, we intersect the highway. It's about two o'clock in the afternoon now, and the children are getting out of school. Quickly we acquire a fairly large following, because by now, the word has spread that there are some white people in the mountains who are giving out bombo (candy) and rubber handballs.

On Emanuel's advice, we give the group of boys a few of the balls and the group of girls some balls. He has told us that this is necessary because they are not allowed to play together at school.

Where we have intersected the highway, we are about a mile up from the church. We are able to walk at a good pace on this level piece of pavement, and it feels good to stretch the cramped muscles in my legs. I think this is the first time today we haven't either been going up, or coming down a mountain trail. As we travel down the highway, I see a man sitting on a log footbridge across a barrow ditch, and he is reading one of our testimonies. I call Emanuel's attention to it, so we stop to talk with him. He says we witnessed to a friend of his earlier in the day, and the friend shared the testimony with him. We ask him if he knows where the Eglis Bautist Shyrongi is, and he says yes. I tell him that I will be preaching the word of God there at four in the afternoon, and ask him if he would like to come and listen. He nods that he would and says he'll be there if he can.

Our lunch fare is the same as yesterday; only today we are invited to the open-air kitchen behind the houses to watch how it is cooked. This is an experience. Everything is being cooked either on or in the open fire in big black pots. The potatoes are roasting in the coals, while the pots bubble with rice, cabbage, beans, etc. All the while, kids romp and play around the pots, and chickens scratch the ground nearby. It doesn't look any more unsanitary than camp cooking, though, and I've certainly done enough of that to know that a little debris from the fire doesn't hurt the food any. Like they say, if it's cooked, it's edible. Besides, I'm sure that if anything big like a grasshopper, or a bird flies into it, the cooks will fish it out.

After lunch, we decide it's too late to go back out visiting, so we ask Jean Claude if they would like to have a Bible study. This pleases them no end. They don't have Sunday school, and they don't have the opportunity to discuss the Bible in their church service. They are full of questions, and Jeanette and I try to answer them the best we can. Sometimes I have the answer, and sometimes Jeanette does. They seem to enjoy taking part in looking up scripture that will help answer some of their questions. Some of them already have their own Bibles, but most don't; so again, we assure them that before we leave, they will all have a Bible. We encourage them to start home Bible studies, and they get very excited about this.

At this afternoon's service they are singing a different song. It's not quite as wild as yesterday, or maybe I'm just getting used to African singing. Anyway, the primitive beauty of it still thrills me and makes my blood rush. I catch myself tapping out the rhythm of the drum on my Bible, and trying to do their shuffle dance step, but I'm four or five shades too light to get the rhythm right. It's a catchy tune, if that's what you'd call it, done in counter-point, as is much of the music of Africa. One person sings out the chant, and the chorus responds to it. Emanuel tells us the words mean, "Believe in the Lord Jesus, and you will be saved."

I'm not too nervous this afternoon. I can actually look up from my notes on several occasions, and it seems like Emanuel and I are more in concert than before.

Marvin shows up just as we're finishing up, and gets some video tape of the church and people. I hope I can talk him out of a copy. We all climb into the truck exhausted, including Celestine. He has spent all day with us again, and now, he has to go back to the mission to guard again while we sleep. Bless his heart, when the meek inherit the earth, his kingdom will be massive. I'm glad to call him friend.

This evening, we make arrangements with the Ogles to buy the Bibles for us. We're gone from seven in the morning until seven at night, so there's no chance for us to do it. We discover that with the money we have, we can buy two hundred twenty-five New Testaments or one hundred ninety-seven complete Bibles. We believe the need is for the complete Bibles.

Jeanette and I make a big decision tonight. We're tired of eating tuna fish and crackers, so we decide to brave the little African café a couple of blocks down the street. It looks clean enough, and as long as we don't eat any raw vegetables or fruit, we should be okay. We order spaghetti bolognaise and wait for over an hour for it to come. We figure that they probably don't have steam tables like American restaurants, and so don't prepare the food until it's ordered. When we do get it, it's pretty good, and we eat like we hadn't had a gigantic lunch.

WEDNESDAY, FEBRUARY 17

It has become a ritual now to walk out in the garden to watch the sun come up with Celestine. I wonder if he'll miss it as much as I will. I'm developing such a love for this country and these people. I've always loved Africa. That is wild Africa, safari Africa, lions and elephants and crocodiles Africa with its dusty savannahs and thorn trees; but this is a different Africa. There are no wild animals here. Oh, there are mountain gorillas in the north, but we can't go there. There is fighting there. Here there are only people, people and mountain farms; people who are hungry to hear that Jesus loves them, people who want a Bible of their own, people who have stolen a little piece of my heart. One of them is coming up to me now. His name is Emanuel, my brother Emanuel, my brother in Christ, my black brother.

"Mwaramutze, umeze ute?" I grin. I'm showing off a little bit now. Emanuel is pleased.

"If you stayed another week, you wouldn't need me. You would be speaking Kinyarwanda fluently," he says.

Celestine climbs into the truck. "Are you going with us again, Celestine?" Jeanette asks. He smiles his shy smile and nods when Emanuel translates for him. Jeanette shakes her head, "You guard the compound all night and then go with us all day. When do you sleep?"

Emanuel translates his answer, "He says his day off is Thursday. He will sleep tomorrow."

Marvin joins in, "He and the other guard take turns napping during the night," he explains. "He's the leader at the Kyuga church (pronounced Chuga), you know. He wouldn't miss this one."

No, I didn't know. He works ten hours a night guarding the compound, keeps a farm some five miles away on that distant mountain, leads the church at Kyuga, and yet feels that what we are doing is important enough to put his other life and family on hold to be a part of it. It's humbling to be in the presence of a true saint.

The road over the bridge is familiar territory to us by now. We smile and wave at the guards at the roadblock, and they wave us on through. We go like we're heading for Jari, but when we get to the turn, we continue north for another mile or two, and then turn up another dirt road. It's better than the track to Jari, but it's still narrow and full of ruts. It gets too narrow for us to drive on into Kyuga, so Marvin lets us out some two hundred yards from the village, and we walk the rest of the way. In the center of the village we pass a small bar and out front, right in the road, there are four or five men sitting around a homemade wooden table, drinking beer. They stare at us a minute, then one shouts, "Hey, who are you people?"

Emanuel tells them, in Kinyarwanda, "These are Americans who have come to Africa to tell our people about Jesus."

"Well, why don't you start with us?" the bold one says.

Emanuel grins, "Good, come on into the church, and we will."

How can I describe the Eglis Bautist du Kyuga? First, let me say

I've seen adobe cow barns on the Navajo reservation back home that are better than this building. It's only about eight feet square. Inside, it has four wooden benches around the mud walls, and a tiny wooden table in the center of the dirt floor. For light and ventilation, it has a front door and a back door. No windows. The rafters are exposed poles on top of which is nailed a tin roof with daylight showing through in several places. I guess that's to give the lizards a place to escape. Next to this place, Jari is a cathedral.

Into this small space crowd the original church group of about ten and the men from the bar. It's so crowded, several of the church members have to be asked to wait outside. They do, but not to be left out, they fill the two doors. *So much for light and ventilation.* We spend about half an hour reading our testimonies and playing the record. Emanuel wants to play the one entitled, "Are you afraid?" He thinks it is appropriate for this group and these times in Rwanda. The men have some questions, and the bold one seems particularly interested. When Emanuel asks them if they would like to pray, to accept Jesus, they answer yes. Then when we get ready to start out on our visits, the bold one leaves his friends at the bar, and follows us up the trail.

Just as we are leaving Kyuga, from up on the mountainside, we hear *pow, pow-pow-pow.* Emanuel jerks around and looks at us, and on his face I see stark fear. I've seen enough around here to know that there is no hunting, so I have to wonder what's happening. I'm sure each of us is wondering if the fighting has gotten this far south, but we don't hear any more shots, so we dismiss it; although, it bothers me for a long time because I know the villagers don't own firearms.

We've been walking for about a half hour now and have already made a couple of visits. I have this real uneasy feeling. I can't explain it. It's just a bad feeling, and I mention it to Jeanette.

She looks at me funny and says, "I've had the same feeling for a while now. I just thought it was me."

I figure we're just feeling jumpy about the shots we heard earlier, but I mention it to Emanuel, anyway. He nods gravely.

"This is a bad place," he says. "There are many forest doctors in this valley. Much witchcraft."

While we're walking a path between two banana fields, we see some people working in one of the fields. A woman looks up and sees us, runs down from where she is working and hugs Jeanette and starts talking rapidly. Emanuel seems nervous, or agitated, or something, and just keeps walking without speaking to the woman.

"Emanuel, what is she saying?" Jeanette calls.

He comes back down the path and finally speaks to the woman, then shrugs and shakes his head. "She's not saying anything. She's just talking foolishness, gibberish." She follows us along the path until we come to the house where we will visit. The family and some friends have gathered in the yard because there are too many of us to go in the house. There are now a dozen or more. Jeanette is going to do the talking here. We alternate, and if there are more women present than men, she does it. If there are more men present, I do it. Seldom are there more men that women, unless we stop someone on the trail, or as in one case, we stopped to talk to a group of men building a house.

The crazy woman listens to the testimony, although she jabbers continuously, smiling and giggling to herself, but when Jeanette leads in prayer, her face becomes as hard as stone, and hatred flashes from her eyes. She refuses to bow her head, and sits in stony silence, glaring at Jeanette until the prayer is over. Then, as if nothing has happened, she resumes her babbling and giggling. I don't know that I've ever seen a possessed person before, but I'm convinced that one is in our presence now, and I can truly say that I'm a little afraid. The woman follows us to the rest of our visits, and at each one, the scene is the same. It's un-nerving.

By midday, we've made several visits, and it's time to head back to the church for lunch. I'm not looking forward to eating in Kyuga's dirty little church. When we get there, lunch isn't ready, so we wait outside on some benches and sing hymns in Kinyarwanda. One of the ones we sing is the one I tried to learn yesterday. Today I pick up a few of the words, but I still get left behind. We go inside to be served, and the cooks have spread a colorful little cloth over the table and made some flower arrangements for the centerpiece. I feel real bad about having uneasy thoughts about eating lunch here. The people have gone out of their way to make us feel comfortable.

Guess what's for lunch? How did you guess? Rice, sweet potatoes, beans, and that delicious cabbage/collards concoction. I'm really getting to where I'm enjoying it. It beats a can of tuna, and there's always more than enough. I get up from the table stuffed.

By late afternoon, after our visits, we're on our way back to the village, when a man coming down the trail stops us, and from his gestures, I get the gist of his conversation with the Africans. He points toward the mountain, says, "Bang, bang!" and grabs his thigh.

After he has gone Emanuel translates: "The soldiers caught a Montagne (rebel) in the mountains this morning and chased him through the banana groves and fired at him. He got away, but they caught him again, hiding in a hut, and when he tried to run, they shot him in the thigh." So the rebels have infiltrated this far south, even if only two or three at a time.

This afternoon, we decide that because the Kyuga church is so small, we'll head back to Jari for the afternoon service. Even though I can't see the village from here, we're actually standing at the base of Jari mountain, and right up there to my right, only a couple of miles, is Jari.

We're going to walk back down to the highway, which is a good two and a half miles, to catch a taxi another three or four miles to Jari. Some of the group are just going to climb the mountain, and I tell Emanuel we can all do it. He casts a glance over at Jeanette and shakes his head. After all the walking we've done, I can't see the big deal about walking another two miles up a mountain, but I don't argue. Maybe he's tired and doesn't feel like walking it himself. Actually, Jeanette tripped on the trail a while ago and twisted her ankle. He's probably just concerned for her.

For some reason, we don't stick to the road we walked in on, but take a path that skirts the base of the mountain. After a short while, we come to a deep ravine with a gushing little stream at the bottom. We have to cross over on a log footbridge. Jeanette has acrophobia, and I can tell she's not real happy with the idea. Jean Marie goes over first, stumbles, and nearly falls, but he catches his balance like a tight-wire walker, and continues on over. Several others go over without incident; then, it's our turn. The log is so narrow, there's no way we can go over together, so I go right behind Jeanette to hold her hand, and give her a little comfort. We both go over without either of us falling into the ravine. Just beyond the bridge, the others say, "Mwiriway," and strike off up a trail that seems to go straight up the mountain, no switchback at all. I can see, now, Emanuel's apprehension at our trying it.

When we get close to the highway, Emanuel deposits us at the house of a friend and goes on out to the highway to try to stop a taxi. It's a real nice house with real furniture. I wait outside with what's left of the group, and the woman who lives here asks Jeanette to come in for a cold drink of water and to look at some photographs of other missionaries who have visited her. Her husband is at work at a factory down the highway. He's one of the few who has a real job which pays real wages. That explains the fine house with real furniture.

After about an hour Emanuel returns with a taxi. A taxi over here is actually a van with four rows of seats. We all crowd into it and start off up the road toward Jari.

Primitiva, a pretty little teenage girl who has been with us since Monday, starts to sing the crusade song, and right away, the whole group joins in. Before long, the van is rocking from side to side, and people we pass turn to see what all of the commotion is about. Hearing the words, they grin and wave. Today, as we approach the church, the racket is not coming from there. It's coming from us. Those who walked up the path have been waiting for us in the church and hearing the racket, they all come pouring out, clapping their hands, and grinning.

We ask the driver and fare collector if they'll come back for us at five, since Marvin can't pick us up this afternoon. The driver shrugs and says they'll just wait for us. Of course, we invite them to come in for the service, and they accept.

I've prepared a goodbye message for them, since this is the last day we'll be working with Innocent and the Jari group. Tomorrow, we go to Masoro to work with Pastor Denys Rutayigirwa.

My message is about planting seeds and the work that needs to be done after the seeds are planted. I use Jesus' illustration of the farmer who sowed his seeds and some fell on stony ground, some fell on the side of the path, some among the thorn bushes, and some on good, fertile ground. Of course, my point is that we've had a good time together planting the seed, but now, we must move on, and it's up to them to take care of the harvest. It's a sad time for me. It's a message that comes straight from my heart, and I believe, for the first time, I'm really delivering a sermon.

Innocent is beside himself with joy. The chief of Jari district is visiting in the service this afternoon. This is such an honor for him and the little church, to have such a distinguished visitor present.

When I give the invitation, several come forward to receive Jesus, including the two taxi drivers and, to everybody's joy, the chief comes forward, the big Umwami himself. After he has prayed the prayer and asked Jesus to be Lord of his life, he turns and addresses Jeanette and me. He tells us how glad he is that we have come to Jari to witness to his people and thanks us for what we are doing with the African people.

We have brought along a few of the Kinyarwanda Bibles, and on the spur of the moment, Jeanette and I decide to make a little ceremony to present him with one of them. Innocent is so pleased, I'm thinking he's going to be raptured right here on the spot. He's jumping up and down from one foot to the other, shouting "hadaduya, hadaduya!" When the chief has had his say, we present the church with the rest of the Bibles and explain to them that we couldn't carry all of them with us, but that Innocent will have more to distribute later. They end the service by giving us a couple of going away presents which consist mostly of Bible verses. We mark them and annotate them as gifts from Jari, and now every time we read them, we will remember our friends here. They have little other to give us, but one of the gifts they give us is two of the little round grass rings they put on their heads to carry their loads. One of the women has made them especially for us. They are worth nothing, of course, but I wouldn't sell them for a thousand dollars apiece.

As we pull away in the taxi, they walk along beside to the outskirts of the village, and I realize we won't see most of them again this side of heaven. It's a quiet, thoughtful ride back down the mountain.

The security at the river has been beefed up considerably, and now French soldiers are checking papers. It takes us a good five minutes to cross the bridge. Refugees are everywhere. We have been told that right outside of Kigali, the government has set up a refugee camp for nine hundred thousand refugees. As I have said, they are coming out of the north with only what they can carry on their heads.

Jeanette and I decide to have spaghetti bolognaise at the restaurant again tonight. When we get back to our room and crawl into our separate bunks, in my drowsiness I hear Jeanette say, "I'm afraid. Every time I close my eyes, I see rebels breaking into the compound and finding us here. Can I get in bed with you?" We spend the night coiled tightly together with tightly coiled muscles. It was a long, fearful night.

THURSDAY, FEBRUARY 18

Masoro is in the other direction from the Jari district. It's east of town, out by the airport.

We have told Marvin that we will take a taxi this morning. Catching a taxi in Africa isn't like catching a taxi in America or Europe. You don't just pick up the phone and say pick me up at such and such address. We have to walk the four or five blocks from the mission to the depot, find a taxi that is going in our direction, take a seat, and then wait until they have a full load. Full load means at least eighteen people or more, and they don't depart until they have a full load.

While we are waiting, a young man near Jeanette seems fascinated by her, and just keeps staring at her. Finally, she smiles, and not being able to talk to him, hands him one of her testimonies. He reads it through and then starts trying to talk to her in Kinyarwanda. She calls back to Emanuel, who is in the back of the taxi, to talk to the fellow. The young man, figuring out that Emanuel is with us, gets out of the van and walks back to where he can talk to Emanuel through the window. Going over the testimony with him through the window, Emanuel leads this young man to Christ before we leave the depot.

Even though it's only five or six miles out to Masoro, it's a very long trip. Not only are there eighteen people in this van, they all have enough luggage to fill the forward cargo bin of a 727. I love Africa and its people, but if the deodorant industry had to depend on them to stay in business, well, there wouldn't be a deodorant industry.

After making a good dozen stops, the van finally comes to our stop, and we climb over the other passengers to get out. An elderly woman who has come this far also gets out, squats right beside the van and relieves herself. Jeanette and I seem to be the only ones who notice, and we try not to.

On our right, up the hill about two miles, is the airport; and on the other side of the highway, across the only level field I've see in Rwanda, and up the hill, is Masoro. Emanuel points to a small brick building at the top, and says, "There's Masoro church."

It's built on the same order as the church at Shyrongi, and by the same people from Maryland. It's a roomy little church with big double doors in front and two small doors on the sides. I would guess it could seat about one hundred people, well packed. Because we had to wait so long at the taxi depot, all the church members are already there, singing the crusade chant and beating the drums. I'm used to the sound now, and it doesn't scare me. Denys has about six who are going out with us. We move up the hill toward the village of Masoro, and my first impression is that this is a much more prosperous area than Jari, and much, much less remote than the mountains behind Shyrongi.

The village consists of a main street with about twenty to twenty-five houses on both sides, and a small store that sells fresh vegetables and Fanta. Fanta is the soft drink of Rwanda. It comes in citrus and tropical fruit flavors.

The houses here in Masoro are mostly square with either tin or wood shingle roofs. We stop in the front room of one of the houses. The family who lives here already has eight to ten people seated on the dirt floor or on grass mats all along the walls. They have been waiting for us to show up.

We go through our testimonies and about half way through the record, two or three more come in, so we read the testimonies again. I can't say how many decisions are made here... several. Before we are finished, the ones who made the decisions get up and leave, and a whole new group files in and sits against the walls. We go over everything again, and before we finish with this bunch, still more come in.

One woman comes in, makes her way past several others, finds a place against a wall, and sits down. As it turns out, she wasn't invited. While she was passing by on the road, she saw all of the people coming and going and came in to see what all the commotion was about.

As I am doing the speaking, Jeanette is just watching the reactions of the people, and this uninvited guest asks Emanuel, "Why is she staring at us?"

Emanuel translates for Jeanette, who just smiles and says, "I want to memorize your faces, so that when we meet again in heaven, I'll remember you."

There are more decisions made at this meeting than we've had at any one place since we got here, and Jeanette has made a friend for life.

We stay so long in this one place that we are only able to make a couple more visits before it's time to stop for lunch. Today's lunch is at the home of one of the deacons, and it's basically the same, except that here, we have a few chunks of very tough stew meat, some fresh avocados, and mangos.

As we are sitting here waiting for the food to come in, I'm humming the crusade chant to myself. It's been going through my head all morning. I've even gotten a couple of the words now. At least, what I think they sound like. Emanuel laughs at me and makes a little joke about my trying to sing in Kinyarwanda, then he writes the words down on a scrap of paper. He and Denys get a big kick out of trying to teach us to sing it. After lunch, as we climb the mountain for our afternoon visits, I practice the song to myself.

From the top of the mountain, we can see the airport to the east, Kigali to the south, and Jari Mountain in the distance to the north. We stop on the trail to watch some men building a house. It is an unprecedented house for this area. It has to be close to a thousand square feet with windows, vigas, and a tile roof. It reminds me of some of the adobe homes in New Mexico. Denys tells us it belongs to a very rich man.

On our way back down the mountain, we stop at a home just outside of the village, and it, too, is a nice house. We go into the front room, and they actually have a couch and two or three chairs, a nice dinner table, and a battery-powered radio. The young woman here is polite to us, but seems nervous to have us here. She says her husband, who is at work, is Catholic and wouldn't want us here talking about religion. We try to explain that we are not here to change their religion; we just want to talk to them about the gift of salvation that Jesus has to offer. We ask her if she has ever accepted Him as her personal savior. She won't answer or make any commitment, but says if we want to come back when her husband is home, we are welcome. Denys tells her that he will come back to talk to her husband and then invites them to come to the service this afternoon. As we leave, I have a sad, empty feeling. I feel that even though she says they belong to the Catholic Church, she has never made a commitment to accept Jesus as her Lord and savior. It distresses me. I can't help thinking, the more affluent people are, whether they live in America or Africa, the less they are willing to listen and accept; the more impoverished they are, the more they want to hear and know that there is a God who loves them. In my mind, I compare this home with the crippled old chief at Jari. I remember the light of joy that came into his eyes, and now I see nothing but fear and doubt in hers.

We arrive back at the church about an hour late, but it doesn't really matter, we're on African time. When they start to sing the crusade song, I sing right out and take everybody by surprise. I've nearly even got the African shuffle down.

The first forty-five minutes of any African service is taken up in singing, and even though we're getting started an hour late, today is no exception. I get the biggest kick out of the children's choir. The missionaries in Kigali have given them Royal Ambassador T shirts, so they are all in uniform. The little drummer is so good and has such rhythm, I can't believe it. Their leader is about ten, but he directs the music like a professional. He has to have been taught by a real music director at some point.

It's close to six by the time I finish my message and give the invitation, and we all start trudging down the path to the highway. Most of the trails we've been on have been through banana fields or thick tropical forest, but this one is so overgrown with jungle, that we're walking through a living green tunnel. We can't see past the canopy on either side or the top, and the sun filters down in shadowy green strips.

When we get to the highway, we're just hoping that a taxi will come past that we can flag down. We don't have to wait too long before a sure enough regular sedan taxi cab comes by. It's the first one I'v seen since we've been here.

There are so many of us, Jeanette has to sit in my lap in the front seat with the cab driver and Emanuel. In the back, they are so crowded they can't get the door closed. They try twice, and then Denys has to lie across the others until they get it shut. They all seem to squirm around until everybody is more or less sitting. We laugh and talk until we get to where we let Denys and a couple of others out. All this time, the driver has been very quiet and has not joined into our conversation. Now Emanuel speaks to him, and almost reluctantly, he tells a chilling story. As he speaks, Emanuel interprets.

"This morning, early, I took someone to Byungo, in the north, to see if their family is alright. Because of the fighting, you know. I was apprehensive, but the fare was so good, I couldn't refuse. After I let them off, on the way back, I was captured by the montagne, and they took me to an empty field and made me get on my knees. They pointed a gun at my head and told me they were going to kill me. I was very frightened. After a while, they talked among themselves, and for some reason they let me go. They told me to return to Kigali. They said for me to tell everyone that they will be in Kigali in a day or two, and then they will kill me and many others."

We have heard many stories of atrocities being committed both by the rebels and the government troops, stories of mass killings, rape, torture, all the bad things that go with war. I've never been in a war situation before, and while I have to admit there's a certain excitement about it, I'm beginning to be a little afraid. It's getting too close.

Emanuel wants us to meet a British couple he is doing some translation work for before it gets full dark, so we pay the cab driver quickly and leave without witnessing to him or even giving him a testimony. After he has pulled away, I could kick myself for this missed opportunity. After all he has gone through today, he needed to be told that God loves him and has a plan for his life. No doubt, God sent him to us today, and we dropped the ball.

We have a nice visit with the couple, and enjoy a bottle of cool filtered water while they tell us about their work in Kigali. Afterward, we tell Emanuel goodnight and walk back to the compound. By the time we get there, it's full dark, and the compound gates have been locked, so we have to call for the guard to let us in. Since it is Thursday, Celestine isn't here, and it's someone we don't know, but he knows us and has been expecting us.

The week's activities are wearing on us, so we nibble on our tuna and fruit and fall into bed exhausted. As I drop off to sleep, I think, *my morning coffee and quiet time won't be the same without Celestine to share it.*

FRIDAY, FEBRUARY 19

This morning, I get up dancing through the guesthouse and singing, "Izere Umwame Yesu numumbona urakira" (Believe in the Lord Jesus and you will be saved). Jeanette gives me a strange look and says, "What's gotten into you this morning?"

"I've got the spirit!" I call back from the kitchen.

"You mean the Holy Spirit?" she asks.

"No," I say, "I've had the Holy Spirit since we got here. This is just the spirit of Africa."

She doesn't feel well this morning, so I convince her to stay in bed and rest. I'm sure it's nothing but exhaustion.

I make myself a cup of coffee and go out for my early morning ritual, and guess who's there waiting for me. You guessed it, Celestine. He has decided to go with us today, even though Masoro isn't in his district. He must have had to rise and start down the mountain well before light to be here this early. I nod and smile, and he nods and smiles, as we lean with our elbows on the wall, and watch Kigali wake up.

The three of us, Celestine, Emanuel and me, walk down to the taxi park and, surprisingly, only have to wait a few minutes before we get a full load and leave.

When we get into the village and walk past the house where we spent so much time yesterday, and where so many people made decisions, I notice that one of Jeanette's testimonies is tacked to the front door. I call it to Emanuel's attention, and he smiles and nods. I have a really good feeling about this. I know this is the home of one of the church members, but still, it's like a sign saying, "Something great happened here yesterday." As we continue on up the road, I notice several people stopping to read it and I know that something great is going to continue to happen here.

Denys has decided to go to the other side of the mountain today, so we have another day of walking ahead of us. It's just as well Jeanette stayed behind, as tired as she is. The sun is hot, and it's humid, and by mid-day, I'm thinking I also need a day's rest.

High up on the mountain, we come to where three different men are building another house. In contrast to the one yesterday, this is going to be a typical African mud hut. They have dug a trench around the perimeter and have laid small logs in the ditch. From what I can gather, they will tie upright poles to these, lace them with saplings, and then wattle the whole thing, using cow dung, water and mud as a plaster -- adequate, but not very sturdy. This is probably going to be the home of a young man who is about to marry and, of course, this is where he will raise his family. When he gets enough kids and some of them get big, they'll build another one next to it.

On this side of the mountain there are several small farms fairly close together. It is considered part of Masoro prefecture, but it's really a small community in its own right. Denys explains that the house we are going to belongs to one of his "disciples," and that he hopes to start a new church here. When we get there, they must have the whole community assembled, and what we have is really a small service out in the yard. I tell them about myself and what we are doing in Rwanda, and then I play one of the records and give an invitation for anyone who wants to make their decision public. Denys is very pleased because he sees this as the nucleus for the new church.

We eat our normal lunch in the same deacon's house as yesterday. Vanese, Denys' wife, has come out from town to have lunch with us. She is a very attractive, well dressed woman. I'm a terrible judge of age, especially women's ages, but she seems much younger than Denys. She has a job in Kigali, teaching French in the primary school. She is trying to learn English, but still needs Emanuel to really communicate what she is saying.

This afternoon we come in late, as usual, and as we drag our exhausted bodies down the mountain, we can hear the singing and dancing coming from the church. It's funny. At the beginning of the crusade when I heard this, it frightened me; now it's a welcoming sound. If a person has a problem with being "charismatic," they won't like African church. As for me, church in heaven will be African church.

Jeanette and the Ogles have driven up from the mission for the service this afternoon. I'm glad to see that Jeanette is feeling better.

We straggle in past the people dancing in the aisles and take our place behind the little wooden table that is the podium. They continue to sing for about another fifteen minutes before Denys stands up and raises his hands for quiet.

I didn't prepare a sermon for today. I was just too tired. I had planned to preach one of the ones I had prepared for Jari, but now that it's time to preach, it's so late I have decided to just give my personal testimony. When I get to the part about my cowboy days, everyone gets a big laugh out of the way Emanuel explains "cowboy." He lifts his shoulders so that his hands hang about hip high, like the movie cowboys when they're about to draw their pistols, and then he begins to strut around and swagger. It is really funny and everybody, including him, breaks up.

Jeanette has brought a battery powered tape recorder and sings a solo for them. I'm certain that some of them have never heard conventional church music before sung in a soprano voice. They seem enchanted by her singing, but then of course, Jeanette has that effect on American churches when she sings.

After our part of the service, Denys invites anyone who has an illness to come forward for special prayer, and a dozen or so come to the front. One of the people who comes down is a frail woman whom I recognize. She was with the group who made decisions in the house in the village yesterday, and her frail beauty impressed me. So many of the people here are sick from parasites in the water, malaria, and even AIDS. Of course, I don't know what this woman's problem is, but when Denys starts to pray, I feel led by the Holy Spirit to walk down and place my hand on her head. I wish I had the faith to shout, "In the name of Jesus, be healed!" But I'm not that bold. I've come a long way in my walk with Him, but I have a long way to go.

It is late by the time we take Denys home and get back to the compound so, again, we have to honk to be let in. All we want is to go to bed.

SATURDAY, FEBRUARY 20

Today as we walk through the hills around Masoro, we can look over and see the airport. There is much military activity. French military planes are landing every thirty minutes or so, and we can tell that something big is happening. Over here at Masoro, we've been somewhat removed from the presence of war, or maybe I should say, the awareness of war; but now, seeing the planes, we are reminded that we are in a country at war. All day, as we visit, we watch the airport, wondering.

This afternoon I give my message, and Emanuel keeps up a rapid fire interpretation. I don't even have to pause to let him catch up now. We have become a good team, but we are worn out. When I'm through, I turn the service over to Denys. He begins to speak to the congregation in Kinyarwanda, and without thinking Emanuel stands up beside him and starts interpreting into English, which the congregation can't understand. Someone in the congregation starts to giggle, and before long, we're all laughing.

Celestine reports to us that the chief of Jari sends his greetings and wants us to know that he is going to have Innocent start a Bible study for the children. I know that because he is the chief, attendance will be mandatory. It wouldn't have to be, though; the children will love it.

We have brought a tambourine and a dozen Bibles to present to the church, and they have some gifts for us. They give us a grass sleeping mat, and then the little drummer from the children's choir comes up and gives us his goat skin drum and another of their instruments that is nothing more than a cooking-oil can with holes punched in it and filled with pebbles. It's crude, but when they shake it, it adds to the rhythm of the drum.

Then the woman who asked Jeanette why she was looking at her comes forward and places two hen eggs in a small paper bag on the alter and points at Jeanette. It's a good thing neither Jeanette nor I are required to speak at this time because neither of us is able to say a word. All I can do is try to swallow this lump in my throat and nod my head in appreciation. I look over at Jeanette, and her eyes are brimming with tears. It's a very emotional time for all of us. We'll see some of them again tomorrow, but we know that our time with them is coming to an end. I have mixed feelings. I'm tired, and I want to see my grandbabies, but I know the work isn't finished. I'm afraid because of the war, but I don't really want to leave.

On our way back to Kigali, we turn north to take Celestine and Primitiva down to the river. It'll cut about a half hour off their walk back to Jari. We pass several troop trucks filled with French troops and a couple of trucks pulling mounted howitzers. We've become used to seeing Rwandan troops around town, but this is the most military activity we've seen since we've been here. At the bridge, French and Rwandan troops have dug in on the hillsides above the river, and we can see machine gun nests all over the place. When we get back, Larry Randolph, the Baptist missionary, has called a staff meeting and invites us to attend. Since we are Americans, he thinks we should hear what he has to say. He has spent most of the day in a meeting with the American Ambassador. Conditions are critical. The Ambassador hasn't come right out and ordered all Americans out of Rwanda, but he has pulled all of the Peace Corps volunteers out of the countryside to be ready for evacuation on a moment's notice. Larry advises the Ogles that the decision to stay or leave is theirs at this point, but the Ambassador has asked that all non-essential personnel volunteer to leave. The Rwandan army cannot keep the rebels out of Kigali. The French have been called in to secure the airport and a corridor from Kigali to the airport in case evacuation of non-Rwandans is necessary. The rebels are better armed than the Rwandans. Someone is backing them. Someone big. The general opinion is it might be Kadafi or even Iraq. They are within fifteen kilometers of Kigali now. That's only about seven miles or so. If they decide to take Kigali, it's theirs.

We go to bed with stones in our stomachs tonight and neither of us sleeps well. I'm listening all night for firing or the sound of heavy equipment moving across the river.

SUNDAY, FEBRUARY 21

It seems like a month since last Sunday. So much has happened. It seems like I've lived a whole lifetime in one week. I dreamed last night that the compound was being overrun by soldiers firing and blowing up everything. I keep seeing Emanuel, Angela, and their two little boys out on the highway with a thousand other homeless refugees trying to make the safety of Tanzania. I'm relieved when he shows up this morning with that big white smile of his. Black people have such great smiles.

No visiting at Masoro today, just a church service and dinner at Denys' house. Mrs. Randolph has decided to come to Masoro with us to hear me preach, so she drives us out. My message is one of encouragement again, like at Jari. I tell them what a great joy and privilege it has been for us to come and work with them, but that they must now finish the work that we've begun together by themselves. Several times I have to stop and get a grip on my emotions.

After the service is over, the people mob us wanting to hug us and say goodbye. Of course, we can't understand what they are saying, and Emanuel can't interpret because everyone is speaking at once. The woman who gave Jeanette the eggs comes up and takes both of her hands, and they share a silent communication of love. There are lots of tears this afternoon, theirs and ours. As we drive away, Mrs. Randolph tells me what a great message it was. Do you think I've become a preacher? No, the Holy Spirit has used two willing subjects to spread the Gospel; what a privilege and blessing.

Dinner is very nice. Denys and Vanese, Emanuel and Angela, and Mrs. Randolph share it with us. It's not the normal fare. Vanese has cooked some beef that's not near as tough as that up in the mountains. We have fresh fruit and vegetables and an omelet made from Jeanette's two eggs. Knowing that this is the last time we'll be with them makes it bittersweet.

This afternoon we are having our rally. The other teams will be coming into Kigali out of the surrounding country with pastors and church members. They have been in the south working out of Butari and aren't even aware of the developing problems here. They are surprised at all of the troop activity around us. When we find out that the Flinchums haven't had lunch yet, Jeanette and I take them down to the café to drink a Fanta while they eat. Besides, we want to say goodbye to our little café.

Our rally is a good time together, sharing what we've experienced. We discover that over eight thousand seven hundred people have accepted Jesus into their lives because of the combined efforts of the crusade members. It's been a good week; one that will live in my memory for as long as I live.

Innocent and a few members of his church are now leaving, carrying loads of Bibles back to Jari. Jeanette is openly weeping now as they leave, hefting the boxes onto their heads for the very long trek down this mountain and up the next. She feels badly that they have to walk such a long distance carrying such a load in the dark. She has learned to love them very much. It's difficult to say goodbye.

Rodney Smith tells us in private that he has had a hard time over at Gitarama. His interpreter can't speak English very well, and Rodney has had a terrible time getting his message across. I have to laugh, though I know it's not funny to Rodney. I can't imagine doing this without a capable interpreter. I silently thank God once more for giving us Emanuel.

During the rally, Rodney's interpreter gets to feeling ill, although I think he's just embarrassed here with the other good interpreters, so I ask Emanuel if he'll help Rodney out.

It's past our normal bedtime. It's well after nine by now, but we're all sitting around the guest house, swapping stories and eating up the last of the tuna and canned fruit. This is the first time in a week some of the members have been able to sleep and eat inside a house. The Flinchums spent the entire week living in a tent. We had it good.

It's good to have them all back, and to know that everybody is safe. Only one member isn't back yet. Lewis, from Las Vegas, Nevada, has been over by Kibuye. This isn't in one of the battle areas, but we're still concerned. It's bad enough just to be out on the road after curfew. The Rwandan troops are on edge enough to shoot you and ask questions later. Before we get ready to turn in, he and his interpreter come in, obviously beat. They tell us how they were stopped and questioned at the river and then finally released. Rodney relates a similar story about himself and his interpreter.

MONDAY, FEBRUARY 22
Never in the thirty-five years that I've been traveling space available on the airlines have I had them call me at home to tell me that a particular flight was full, and that I wouldn't be able to get on, but Sabina Airlines called me here at the mission yesterday afternoon

to advise me not to come out to the airport to stand by. They say that we'll have to try to get out on Thursday. I can't wait until Thursday. Kigali may be in rebel hands by Thursday. The flights are all full, they tell me, because everyone is trying to get out of Kigali before it falls. I've convinced them to reroute me through Nairobi, so I have to go to the Sabina office today to get my tickets re-issued. They have tried to tell me that even if we do get on here, we'll be bumped in Nairobi. That's fine with us. Kenya's not in civil war.

Emanuel has shown up to go with us in case we need help talking to the Sabena agent, but as it turns out, she speaks excellent English. She is very cooperative, and we get our tickets straightened out without any further trouble.

When we get back to the compound, the teams have decided to go look over Kigali and do a little shopping. We've been here for more than a week, and nobody has done any sightseeing or shopping. That's okay. We came here to work, not to be tourists.

Our flight leaves here at nine tonight, and I can't enjoy sightseeing for worrying about having to stay here for--who knows how long. We have decided that if only one of us can get on, Jeanette will go and I will stay. It's not like I'd be here alone. The Randolphs and the Ogles will be here, and Rodney is not leaving until tomorrow. I know that my worries are unfounded. If Kigali does fall, the French army will make sure that all Americans and Europeans get out safely --- won't they?

It's dark now, and we're loading the van to go to the airport. I stop and go to the back wall to look out towards Jari. There are no lights to indicate that there's even a village up there. Everyone is in their huts, lying on their sleeping mats on the floor. Night comes early in the tropics, and once it gets dark, there's no reason to stay up. There's no TV. There's no electricity up there to run one, if you had it. I lift my hand in a silent farewell, and my heart fills with the love I feel for them. I repeat their names as I say goodbye: Innocent, Jean Claude, Jean Marie, Eugenia, Primitiva, Maurice. Then there are the nameless ones, the family who wanted the Bible so the father could teach his family about Jesus, the woman at Shyrongi who pleaded with Jeanette for a Bible of her own, the crippled chief. They all parade before my mind's eye as if saying goodbye themselves. Celestine is here, so I can tell him a personal goodbye. When we get to the airport, some of the Masoro group is here. They have walked the three or four miles up the hill and have been waiting for us to arrive. Denys, the big bear, gives us a hug.

As glad as I am to see them, I wish they hadn't come. I'm really worried for them. It's already past curfew. I want Denys to take some money for a taxi, but he refuses. Then Marvin says it's okay. He'll load them in the van and take them home. I feel a lot better and can enjoy having them here now.

After a time of prayer with all of them, we have to go into the passenger-only area, but the group doesn't leave. They stay out in the general waiting area and continue to pray for Jeanette and me to get on the plane because they know there is a very good possibility we will not get on. We spend the next agonizing hour waiting to see if either of us will get on. Just at nine o'clock, after everyone else has already boarded, the Sabena manager comes over and tells us there are two seats left, but they are only to Nairobi. I breathe a sigh of relief, and say a silent thank you to God. Then I have a pang of guilt as I remember the young lady who works in the mission office. Before we left, she came to us and said, "Please pray for us. We can't get on a plane and leave."

Our flight path takes us out right over Masoro, and Jeanette has her face pressed up against the window. I suspect she might be crying, but I don't say anything. I can't.

Well, it's past midnight now and we're out of Nairobi, winging our way to Brussels. We got off the plane at Nairobi, but we were re-boarded with the rest of the team. Tim Davis says he was never worried. He says he prayed about it, and he knows God has connections in high places. I'm sure glad of that, though I wondered at the time he said it, *who has higher connections than God? Maybe he just said it wrong.*

I unfold the paper that Jean Marie gave us on Sunday and read it again. I'll share it with you now:

"Dear Brethren, I am Rwililiza, Jean Marie Vianney. I am happy to give you my testimony. I was born in a nominal Christian family. I completed my primary school, after that I was charged to look after the flock of my parents. In that situation, I started to practice sins, but God was having a good plan for my life.

At 28 years old, I heard the message about salvation. Then I accepted Christ in my life. Satan didn't stop to tempt me. Then he caused me to suffer stomach problems. I went to the doctor. After being treated, he gave me an ordinance for my medicine, but the medicine was very expensive while I could not have money to buy them. I prayed for it. Then someone, prepared by the Lord, gave me it. After having used it, I became healed. Now I have three years feeling well. I healed also the knee problems. Therefore I praise the Lord for my miracles that the Lord did for me. I am the leader of the choir Urumuli (Light). The first choir of Jali. I am a single who praise God.

I want you to pray for me so that I must be strong in faith in the Lord, and may have opportunity to be married.

May God bless. I give you this scripture: Luke 21:36 and Collosions 3;12-17.

Good by."

I lay my head back and close my eyes. Goodbye, Jean Marie. Goodbye, Rwanda, my "land of a thousand hills." I love you.

In the Brussels airport, we sit at a table in the coffee shop and watch the sun come up. We have parted company here with the rest of the teams who have all headed home by different routes. I've told Eleazar Ziherambere, who is General Secretary of the Rwanda Baptist Union, that Jeanette and I want to be Emanuel's sponsors for seminary training. He says he'll look into what it will take and let us know.

Well, the adventure is over. I'm home now, home with family and normality. No more ten hour treks through lush tropical mountains. No more visiting folks in mud huts with grass roofs. No more war. Can I adjust to this? I wonder.

I haven't been able to get any news about the war over there. Americans don't know anything about a war in Rwanda. They don't even know where Rwanda is. When I tell them it's where the mountain gorillas live, they nod their heads. Most have seen the movie, *Gorillas in the Mist*, or read in *National Geographic* about Dianne Fosse's work.

There's not a day of my life that I don't think about my friends and pray for their safety. It's been three months now, and I still catch myself singing "Izere Umwami Yesu."

NOVEMBER, 1994

The news from Rwanda isn't good. After I wrote my last entry, I discovered that the rebels halted their advance where they were when we left. They were in negotiations with the Hutu government when the airplane carrying the presidents of Rwanda and Burundi crashed while landing at the Kigali airport. The Tutsi rebels were accused of shooting it down, and one of the worst genocides in recent times began. At this writing, close to one million people have been killed. Of my friends, I have heard that some of Pastor Denys' family was killed. Primitiva married Marcel, and then she and her baby died of typhoid in a refugee camp. Marcel was captured and beaten, but I understand that he escaped and is well. I have been told that Celestine and his family were killed, but I haven't been able to verify that.

Shortly after the killing started, Angela, Emanuel's wife, called to tell us that they were hiding out in the mountains and were afraid for their lives. We were able to help them get out of the country, and they are now safe and well at a Bible college in Mwanza, Tanzania. It was through them that we got news of the others.

If I'd known how it would all turn out, would I still have gone? You bet! I will never forget my beautiful Rwanda and the wonderful friends we made, and I thank God daily for all of those who accepted Jesus as their savior. I will see them all again someday, and we'll sing "Izere Umwami Yesu" t

CHAPTER 6
ONWARD AND UPWARD

MARCH 27, 1997: AN OPEN LETTER FROM JEANETTE TO
ALAMEDA BAPTIST CHURCH

Dear Church Family,

As some of you well know, for several years Ralph and I have said that upon retirement we would like to go to Africa as volunteer missionaries. Our future has arrived, although it is earlier than we anticipated. In January Ralph called me at work all excited. It seems that he was throwing away a bunch of old magazines from under the end table and ran across a Global Outreach newsletter. As he flipped it onto the pile to be thrown out, he saw an ad for a couple to come to Jinja, Uganda to relieve Wayne and Bonnie Sue Walker, the administrators of Good Shepherds Fold Children's Home. It seemed it had our name all over it. We immediately expressed our interest, even though we had not yet begun to think about retirement. We prayed fervently that if this particular opportunity was not of God, He would close the doors. The doors have not closed, and we have been approved for a six month to one-year appointment.

It is with great excitement and some fear and trembling that we have accepted, and we hope to be on the field by the first of June. After continued prayer, we strongly believe we are going to Jinja in obedience to God's leading. The orphanage presently has 106 children who range from toddlers to a thirteen year old girl. Just imagine being grandparents to 106 of God's precious little children and being able to share Christ's love with them! Wow!! We understand that 65 of the children have made professions of faith and desperately need to be discipled to help them grow in our Lord.

We realize that our strength and ability will only come from the Lord. The foundation of any effective ministry is prayer; therefore, we are asking you to consider being one of our "rope holders," a part of our prayer support team, as we launch out in this faith ministry. We estimate the cost of our living in Uganda will be $800.00 per month. If the Lord lays it upon your heart to support us financially as well as prayerfully, please make checks payable to Global Outreach. They will be handling our finances for us while we are in Africa, and one hundred percent of your gift goes directly to support our ministry; nothing is taken out for administrative costs. We understand that as our needs are presented and people respond under the leadership of God, our needs will be met according to his will. A monthly gift would be helpful, but a one-time gift would be a tremendous blessing and help us as well. We sincerely believe, as did Corrie ten Boom, "I'd (we'd) rather have a dollar which the Lord directs you to give than a thousand which he hasn't." Any such gift will be much appreciated, and all gifts are tax deductible.

We have selected you for this request because we know you to be mission-minded Christians and longtime friends. May the Lord bless you abundantly as you join us in this exciting ministry for Him in a third world country. As we go, we remind ourselves of Joshua 1:19: "Be strong and courageous. Do not be terrified; do not be discouraged, for the Lord your God will be with you wherever you go."

In His grace,

Jeanette

MAY 1, 1997

Today is the first day of the rest of my life. No more getting up at 3:00 AM to scrape frozen windshields. No more cancelled flights. No more irate passengers with damaged luggage. *I'm sorry ma'am.*

It looks like normal wear and tear to me.
Oh, I'm sure I'm going to miss some of it. No doubt I'll miss my friends, both those I work with and some of my "special" customers, but I'm ready for retirement. I've been ready for a couple of years now.

I'm looking forward to this new era of my life, working in the orphanage, perhaps doing a little writing, whatever the Lord has lined up for me.

MAY 24, 1997
We've been so busy trying to get ready to go, I don't know if I'm enjoying retirement or not. We've had luggage to buy, shots to take, preparations to make concerning the house and car, and trying to see everyone one last time before we leave.

I knew saying goodbye to the kids and grandkids would be hard. Everyone had held up pretty well, including our three year old grandson, Tyler. When we hugged and kissed him goodbye he looked at his mom with damp eyes and trembling chin, but he was holding it in. Then as we started down the jet-way, we could hear him screaming, "Papa, Lala," and sobbing so loud, we could hear him even after we boarded the airplane. Of course, we were also crying. As we went into the airplane, the flight attendant who could hear him as well, put her arms around us and started crying, too. She didn't even know what she was crying about until we told her we were on our way to Africa to run an orphanage. Then we all three stood in the galley and everyone in first class had a good old cry as we listened to Tyler's broken hearted wailing.

Saying goodbye to Greg, Heather and Eric, our kids out in California was hard, but they were more excited about our going than they were sad. Saying goodbye to Justin, Mason and Randi our grandkids out there, was much harder.

We have decided that we can't make it out of here on the 28th, as planned. There are just too many loose ends to tie up. We are now shooting for June 5th. I just hope we can change our hotel reservations in Cairo without losing any money.

MAY 29,1997

We packed our suitcases today, and leaving my chest-of-drawers and closet almost empty finally makes it feel real. We've spent so much time "getting ready," it was beginning to feel as if we were just going through some kind of drill.

We're going to have to buy another Rubbermaid Rough-Tote for the orphanage stuff. We've had so much in the way of toys and clothes donated, we can't get it all in the luggage we have. I'm afraid we're going to have beau-coup excess baggage now.

JUNE 3, 1997

One day and a wake up, as they say in the army.

Jeanette and I are about to drive each other nuts checking and double checking. I guess, whether we're ready or not, though, tomorrow we're out of here.

On Sunday, Pastor Jim preached a sermon from the first chapter of Jeremiah about being called out and consecrated. It was directed specifically at Jeanette and me. Then he brought us forward and called for a laying on of hands. Many of the congregation came up, laid their hands on our heads and prayed with us. It was a very meaningful service, and an emotional one. Our good friend Barbara Weaver came forward and read a poem she had written, then gave it to us.

It reads:

Our Call

Long ago in a naïve childhood,
I learned Africa was over there,
mysterious, frightening, far away,
 shadowed apparitions everywhere.
Whispering, "It's the dark continent."
See the map, "even skull shaped," they said.
Uncivilized, wild, wild things, huge snakes....
Shivering, I snuggled safely in bed.

93

As I grew, learned to read, listen, think,
the world inexplicably grew.
Africa, a real place, real people.
Realization!
Lord, you love them too!
No longer vague speculations,
demanding sights, sounds thrust in my life.
The need so great! The call so clear!
Lord, how can I help ease this pain and strife?
My dear friends, Lord, you wisely have chosen
to show your love, to carry the light.
One by one, the ageless method,
illuminating that hopeless night.
"Physically challenged children,"
politically, correctly we say.
You see them as beautiful children,
needing love on their difficult way.
You showed people your plan for helping,
called some to carry on your design.
We can all be part of your program;
prayer and love linking through space and time.
Their sacrifice will not be easy;
they rely much on love, faith and hope.
Jeanette and Ralph soon will be going,
But Lord, you've called us to hold the rope.

JUNE 4, 1997

Saying goodbye to Mom and our son Mark wasn't too hard. We were so rushed getting all the luggage checked in (without an excess baggage charge, I might add) that we didn't have time to drag it out. It's best that way, I think. Mark has been very positive through the whole thing, but before we boarded the airplane he pulled his mom aside and said, "You know, if it starts getting hot over there, I want you to promise me that you'll get out. Don't think about what will happen to the orphans. Remember the kids and grandkids you have over here." I guess he remembers how it was in Rwanda.

I was afraid of that; we didn't make either of the flights out of St. Louis to New York Kennedy, so we had to catch one into LaGuardia. You see, we were flying on an airline pass, space available. It wasn't too bad, though. Our luggage did catch the first flight into Kennedy so we didn't have the hassle of claiming them, carrying them out to the curb to catch Carey Limo and lugging them across town. The ride from LaGuardia to Kennedy was kind of pleasant. It gave us a chance to see some of New York besides the airport.

It's about 7:30PM. I'm sitting here in the nose of this Boeing 747 waiting for them to close the door and get us on our way. I'm so tired already, I can't imagine how tired I'll be after being up since 0 dark:30 and flying all night. Actually I can imagine it. I've done it enough times, and I remember all too well how tired I'll be.

They just loaded the galley, and I realize, also, that I'm starving to death. All I've had, since a taco in the St.Louis airport, is a nectarine.

First class isn't what it used to be in the glory days, but it's still great. Our menu tonight gives us a choice of either Chicken Marsala or salmon. I long for the good old days when TWA served buffalo steaks, shrimp cocktail, and a dessert tray that would put a fine restaurant to shame.

JUNE 5, 1997

I've hunted grizzly bears in Wyoming, shot the Rio Grande Box in an inner tube and ridden a Brahma bull in the Saturday night rodeo, but I've just decided that the most dangerous thing I've ever done is ride a taxi from the Cairo airport to the Oasis hotel.

To begin with, the Oasis is out by the pyramids, which is about 40 miles from the airport and our driver speaks not a word of English. All I know in Arabic is "la'a shokran, no thank you." That's what I should have said when they put us in this taxi.

Our route takes us right through the middle of Old Cairo, which is something to see. The road is four lane, then drops down to two lane through the city and goes back to four lane on the outskirts. On the four lane portion, the cars race along, five and sometimes six abreast, jockeying for position, the right of way belonging to the car with the loudest horn.

So here go the five cars, looking for all the world like the chariot race in Ben Hur, and right in the middle lane, there is a donkey-drawn wagon. The poor donkey (a tiny skeleton covered with a scabby hide) is trotting along, pulling a wagon filled with 50 gallon drums of something, trying valiantly to keep up with the traffic. All the while pedestrians are darting in between the cars, trying to cross the road.

Jeanette keeps looking at me with huge, terrified green eyes and squeezing the blood out of my hand.

Our driver has had to work his way over from the middle of traffic and stop at the curb five times. Once to pump up a flat tire with a hand-pump, and four times to ask for directions. At one point, we were so lost, we thought we were going to have to return to the airport, if the driver could find his way back, and start over.

We arrived at the airport at 3:45 this afternoon and were met by my friend G.R., who is the station manager here in Cairo. He did a super job getting us through customs with all of our luggage and putting it in storage for us. We left the airport at about 5:00 and have finally arrived at the Oasis grounds at 7:00. The hotel is very nice. Actually it's not a hotel at all; it is individual cottages, with mini-parks scattered all around, each with their own little fountain and pool. We had wanted to do a little sightseeing but we are so tired and our nerves are so frazzled, I think we'll take a nap until supper.

JUNE 6, 1997

After supper last night we went to the light and sound show out at the pyramids. It was interesting, but we were both so tired, we didn't really enjoy it.

The plan for today is to walk back over to the pyramids and do some exploring. This evening, we've been invited to have dinner with G.R. and his wife at their home; then he is going to take us back out to the airport and help us get checked in for a 3:15 AM flight, and another all-nighter down to Entebbe. We have come so far already, but really, we're just a little over half way to our destination, maybe two-thirds. We still have another 3,000 miles to go, straight up the Nile River.

Right now, I'm sitting at a little table in the park right outside of our cottage, watching a magpie bathe in the fountain. He's really getting with it. He completely submerges himself in the water, climbs out onto the rim to ruffle his feathers, and then plunges back in head first. I've never seen anyone or anything enjoy a bath so much. It's almost like he's doing it to entertain me. He's quite the clown and fun to watch.

It's noon now, and HOT. I think we're going to bag walking around in the desert and just sit by the pool and relax until time to go out to G.R.'s place.

Cooking Lunch

GSF Welcome

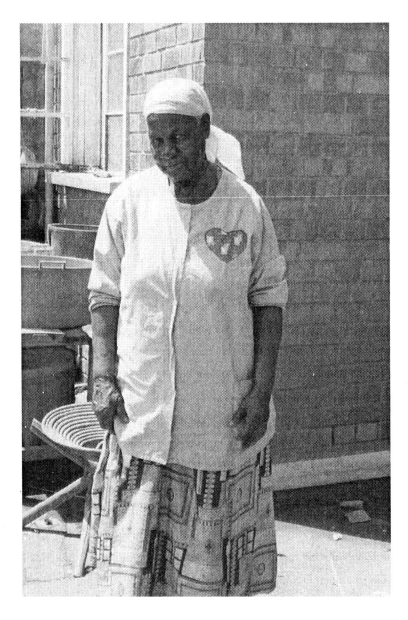

Jja Jja Mary

Faithie's Bad Hair Day

Outdoor Kitchen

Tall Mary

Field Day

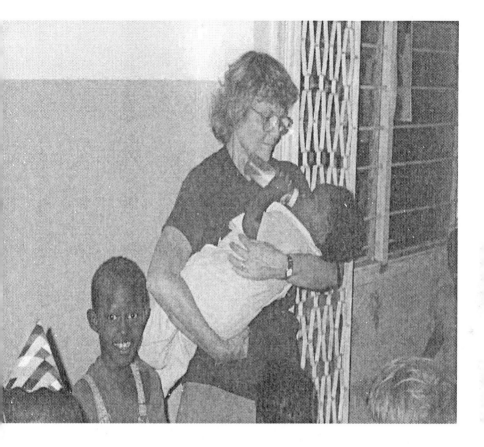

Jeanette with baby Michael

Jeanette giving vitamins

School Assembly

Charles as Aunti Jeanette

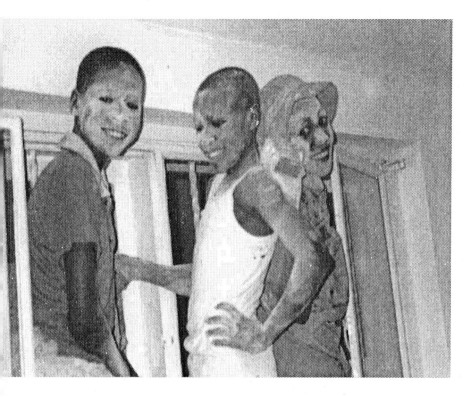

We're Wazungas

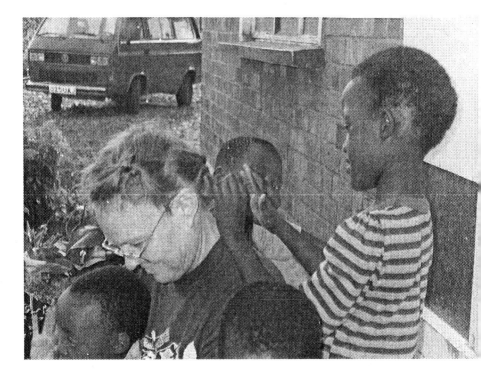

Playing in Jeanette's Hair

Ralph's birthday party

Snettles

Farewell party

Kagje under the bougainvillia

Children's village

CHAPTER 7
THE ULTIMATE CHALLENGE

SATURDAY, JUNE 7, 1997

As our plane drops through the clouds and begins its final descent to Entebbe airport, I gaze out the window at the enormous, incredibly beautiful lake below us, and a thousand thoughts race through my head. Foremost of these is the same old feeling of anxiety, inadequacy and fear that I had experienced in Rwanda. Again I ask myself, *What have you gotten yourself into now?* And then I reason with myself, *How bad can it be? After all, you've already gone through the culture shock in Rwanda. Africa's not new to you. You've seen both Africas.*

Kevin and Heather Van Pelt, our counterparts at the orphanage, have picked us up in front of the terminal. It seems they were not allowed into the customs area to help us get through the maze. It would have been helpful since they had been through it all just a couple of months before.

Clearing customs was no easy matter, either. In addition to our luggage, we had two big Rubbermaid Easy-Totes filled with donated clothes and toys for the children at the home. To assure that they made the trip without breaking open somewhere over the Atlantic, I fastened the lids down with screws and then taped them all around with strapping tape. I might as well have painted a sign on them, "Warning!!! Contraband!!!" The customs official asked me in Uganda English, which I hadn't gotten the hang of yet, "Wha 'tis in the boxes?"

I answered, "Oh, only some clothes and toys."

"New or old?"

"New."

He got a very perplexed look on his face, called over another official and in rapid-fire Uganda English, which I couldn't even begin to understand, conferred with her. After a few minutes, they decided that I must be bringing the stuff into the country to sell, since it was obviously not for my own use. At first, they thought that if I paid an astronomical duty on it that it would be okay. Then when I balked, told them the stuff wasn't even worth what they wanted to charge me, and that before I paid an amount like that, I'd just leave it there, they decided they better call in a supervisor. It had been nearly an hour in this stifling hot room. By now I was ready to just put it all back on the airplane and go home.

The supervisor finally came over to me and asked why we were carrying all of the new children's clothes and toys in our luggage. I took a couple of deep breaths to calm myself down, said a quick prayer and replied, "Sir, I'm going up to Wairaka to help run an orphanage. The toys and clothes are gifts from people back in the United States for the children of Good Shepherds Fold."

I waited for the inevitable shaking of the head and calling the Minister of Tourism, but he only smiled and asked, "Global Outreach?"

I could have kissed him! "Yes!!" I beamed.

He waved away the other two officials and said, "Have a nice day sir, sorry for the inconvenience."

By now, after an all night flight from Cairo and the hassle with customs, we are zombies again. As we drive the eighty kilometers from Entebbe to Jinja, the abject poverty and hopelessness of Africa begins to overwhelm me. I thought I wouldn't go through the culture shock this time, but I was wrong. As we pass the women walking along the road with their burdens on their heads, an mtoto (infant) strapped to their backs and a toddler in a ragged T-shirt holding each hand, I start to get a headache, my stomach begins to churn, and the old familiar chant starts running through my head, *what am I doing here? I can't do this!* Then my daughter's words return to me. "But Dad, aren't there people right there in Albuquerque who need saving. Why do you have to go to a place like Uganda to serve? Aren't they still in civil war there?" Well, there is still some fighting up around the

Sudan border, but it can't be called a civil war, and in all honesty, I know that Uganda has a very stable government for Africa.

The country is beautiful in its own tropical, backward, third world way and I have the mixed emotions of anxiety, pity and eagerness to do what we've come to do. Not that I'm at all sure what that might be.

As we drive between two massive rock pillars into the driveway of the orphanage compound, I see a large, old, two story, red brick home, run down to be sure, but impressive none the less. I guess at this point my spirits do raise a little. It really isn't all that bad. There seems to be about a half-acre front yard with several giant trees, some swing sets, and tied out in the grass there is a small grey donkey who raises his head and brays a welcome to us as we pass. *Hmmmm, I might like this place after all.*

Then we drive around the side into a courtyard, and there on the parking pad, between the main house and a small cement building, are over one hundred children of all ages and about a dozen African women waiting to greet us. Now, you might think this is a positive thing, and maybe it should be, but I am completely overwhelmed by the enormity of the job ahead of us.

I open the door to the Volkswagen van, step out into a huge mud puddle, and a stench like something dead engulfs me. I can feel the bile rise in my throat, and I pray, *God, please don't leave me. I need your strength right now. Please don't let me throw up here on my first day.* I look around at the smiling black faces surrounding me, and all I can feel is helplessness. I see a one-legged girl standing shyly away from the group with a crutch under her arm. I see a girl slumped over in a wheelchair with drool running down her chin and on the ground at my feet; there is a boy about fifteen years old, his deformed legs and left arm trailing behind him as he drags himself toward me with his one good arm. I want to jump back into the van and slam the door, but I look over at Jeanette and, although I see the helpless terror in her eyes, she flashes her most radiant smile and cries out, "Hello, we're so glad to be here with you. We're so looking forward to getting to know you all by name. My name is Jeanette, and it won't be long before I'll know all of your names." *My wife!!!* Once again I'm astounded at the strength of character in this woman that God has given me to be my partner through life.

At the end of the parking area, there is another cement building and on the porch there is a family of five or six and a woman with a couple of kids. Jeanette smiles and waves at them by raising her hand and closing her fingers to her palm quickly two or three times. The woman looks at her questioningly for a moment, then steps off the porch and comes to stand in front of her, waiting. Kevin laughs and Heather explains, "In Uganda, that's not a greeting, it means come here." We all get a laugh out of this and it seems to be a tension breaker.

Kevin picks up a couple of pieces of our luggage and says, "Come on, I'll show you where you'll be calling home for the next six months." He leads us over to the little cement building across the parking pad from the main house. It's about 30 feet long and is divided into 4 rooms. On the door in the center room there is a hand lettered sign, obviously made by the children, which reads, "May God bless Uncle Ralph and Aunt Jeanette. Welcome to Uganda."

He takes out a gigantic iron key, unlocks the door, then hands it to me. "You probably ought to keep it locked when you're not in there. I'm sure all of the staff are honest, but the children are very curious, and you don't want them pawing through you're stuff."

When we step inside the room and look around, I almost chuckle. If it wasn't so deflating, it would be comical.

Our new "home" is a cement cell about eight feet wide and ten feet long with a door on the front wall and a window on the back wall. I call it a cell because that's what it reminds me of, a monk's cell in a monastery.

Outside of our window, about 15 feet away, is the children's latrine. Today it is hot and steamy, and the aroma from the latrine drifts through the open window and fills the room.

On one of the side walls there are two wooden shelves about four feet long and six inches wide. On the opposite wall, there are eight or ten nails. There is no bathroom and, of course, the closet is the shelves and the eight nails. The furniture consists of an old iron bed with a four inch foam rubber pad on a sheet of plywood, a wicker chair, a bedside table, and a rattan bookcase with three shelves.

"Uh, where are the facilities?" I ask.

Kevin grins, "Well, during the day, you can use the bathroom in the main house, but at night we lock up the main house, so you'll have to use the one around back."

"Is that the latrine right outside our window?" I ask.

"No, come on, I'll show it to you."

We walk around to the back of the little building, side-stepping, or stepping over the mud where a drain pipe has broken, and at the end of the building, we come to a small room just big enough for one person to stand in, and in the middle of the floor there is a hole with flat rocks on either side. "African toilet," Kevin says.

"Yeah, I know," I nod. "We've used them in Rwanda." Someone has used this one recently and left their calling card on the standing-stones.

We continue on around to the back side of the building and discover another room about the same size only this one has an honest-to-goodness flush toilet. Of course, your knees would rub against the wall in front of you, if you were sitting on it, but you could sit on it and not just straddle a hole in the ground. At some point in history the cement walls were painted with white enamel, but now the red mud has streaked the walls in big rusty looking splotches, and there is a good-sized spider web behind the tank. There is probably no need to sweep it out. It would only reappear by nightfall. Not only that, I'm sure a resident spider keeps the mosquitoes down a little.

I look at Jeanette. Is she really going to come around here in the middle of the night to use this? She returns a rather queasy, frightened look. She hates spiders.

Added onto the building next to this commode room there is a mud brick lean-to. Inside, a water pipe runs up the wall to about head high, with a shower head attached to it.

The tin roof slants off of the building wall and extends about six feet to a wall that is around five and a half feet high. Since the roof is attached to the building about seven feet high, and slants down to this wall, I can stand here and look over the top, or someone could stand on the outside and look over. Of course, there's nothing to see on this side except the children's latrine, and most of the children are too short to see over it.

The door is made of three one by six planks nailed to two by fours placed in a Z pattern. I can see where it might give you some privacy but there are some pretty large gaps between each plank and it only reaches down to about knee high. A person could easily watch everything going on outside, or stand outside and watch everything going on inside.

Standing here looking around in the dim light, because there's no electric light out here, I shake my head. There's no way Jeanette is going to shower in here. First off, the walls are made of mud bricks that have never seen plaster or paint. Secondly, they are covered with very large mosquitoes, and there is a toad as big as a baseball cap enjoying the standing water on the floor. You see there is no drain, just a hole in the bottom of the front wall for the water to run out. That explains some of the mud we had to come through to get here. Third, since our room is on the other side of the building, we will have to enter the shower fully dressed, hang our clothes and towel on the nails in the wall and shower with them in the shower with us, then dry off with a damp towel, redress in damp clothes, pick our way past the outdoor kitchen, through the mud from the broken soil pipe and shower run-off, cross the parking pad, which is always filled with playing kids, and back to our room, shivering the whole way, I'm sure, from the cold shower.

Kevin reaches down and removes the jerry can someone has left there to catch the drip from the faucet. "We can get a hasp and a padlock," he says. "I've told the kids not to use this one, but ---."

"I don't guess there's any such thing as a lavatory around here?" I am trying to make light of it all, but I know my frustration is showing.

"There's one in the main house," Heather says. "That's what we use."

"And the main house is locked after dark," I add.

She just nods grimly.

Kevin says brightly, "Come on, and we'll show you the main house."

We had seen the main entrance with four wide steps leading up from the yard to the porch when we drove in, but we enter the house through the kitchen, just across the parking pad from our room. I guess here is as good a place as any to tell you the difference between the indoor kitchen and the outdoor kitchen. The indoor kitchen is pretty much a regular kitchen for a house this size. It contains a gas range (propane), a work table, and a double sink. This is where some of the kitchen staff prepares the formulas and special food for the babies, and where the dishes are washed, in cold water, of course. It is also where the medicines are stored and dispensed. In other words, it also serves as the clinic.

The outdoor kitchen is a large pole barn across from our bathroom and shower, where the food for the rest of the orphanage, including the staff, is prepared. It is also where hundreds of liters of water are boiled for twenty minutes every day for each day's use.

There are four wood-burning stoves out here, each one bubbling with something different. They are unique. I don't think I've ever seen any quite like them. Kevin says they are made of clay. They are round, with a hole in top where very large pot is placed over the fire, and there is a hole in the side near the bottom for the firewood.

We've only been here an hour or so, but the bulk of the activity seems to be either the outdoor kitchen or the parking pad right outside our door. This seems to be a favorite place to play jacks, jump rope, wash clothes, or just sit on our front step and hang out.

As we pass through the indoor kitchen, Heather introduces us to four women working there: Rita, Rebecca, Betty and Tall Mary. Tall Mary is just that, she's close to six feet; but Rebecca is tiny, very pretty, and ducks her head shyly when she's introduced. Rita is working over something cooking on the stove and says, "Your lunch will be ready in a few minutes." I try to smile appreciatively, but truthfully, I'm still a little queasy from the travel, and I'm not sure I can eat lunch.

Our little tour moves from the kitchen into a narrow foyer. The front door is on one side and a staircase to the second floor is across from it. All along the floor beside the staircase, and against the other wall on the floor are probably 15 straw baskets. "This is where the babies sleep," Heather explains.

Also against the wall, surrounded by the baskets, an African woman is sitting on a beat up old couch, holding a small child. "Rose," Heather says, "this is the Reaves." She doesn't have to explain who we are. Everybody in the compound has been expectantly awaiting us for over a week. Heather reaches over and feels the baby's head. "Rosie is very sick with malaria," she explains.

When we reach the top of the stairs, we turn right and go into a large bed room. The walls are lined with bunk beds, stacked three high. It looks to me like this would sleep around fifteen to eighteen kids. "This is the girl's room," Heather says proudly.

From there, we go across the hall to the boy's room, about the same size, also lined with triple-deck bunk beds. The smell of urine almost knocks me over when we enter. "Some of the smaller ones wet the bed at night," Kevin says. "We try to have them sleep on the foam pads on the floor. Then in the morning, we put the pads out on the veranda to air out."

"Do you ever try to hose them off?" Jeanette asks naively.

Kevin shakes his head and I can hear him thinking, *Boy, do you have a lot to learn.* But he just says, graciously, "No, we thought about it, but they'd never dry before night, and they'd be rags after three washings."

I look out on the veranda and see that they are not much more than rags now.

Between the girl's room and the boy's room is a smaller room with cribs for the older babies. Over each crib is mosquito netting, quite full of torn places big enough for the mosquitoes to get inside to the babies. There is a door in this room leading to a large veranda overlooking the front and side yards. The railing around the veranda has a mesh fence to keep them from falling two stories to the gournd. This is the babies domain and where they spend the majority of their day.

Rita yells up, "Your lunch is ready."

She and the other kitchen staff have laid out a beautiful lunch on the screened porch that looks out over the front yard. I don't know what some of it is, but it looks good. I recognize the rice and beans, of course, and the fresh fruits, but there is a bowl of some pale yellow vegetable cooked with tomatoes and onions that I don't recognize. "What is this?" I ask.

Rita beams, "That is the national food of Uganda, matoke, and I cook it better than anyone else in Uganda."

I'm able to eat a little even though I have no appetite, and she's right, the matoke is quite good.

"If you guys don't mind," Jeanette says, "I think we need to rest a while. This has been a little overwhelming."

Heather smiles, "Yes, by all means, go and get settled, take a nap, whatever. When dinner is ready you'll be able to hear the dinner bell." She points through the screen to a tree in the yard. There is an old car rim hanging from a limb, and hanging from that is a jack handle. I guess that's the dinner bell.

We have stacked our two big trunks against the wall at the foot of our bed. It gives us a small lane between the bed and the suitcases to walk, and there is a lane on either side of the bed about two feet wide. I look around and see that they have placed a grass sleeping mat on each side of the bed so that we don't have to walk on the bare cement floor, and there is a vase of flowers on the end table. Pretty curtains, which match the bedspread, flutter at the window. They have gone all out to make it homey and try to make us feel comfortable. Heather has told us that Big David, the oldest of the orphans here, and also the home's resident tailor, has made the curtains and the bed spread especially for our arrival.

I push back the mosquito netting on the bed, flop down and throw my forearm across my face. My eyes fill with tears, and run down the sides of my face. I just want to go home. I feel Jeanette sit down on her side of the bed, and in just a little bit I turn and glance at her. She has her face buried in her hands and is crying.

My mind just keeps repeating, *Please, Lord, I want to go home.*

Clang, clang, clang, clang!! I sit straight up in bed. I'm confused. *Where am I?* I don't know what time it is. It's still light out. *Oh, yeah,*

I remember now.

I go to the door and look out. There's a half-pint kid out there who can barely reach the wheel rim, whacking away at it with the tire iron. **Clang, clang, clang, clang!!**

"Must be suppertime," I say. "That's good. I'm finally hungry."

The kids are racing in from every corner of the compound. They grab a bowl, one of the kitchen staff ladles some beans and rice into it, and they race into the big dining room to sit down at one of the long tables. Some of them are eating with spoons, but most of the younger ones are just shoveling it in with their hands.

We get our plates and ladle on some beans and rice and sit at the little table on the porch. It's a pleasant evening and now that I've rested, I can see that the area is beautiful. It's very green ---- and red. The soil is as red as blood, and looking at the buildings and Jeanette's white tennis shoes, it stains anything it comes in contact with.

We can look across the valley in front of us and see Lake Victoria about a mile away. The valley is filled with little shambas (farms) with their fields of maize and beans, their banana, avocado, and mango trees. Ruben, the donkey, has laid down for the evening and Solomon, the pet crested crane, flaps his wings and soars to the top of the house to roost until morning. Except for the clamor in the dining room, it could be quite tranquil.

Kevin gets up and goes to the pantry and brings back an arm load of condiments. "Here," he says, "help yourself. It makes it a lot better." He pours chili powder on his beans and curry on his rice. I do the same. It does make it tastier.

When we have nearly finished, I glance up at the door to the main dining room and see two little girls, maybe eight or ten years old. They seem to be waiting expectantly, almost hovering. Heather scolds. "You girls go on now. You can come in after we leave."

"What's that all about?" Jeanette asks.

"Oh, they're supposed to take the dishes into the kitchen to be washed, and they get to finish up whatever is left in the bowls."

As we walk out, they rush in, and like starving little animals, they fight over the scraps in the bowls and on the plates. Kevin shakes his head. "It's not like they don't get enough to eat here. There just seems to be an inherent greed. I guess it's just their nature. They are so used to doing without and not having enough. They can't get used to not grabbing and scratching for every morsel."

It's about 11:30 PM now and I'm so exhausted, I'm shaky. We just finished sing time and putting the children to bed, and putting the children to bed, and putting the children to bed.

After supper, all of the kids either help in the kitchen cleaning up the dishes, or go out and "pick the compound." That means going over all of the area that is fenced, which is about an acre in size, to pick up all of the debris from the day. With 115 children, that can be considerable.

After that, between 7:30 and 8:00 PM, everybody goes into the main dining room for sing time. When I first heard it from our room, with the drum beat and typical African sound, it was very reminiscent of Rwanda. Once I was inside, however, with over 100 kids jumping up and down and yelling their songs at the top of their voices, it was more a deafening racket to my ears than music. It really began to get very hot and sweltering in the room, and I realized that Luka, our night watchman, had closed the windows tight against the mosquitoes and who knows what dangers the night might bring. To make things worse, the electricity had gone off, so we were using candles, or as they call them, paraffin torches. The heat, noise level and exhaustion were just about to do me in, so I went out onto the front porch to get some fresh air. While I was standing there, I noticed a movement out in the yard. When I looked closely, I saw that Luka was just standing out there by the big tree, listening. I called out to him, "Jambo, mzee (Hello, old man)." Even though he was a good 20 feet from me, and it was dark, I could see the big grin come over his ebony face. "Jambo, Bwana," he answered, and bowed with his arms held straight by his side.

Let me tell you the little that I've learned about Luka from Moses, one of the older boys. He is an Acholi warrior from up north; that's why he speaks Swahili. The Acholi are known for their height. Luka stands well over six feet tall. As Moses says, "They are very fierce warriors. Everyone is fearing them." Luka defends our compound at night with a homemade bow and arrows and a couple of short spears, yet with him out there, I feel very safe. I don't know everyone here yet, of course, but I know I'm going to like Luka.

SUNDAY, JUNE 8

What a terrible night! We were up half the night with little Rosie. She's the one who has such a terrible case of malaria. She was running a temperature of 104 all day yesterday and most of the night last night. When we put her to bed, we made the decision to take her to the clinic in Jinja this morning. Then, about 2 o'clock she went into convulsions, and we knew we should have done it yesterday afternoon. If this went into cerebral malaria it almost certainly would kill her, or at the very least, cause severe brain damage.

We bathed her with cool water, but her temperature just wouldn't budge. We knew if we were going to save her we would have to get immediate help, so we agreed that one of us should go up to the YWAM (Youth With a Mission) compound, wake the nurse who lives up there and ask her to come down and treat Rosie. She very graciously left her bed, rode down the hill with us, and gave Rosie a shot. By the time Rosie's temperature came down to a safe level and we took the nurse back to YWAM, it was close to 4 AM. It was a very short night.

If I was ready to go home yesterday, I'm doubly ready this morning. I truly don't have what it takes to do this.

The compound has been fairly sane this morning. Kevin and Heather loaded up the Volkswagen with ten or twelve of the kids, including four or five wheelchairs, and took them down into Wairaka to the Nazarene church. Some of the older ones walked up toward Wanyange to "Victor's Church." That leaves Jeanette and me with only the kitchen helpers and the babies, maybe twenty or so. Rosie is up playing with the other kids. I'm astounded at the resiliency of a four year old.

After church we took Rosie and Peace, another one of our toddlers, to the clinic. They gave Rosie another shot and told us she would have to have three more over the next three days to kill the malaria parasite in her blood. They gave us a syringe and the medicine, so that we don't have to bring her back into town every day. None of us has ever given a shot before. This should be fun, but I guess not for Rosie.

Since it was lunch time, and we were all hungry, including Rosie, we went to an Indian restaurant to eat. It was good, but I've never particularly liked Indian cuisine. Talk enchiladas and chile rellenos to me, though, and you have my undivided attention.

We have decided, since we're in town anyway, to take care of some other business we have. Jeanette and Heather have gone to Starcom, a small boxcar-like building, where we can send faxes and make long distance phone calls. We are unable to make long distance calls from the orphanage. We can receive them, if anyone happens to be near the little room that's called the office to hear the phone ring, but that's not likely. I'm not kidding; the noise level around the office is so bad you have to be right next to the phone to hear it. None of us like to stay in the office much. If you go in there, you have 25 little people lined up at the door begging for paper and pencils to draw, coloring books to color in, or just to look at the *National Geographic*. Not only that, but we don't normally have the luxury to just sit in the office. But I digress.

Kevin and I, and Philip, the orphanage handyman, have come to the open market to buy a few items for the kitchen. We'll do the main shopping later in the week.

I can't really describe the open market here, unless somehow I could make this paper scratch and sniff. It is much larger and more crowded than the Nanyuki market. There is an open trench that runs right through the middle of it with who knows what flowing in it. Whatever it is, the smell is about to turn my stomach. It's somewhere between human waste and rotting garbage. It's probably both.

There are hundreds of little stalls with everything from vegetables to clothes to hardware. Then there are the merchants who can't afford to rent a stall who just pile their wares on the ground in little pyramids: pyramids of tomatoes, potatoes, onions, avocados, mangos, papaya, hen's eggs and tiny dried fish laid out on newspaper. Toward the back of the market is the meat section. Here, the stalls have fly-encrusted goat carcasses, sides of beef, and live chickens hanging from the rafters. We go a little farther and come upon a man who is cooking something that looks like New Mexico Indian fry bread on a wok made from a scrap of oil drum, over an open fire.

Kevin asks Philip, "You want a chipâté?" Philip nods eagerly.

"None for me," I'm able to get out around the gorge in my throat. "I'm still full from lunch."

We buy a hundred kilo bag of rice and one of beans and hire a couple of men to carry them the two or three blocks to the Volkswagen for 100 Uganda shillings, or about a nickel apiece. Remember, a hundred kilos is around 220 pounds. They hoist them on their backs and take off at a trot behind Philip. Kevin and I go outside the market area to a hole-in-the-wall shop to buy some needed medicines for the orphanage, then collect the girls at Starcom and head down the pothole-filled, pedestrian and bicycle-clogged eight mile journey back to Good Shepherd's Fold. We have to go through the little villages of Bugembe, Wanyange, and Wairaka, and at each village we have to slow to a crawl for the people walking in or crossing the road. It takes us over a half hour to make the eight mile trip.

Supper time and guess what's on the menu. You've got it, beans and rice. Since we bought a hundred kilos each of beans and rice at the market today, I have a feeling it'll be beans and rice again tomorrow, and rice and beans day after tomorrow.

"When are we going to have some more of that matoke stuff?" I ask.

"We'll take the lorry in Tuesday and do the real shopping. We'll get a couple of stalks of matoke then."

"How often do 'we' have to do the real shopping?" I ask.

"We generally go in on Tuesdays and Fridays, unless, like today, we have to make a trip in for some other reason. We try to drive as little as possible. Gas is a little over $4.00 a gallon."

I'm so tired all I want to do is fall into bed with all of my clothes on. Putting the kids to bed tonight wasn't too bad. Of course, just like with any family, you put them down, and they need to go to the bathroom; then after they go to the bathroom, they need a drink of water. This means going all the way down to the kitchen for a drink. Take a normal family of 3.5 children, multiply that by about fifteen, and you have the experience of putting the boys down at GSF.

The overcrowding here hit me again tonight as I tucked all fifty-five of them in and read them a story. The smaller ones, five to ten years old, are sleeping three to a bunk. Some of the older boys, ten to twelve, sleep two to a bunk; the little guys under five, and there are about a dozen of them, sleep on the foam pads on the floor. The floor between the bunks is littered with little bodies. There is no open space. If somebody gets up during the night there's no way they can cross the room without stepping on someone.

Jeanette finds the same to be true in the girls' room. Sometimes, a few of the older girls will get the floor pads pulled out and covered with a sheet, but most of the time there is no sheet or piece of cloth to cover them. Also the big girls will occasionally help settle the handicapped and smaller girls in their beds or on their pads, but sometimes when she goes up to tuck them in none of the pads are even in sight, let alone prepared for sleeping. When she finally gets them all in their beds, two and three to a bed, sings them a song, or reads them a story, she will be worn out, comes back to the room and literally fall into the bed.

Tonight I push the mosquito net back, collapse onto the bed and take my shoes off. Jeanette looks pleadingly at me. "Would you get me a pan of water from the kitchen before they lock the house?"

We've figured out a way to get around the absence of a lavatory. We brush our teeth out in the yard with a bottle of filtered water, and for washing, we put a little plastic pan of water on top of our stacked trunks. If I'm lucky, I find a jerry can that's still warm from the boiling, and we don't have to wash with cold water. So far, we've gotten by with African baths; neither of us has gotten up the courage to take a shower.

MONDAY, JUNE 9
Brrrrrrrrr, now that's the way to wake yourself up in the morning.

Jeanette went into the house and took a warm bath, but I decided *there's no time like the present; if you've got to do it sometime, it might as well be now.* I thought once I got in, my body would become accustomed to the cold blast of water assaulting it. Not! By the time I was finished, and it didn't take me very long, I was a block of ice. I don't think I'll shower in the morning anymore. I'll wait until late afternoon when the outside temperature is hot and sticky. Even though we're on the equator here, we're also about 4,000 feet high, and the early mornings can be cool.

Jeanette told me that her indoor bath wasn't a fantastic experience, either. The water ran into the tub so slowly that she ended up bathing in about an inch of water. I think she has opted for the early morning cold shower now instead of the bath.

I did need the cold shower this morning, though. We didn't get much sleep again last night. Good old jet lag kicked in about 3:00 AM. We both woke up and lay there for a couple of hours, talking about throwing in the towel and going home at the end of the month when our visas expire. I don't look forward to telling Kevin and Heather. This is a hard job for four of us. I can't imagine how two do it alone, and yet, they've handled it by themselves for over a month now. I have very mixed feelings about it. I keep telling myself that I can't handle it, but I know I can. True, I can't do it in my own strength, but as Paul wrote, "In Christ Jesus, I can do all things." It won't be easy or comfortable, but I can do it.

TUESDAY, JUNE 10

I've spent most of the morning wandering around aimlessly. Jeanette has started going through the trunks to pull out a few new jump ropes for the girls and some balls for the boys. The kids are thrilled with the new toys we brought, but we have determined that we will not hand them all out at once. We'll give them out a few every week or so.

I want to look at the "swamp" problem and see if I can figure out a solution. If you'll remember, our first day here the smell nearly knocked me over as I stepped out of the van into a large puddle of mud. I've discovered the cause of both of these problems. The mud puddle is caused by the drain from the kitchen sink emptying into the yard right under the kitchen window and the run off from the kids washing their clothes on the cement pad. The lake flies swarm around the light on the eve of the house, die and fall into the standing water and rot. I don't believe anything smells any worse than dead flies.

After studying the situation, I believe a French drain, which is nothing more than a pit filled with gravel, will help. We'll have to dig a shallow trench from the edge of the cement pad over under the kitchen window, and then dig a drain-field out into the yard. Once we cover the gravel with plastic, then cover it all with dirt, you won't even know it's there.

Kevin and Philip have already started a ditch from the cesspool out into the yard. At some point before we all got here, the top caved in, so now it's just an open pit filled with sewage.

Another one of the projects he's got in mind is clearing out the storage barn and turning it and the adjoining goat shed into two more classrooms for the school. We have a primary school with classes from preschool through P7. At present, however, three classes are meeting in the dining room. It's very difficult for the teachers to teach when the teacher twenty feet away is also trying to teach in the same room.

WEDNESDAY, JUNE 11

It is *hot, hot, hot*, and it's supposed to be the rainy season, which is also supposed to be the cool season. It's probably only ninety degrees, but the humidity has to be at least eighty-five percent. I'm used to ninety degree temperatures, even one hundred plus, but I'm also used to only three percent humidity.

I feel so useless. There's so much to be done around here, and yet I feel as if we're no help, not yet anyway. We will try to get unpacked today, and then maybe we can settle in and begin to learn the routine.

THURSDAY, JUNE 12

Well, maybe I hit the ground running this morning. When I got up and went around front, Kevin and Philip were already drilling holes in two inch PVC pipe, for the drain-field. It felt good to pitch in and help. Finally, I felt like I might be doing something useful. We hand drilled about a hundred holes in each of five pipes. Since the pipes are ten foot lengths, that will give us a fifty foot drain field. After drilling the holes, we fitted them together, and then rammed the whole length through the dirt wall between the ditch and the cesspool. Hurrah, it drained without bursting out the side of the wall.

My hands are filthy, and I've got red dirt under my fingernails, but I haven't felt this good in a long time.

When the lunch bell rings, I come into the room to wash my hands before lunch. Jeanette is already in here washing. "What are we going to do about the kids?" she asks. She always assumes that I know exactly what she's thinking, and more than half the time, I do. This time, however, I don't have a clue.

"What about the kids?" I respond.

"They never wash before they eat. They just run from playing and eat with their filthy hands. It's no wonder they're always sick."

I nod. She's right. They never wash before eating. They don't really have adequate facilities. "How about if I build some kind of table that we can put several washbasins on?"

"Yes," she says, "and then we can form teams to fill jerry cans and keep fresh water in the basins. We'll make it a rule that no one is allowed to eat until they have washed, and we'll stand out there to help them wash and then dry their hands for them. We'll make it like a kind of game."

After lunch, I take a panga out of the tool room and go off into the forest. I am able to find four tall saplings whose trunks are about three inches in diameter. I have also found a long four-by-four and a couple of two-by-fours in the wood shed, and I'm able to build two long benches, waist high to most of our five or six year olds. They are uneven, and very rough, but they will serve the purpose. Each bench will hold four of the small plastic washbasins, so eight kids can wash at the same time. We will assign two of the bigger kids to each bench. One to haul jerry cans of fresh water, and the other to change dirty water for fresh.

Jeanette calls for everyone's attention during lunch and tells them that they won't be allowed to eat supper unless they wash first. Just like kids anywhere in the world, some grumble, and some think it sounds like fun.

Clang, clang, clang, clang!!!! That's the supper bell, and here comes the stampeding herd, only this time, I'm standing at the head of the serving table with my arms folded sternly. "Show me your hands," I demand. It just so happens that Secunde is the first in line and Kajuna is the second. Their hands are filthy. "No wash, no supper," I say. I have to send the first ten or so back for a wash before the word gets around that they won't be allowed in until they show me their clean hands. We even appoint some of the kids as monitors to help us check the hands.

Actually, it is a big hit with most of the kids, and they love the physical contact of us drying their hands for them. A couple of them even go through the wash line twice just to have the special attention. The only ones who complain are the ones who have to haul and change the water. They'll get used to it, and just like all of the other chores, we will work out a system of rotation so the same ones aren't stuck with it every day. Jeanette notices that Joshua is sitting on the front steps watching the whole process, but with no way to get down to the basins to wash. He, of all the kids, really could use a good hand washing, so she takes one of the basins up to him and washes his hands for him. It fills my heart with joy and love as I notice the big shy smile on his face as she washes and dries each hand.

FRIDAY THE 13TH

Jeanette has become very sick with a high fever and throwing up all night. We don't know if it's fatigue, the water, or malaria. I took a blood smear from her finger this morning, and Heather took it into town to have it tested. The clinician diagnosed it as malaria, but we're skeptical. The incubation period for malaria is supposed to be twenty-one days, and we've only been here a week. Not only that, but we've been taking our malaria medicine faithfully. Heather says they diagnose any and everything as malaria. That's what they know and are used to. I guess, if she's still sick tomorrow, we'll go ahead and start the treatment. She thinks it's the water we drink and says she wants to start buying bottled water. She doesn't even like the taste of the water; maybe it's from being kept in the same old jerry cans all the time, I don't know. But I guess we'll put bottled water on our next shopping list.

We lose electrical power every third night. It's called power shedding. Tonight is supposed to be the night, but since we have lost it the last two nights maybe it'll stay on tonight. It generally goes off around 7:30 PM. It's already 8:45 and it's still on, so maybe. I hope so. I don't think I can take another night of being closed up in that stifling hot room during sing time.

I've really come to love some of the kids. I guess I'll come to love all of them, but right now, I don't even know all of them.

One of my favorites is a 3 ½ year old named Faith. Everywhere I go, she latches onto me. She is just precious, as pretty as can be, and as smart as a whip.

A while ago, I went in to fill a pan with water so we can wash up before bed, and she attached herself to my legs. I leaned down to hug her and asked, "Faithie, why aren't you in singing with the other kids?" She put her hands on her hips, cocked her head and said, "But for me, I am caring for the babies." Here she is just 3 ½, and she's helping take care of the babies.

SUNDAY, JUNE 15

I woke up this morning to a completely overcast sky. This is supposed to be the rainy season, but so far, all we've had is one shower and some pretty impressive thunderheads out over the lake.

Kevin and Philip have taken the big lorry into Kampala-Entebbe to pick up a medical team who is visiting from the states. They will be staying out at Global (that's the shortened version of "Global Outreach African Seminary") which is just up the road from us about a mile. They are supposed to come down here and check out all of the kids and staff. We're in pretty good shape right now, but at any given time, we may have as many as five or six kids down with malaria.

I guess I'll be driving down to the Nazarene church in Wairaka since Kevin is on the road, and Heather has "home duties" this week. This will be my first experience driving in Africa. It will also be my first experience with Uganda church. I'm wondering if it will be like Rwanda church. Of course, Rwanda church isn't all the same depending on whether you are at First Baptist of Kigali or the little mud hut at Jari.

RIGHT AFTER LUNCH

Well, I don't know if it's just Uganda church or the Nazarene church, but it certainly wasn't like Innocent's church at Jari. There were no African chants with loud drums or jumping and dancing in the aisles.

The message was a good one, brought by an African woman. She preached in English, and another woman translated it into Lugandan. I don't know if she preached in English for our benefit, or if this is the way they always do it.

Most Ugandans speak English, but in the villages some of the older people are more comfortable with Lugandan or Lusoga or any number of other languages. I believe I read or was told that there are around a dozen tribal languages in Uganda, and of course, there are no similarities. It's no wonder Africa is lagging behind the rest of the world, when a person from five miles down the road can't understand his neighbor because they're different tribes, and language is only part of the problem. Their customs are also different.

We have decided that we will take a few of the kids on a walk down to the lake.

"Hey, kids, Auntie Jeanette and I are going down to the lake. Anybody want to go with us?" How naïve can I be? Of course, all 115 want to get out of this place and walk down to the lake. Now, how do you choose a dozen out of 115 kids, crowding up so close you can't move, screaming, "Even me, even me!!!?"

Thank God for Heather. She steps in and says calmly, "Okay, anyone who went last week, go play. You can't go this week." Alright, now we only have one hundred to contend with. She waves her hand over the crowd like a magic wand and says, "If you're on kitchen duty, you can't go this week." Another eight or ten drop out.

Somehow, we choose about a dozen of the teen and pre-teens and three or four six and seven year olds and start out the gate to a chorus of wailing left-behinds. I won't do that again. I don't know how we'll choose in the future, but it won't be by making an announcement to the entire compound that whoever wants to go, line up.

The walk down to the lake is fun and enjoyable. The big kids take care of the little ones, and I've made a couple of friends among some of the older ones. There is one boy (actually, he's the brother of Moses) named Godfrey. He has been very helpful in shepherding the smaller kids and leading the way.

The trail winds down through the shambas, or tiny farms, to the highway. It's nice to walk through the maize fields and under the giant mango trees. There is a huge tree, just at the edge of our property that Godfrey tells me is a jacka-fruit tree. The fruit hanging in the branches look like big green hornet's nests. Several of the kids ask me if they can climb the mango tree and pick some of the mangos. I let them.

As we pass through the village of Wairaka, we pass several of our neighbor's homes. The little houses are made of mud, some with tin roofs, some with thatch, all with small children, naked from the waist down, playing among the chickens and goats in the yard. The women working around their outdoor hearths give us scant notice, but the children run to the edge of their property yelling, "Alo mzungus, alo mzungus." The Swahili word Mzungu has several meanings. It can mean stranger or foreigner, but it is generally used to designate a white person. I've learned a couple of phrases in Lugandan, so I respond with, "Oliotia" (Hello).

We pass the two or three ducas (small stores), and the bore hole that constitutes downtown Wairaka, then we pass the Wairaka primary school. This is nothing more than a sign and a handful of students sitting under a mango tree. It makes me proud of our school. Some of the classes may meet in an old goat shed, but at least we have a building for them.

As we approach the lake, there is a large herd of Ankole cattle grazing on the tough lake grass. As are all African cattle, these are as tame as pets and barely step aside to let us pass. Their horns are magnificent. Some are nearly four feet long and as big around as my leg at the base.

The lake is beautiful, but from here, you can't get a true feeling of how big it is. I can see that there are dozens of islands and right across from where we are, the other side is only about five miles away. I don't know the geography well enough yet to discern which direction I'm looking, but I do know enough about the lake to know that I'm not looking across the breadth of it to, say, Tanzania. I don't know if we'll ever be able to take enough time off from the orphanage duties, but I'd love to take the ferry across to Mwanza to see Emanuel, Angela, and the kids.

MONDAY, JUNE 16

There are a couple of the little kids, Faithie being one of them, who think that every time they see me, they have to try to climb me like a tree. I just love them dearly, but, sometimes, it's almost more than I can handle. I finally just had to get away for a while. The only trouble with coming to the room and closing the door is it's twice as hot in here as it is outside.

As frustrating as it is, I have to laugh at Faithie. After telling her to stop hanging on me for the umpteenth time, I finally grabbed her under my arm and started out into the yard with her. "I'm going to take you out there and feed you to that donkey!" I told her. She wiggled, kicked and squealed until I put her down, and then she turned to me, placed her hands on her hips, and with that twenty-year-old-in-a-two-year-old-body look, said, "I'm going to report you to Auntie Jeanette."

TUESDAY, JUNE 17

Jeanette has taken Nicolai into our room so that she can mend his baseball cap. They are both sitting on our bed, and while she sews and tells him Bible stories, he listens with rapt attention. This is almost unbelievable. Nicolai suffers from A.D.D, and is never still for a minute. It's almost like she weaves some kind of spell over him.

I've come to the very small and crowded office to try to write some letters and write in this journal and already, I have at least ten kids coming, asking for paper. I guess I shouldn't complain. All they want to do is write, and, after all, isn't that what I'm trying to do. It seems that as soon as I give one of them a pencil and piece of paper, there's another one standing in front of the desk with their head down, mumbling something. I have to ask them several times to repeat what they've said and, of course, every time I tell them to speak up, they become more timid. I must come across as a cranky old man to them......what the heck; I am a cranky old man.

Jeanette just stuck her head in to remind me that we're supposed to limit the number of kids in the office to five. *Oh, yeah!* I just counted, and there now eighteen scattered around on the couch and floor.

Teacher Sam came in right after breakfast wanting an advance on his salary. He's already had one this term. I gave him 10,000 shillings, about $10.00, for medical expenses for his wife, who is pregnant and due to deliver any day, and five kilos of rice to help feed his other two kids for a week.

I feel so sorry for these people. They have a terrible time making it from pay day to pay day. They make precious little as it is, and they really can't budget what they get. Sometimes I wonder how the ones in the village make it. At least the teachers have a regular income.

WEDNESDAY JUNE 18

The rainy season finally seems to be upon us. It rained pretty good last evening and is overcast and rumbling thunder right now. I wouldn't be surprised if it let loose here in a few minutes and dumped on us.

I'm still wondering what my purpose is here. Kevin and Heather have such a good handle on running the everyday needs, and Jeanette spends a great deal of her day giving out medicines, vitamins and doctoring "supposed" ailments. Sometimes I think the ailments that she has to deal with are just attention seeking by some of the kids. Some of them are real, of course, like the malaria, but many of the same kids come in day after day with "My stomach is paining me," or "My leg is paining me," and when you look, it's a small scratch that any of my grandkids would rub vigorously and go on playing. Maybe I'm being unfair, but it seems to always be the same child with the same ailment.

For me, I seem to wander around looking for something to do. I pray every day that God will give me a sense of purpose and equip me to do the job. Maybe I'm just not being patient enough.

THURSDAY, JUNE 19
Last night we had a staff meeting and made some decisions about duties and responsibilities. I think this is going to help us feel more like we belong here. Jeanette was given the job of medical administrator. Not that she's a medical person by any means, but she has had some nursing training in college.

They asked me if I'd be the school administrator; me, who quit school after my first semester of college. It was all I could do to get out of high school with a diploma. I agreed to give it my best shot. I figure my 20 some years in management at TWA will help me more than a college degree over here. After all, I'll have seven good African teachers and a very competent headmaster under me. I won't be doing the teaching, just running things.

I don't know if I did what an orphanage co-director/school administrator is supposed to do today. I back-filled part of the drain-field ditch, fixed two wheel chairs, interviewed and hired a new teacher, and played a game of baseball with the kids. Why doesn't it sound like a lot when I write it down? It sure felt like a lot as I was doing it.

FRIDAY, JUNE 20
Well, I prayed for a sense of purpose, and the Lord put me to work. Yesterday, me, Kevin, Philip, and one of the boys took the lorry and went to a eucalyptus forest in the mountains for firewood.

We filled the entire bed of the one ton, stake-body truck until sticks were falling off the back and over the sides. It took us most of the day to load it, unload it, and stack it in the shed beside the outdoor kitchen. We go through it so fast; we'll probably have to go again next week.

This morning we brought the lorry, with ten or twelve kids, out to "the land." Kevin dropped us off, and then he and Phillip went back to town to do some marketing.

Some months ago, the orphanage purchased one hundred acres near the village of Buundo. It is in a mountainous region between Jinja and Kampala. Most of the hundred acres is rolling hills. The plan is to eventually build a children's village with several dormitory-cottages for the children, a home for the director's family, a school and a medical clinic, and who knows where it'll go from there.

At present, it is mostly forest, and the area where we are working is down in a swampy valley of thick jungle. Our project is to cut a road through the jungle up to a building site on top of the hill. Apparently, there was a road here at some time in the past because there is a berm raised above the swamp. This is good!! I would hate to be slogging around, knee deep in water, snakes, crocodiles and who knows what all. Whatever road was here, though, has completely gone back to jungle.

I have put the girls to work with pangas, chopping the sides and overhead growth as high as they can reach. The boys and I are cutting down the larger trees and digging up the stumps. Some of them are as big around as my thigh. Luckily, the ground is wet, so it's fairly easy digging.

We got here around noon and have been working for about five hours. It rained on us for a while, but it's hot and I was already so sweaty, it was actually refreshing. So far, the girls have slashed through about one hundred fifty yards of vines and creepers. The boys and I are not making such good progress. We've only cleared about a dozen trees and stumps and made maybe thirty or forty yards.

I'm really beginning to love these kids. They are all hard workers.

There is one girl in particular. Her name is Damali. Her father died of AIDS, and her mother is too sick from AIDS to care for the kids. She is probably thirteen or fourteen and has decided that when she grows up, she wants to be a missionary.

Most of these kids are very spiritual. They have been through so much, and yet they are always cheerful and cooperative.

We have five brothers: Ocham, Francis, Noel, Paul and Ochaki. Ocham is in his early teens, and they range down in age to Ochaki, who is five. When Sudanese troops crossed the border and attacked their village, which is up near Gulu, Ocham ran into the bush with his little brothers and watched as his village was burned and his parents were hacked with pangas and machine-gunned to death. They have every reason to be bitter and angry, and yet, you couldn't find five better boys on any continent.

Ocham just ran up to tell me the lorry is coming back. I can hear its engine groaning as it tries to come into the road we've made. The stumps are gone, but the holes are still there.

I'm glad they're back. I can't remember when I've worked so hard. I'll be ready to jump into the cold shower, grab some beans and rice, and hit the sack.

SUNDAY, JUNE 22

Another Sunday! This is our third. I can't believe we've been here three weeks. It seems like three years.

Yesterday and today Jeanette and I have the compound and all of the kids by ourselves. Kevin and Heather have gone on a two day camp-out, over by source of the Nile, for their fifth wedding anniversary.

I guess it wasn't any more of a difficult day than usual. About noon, Rose, one of the baby care workers, brought her four year old to us with 103 degree temperature and all of the other symptoms of malaria. We asked Florence Wabule, our only resident teacher, to take charge. We then loaded them into the Volkswagen and drove Rose and the baby into town to the clinic for a malaria shot. It's only eight miles into town, but for some reason, it always seems to take four or five hours to go in and get anything done.

Besides doing that, lancing and doctoring an infected finger, interviewing another teacher and showing a group of visitors from Calvary Chapel of Albuquerque around, it was a pretty normal day.

I got a kick out of one of the Calvary visitors. When I showed him our room, he looked at the clothes hanging on the wall and said, "Well, at least you don't have to worry about a closet door taking up valuable wall space." I guess he's got a point, at that. If there was a closet door, where would we put the nails to hang our clothes?

All in all, I'd say the visitors were impressed, appalled, and incredulous. I could tell that after the hour tour, they were more than ready to get back in their van and get out of here. I can't blame them. I still feel that way a lot of the time.

SUNDAY, JUNE 29

I can't believe a whole week has gone by without an entry in my journal. It has been a full week, with lots of things happening.

On Monday I took six of the kids, three boys and three girls, back out to the land. Can you believe it? Where we had cleared one week ago and left the stumps, there were new trees growing out of the stumps. Some were three feet tall, and as big around as my wrist. It's not surprising, I guess. I've actually seen fresh-cut fence posts sprout and start growing limbs here.

I pulled the Volkswagen van up into the road as far as I could, and we proceeded to re-clear what we had already done. About four o'clock, I decided we needed to quit and get back home in time to clean up for supper. Since the road is only about as wide as the van, I would have to back out. It had rained again, so the road was muddy and slick. Now the berm is round shouldered, and as I backed out, I could feel the rear end start to slide. I jammed on the brakes, but that only made it slide faster. The only thing that kept us from going into the swamp is that the rear leaf spring high-centered on one of the stumps we'd left.

After assessing the problem, I determined that the only way we were going to get out of there was for me to lie under the vehicle, in the swamp, and chop out the stump while the boys tried to keep it from sliding down on top of me with long leverage poles. I gave Big Susan a crash course in driving; she'd never been behind the wheel of a car before in her life. I told her, "When I yell you pull this lever down to here and push this pedal." Bless her heart; I think she was more scared than I. Luckily, the van is an automatic, so we weren't dealing with a clutch.

When I climbed down into the swamp and crawled up under the car, I noticed that Godfrey was standing knee deep in the water beside me. "What are you doing?" I asked.

"I'm going to help you," he said simply.

"No, I need you on one of those poles," I told him.

"I put the twins on the pole. I'm going to stay with you." All I could do was nod.

It was very difficult to maneuver under the car the way we were, so it took a good hour before I felt the ax go through. Still the severed stump held like a jack. I yelled, "Go Susan!" She threw it into reverse and jammed down the accelerator while I took a healthy swing at the stump with the back of the ax.

At this point one of three things was going to happen: either the car was going to slide off into the swamp and probably crush me (I had made Godfrey stand clear); it was going to shoot straight across the road and go plunging into the swamp on the other side; or Susan was going to back that car down the road like Bobby Unser.

God was with us that afternoon. The tire on the road caught hold, the stump/jack lifted the mired tire up and out as it toppled, and Susan backed the car about thirty feet onto firm ground, and gently applied the brakes.

Shakily, I pulled myself out of the mud and sat there catching my breath. All of the kids were gathered around me with scared looks on their faces. "You know what?" I said, "I need a group hug." They all broke into big grins and piled on top of me, trying to all hug me while I sat on the ground.

We got out onto the main road, and about four miles from town one of the kids said, "Unca Rrah, (Ugandan for Uncle Ralph) something is smoking back here." I pulled over, and sure enough steam was boiling out of the radiator. (I know Volkswagens aren't water cooled, but this one is.) I put a can of water in it, and we started off again. We got about a mile further before it boiled over again. I goosed it along, maybe another mile, and it quit. The water pump had given up the ghost.

I had been able to goose it to a small village where there are several bars, so I walked down to one of them and asked if they had a phone. Now you have to understand that these bars are just mud huts, and I really didn't expect them to have a phone. One of the ladies of the night told me they didn't have one, but an Indian duka down the road did.

I told six frightened children to stay in the car and lock the doors until I got back. I called GSF from the duka but, of course, by now, it was sing time, and nobody was going to hear the phone in the office. I walked back to the car to try to figure out what to do, and as I sat there, a taxi drove up. I jumped out, signaled to them that I had a fare, and explained what our problem was.

Since Moses was the oldest, I gave him a couple of thousand shillings and told him to go to the taxi park, find another taxi that was going out to Wairaka and bring Kevin back with the lorry. Moses was afraid because by now it was full dark, but he "cowboyed-up," and left in the taxi. The rest of us settled down for the long wait. I knew it would be a long wait because I'd sat in the taxi park for over an hour waiting for a taxi to fill up on many occasions. About 10 o'clock the lorry showed up with Kevin, Philip, and Moses. He had reached the taxi park, decided that the wait was too long, and jogged and walked the eight miles out to Wairaka.

Kevin had brought our cable, but by the time we had it fastened to both vehicles, I was following not more than six or seven feet behind the lorry.

Now I have to tell you, driving on Uganda roads at night is a scary proposition at best. For some reason, the Ugandans don't turn on their headlights at night. I guess they think it runs their batteries down. So being towed on a six foot cable behind a one ton lorry that you can't see around or over is a harrowing experience, but we arrived back at the compound around eleven o'clock safe and sound. When we pulled up in front, and straggled out of the van, Jeanette came to us, hugging each of us with a mixture of joy and worry on her face. She had been beside herself with worry, knowing how dangerous the roads are after dark.

They had kept our supper for us, so I wolfed down my cold beans and rice and headed for the shower with a clean pair of shorts, my towel, and a paraffin torch. If you've never taken a cold shower in a mud shed by the light of a kerosene lantern, you ain't lived, or maybe I should say you ain't lived in Uganda.

Wednesday or Thursday, Kevin and I had to take the visiting medical team and all of their luggage back to Entebbe for their flight back home. This was a good opportunity for us to give them letters to mail stateside. Sometimes it takes two to three weeks to send and receive mail here.

There were four of us cramped in the front seat of the lorry. I was in the middle with nothing to hold on to, so every time we hit a pothole it jarred me from head to foot. I don't think that truck has any shock absorbers, and as I described before, these African roads are all potholes. There are some potholes out there you could lose a Volkswagen in. To make a long story short, I had to spend most of the next day in bed with my back out. When I did get up, I walked around like a crab and suffered considerable pain. Too bad there are no chiropractors in this town. There may be one in Kampala, but that's about as accessible as Albuquerque.

Yesterday was a pretty pleasant day. It was overcast and cool. Kevin and Heather took about fifteen of the kids to Mubule, to another orphanage, so that our kids could play with a different group of kids. They had a great time. Any kind of an outing is a treat for them.

It was a two-fold trip. The second reason for going was to take them some of our food. They only have about thirty children, but they have very little support, had run out of food, and had no money to buy any.

It made me think. Whenever you think you've got it bad, there's always someone who has it worse.

Having them gone for the day brought our compliment down to fifty or sixty, not counting the babies. That's about where we should be, anyway. It was very manageable.

They were supposed to return by one-thirty. When they weren't back by three, I began to get worried.

Jeanette and I had promised to take fifteen of our kids to a soccer match in Bugembe at four-thirty. When four-ten rolled around, and they still weren't back, I called together our fifteen and told them I was sorry, but we weren't going to be able to go. They were crestfallen, but they understood that it wasn't our fault.

At four-twenty, the lorry pulled through the gate. I yelled for Kevin to leave the motor running. They unloaded their fifteen, we loaded ours and without a hello/goodbye we were on our way. Since Bugembe is only about three miles away, we got there just as the match was starting. We all had a ball, and our team even won.

At the last staff meeting, we decided that each couple needed one day off a week to rest and get away from the compound for an entire day. Kevin and Heather suggested that we take Sundays, and they would take Wednesdays. We didn't argue.

This morning being Sunday, Jeanette and I have decided we will go into town and visit the Nile Baptist Church.

Have I mentioned before what it takes for us to go into town now that the Volkswagen is kaput. We have to walk the path through the shambas about a half mile to the road, wait for a taxi to pass, flag it down, and make the eight mile-one hour trip into Jinja. At the taxi depot, we find a boda-boda. That's a public transportation bicycle. You climb on behind the driver, and he pedals you where ever you want to go.

This morning is our first experience going into town this way, but Philip says he is a member at the church, so he will go with us and show us the ropes.

We only have to make five or six stops between Wairaka and Jinja this trip, so it only takes us a little over thirty minutes to get to the taxi park.

Philip is incensed at the horrid amount the boda-boda drivers want to charge us, 300 shillings, or about thirty cents each. He convinces us to walk the one mile length of Main Street.

It's a pleasant walk, and Jeanette and I both enjoy looking in the shops as we pass by. We agree that at some point, we want to come back down here and do some shopping. So far, the only shopping we've done is our bi-weekly marketing for the home.

When we get to the end of town, the Global Outreach truck sees us and stops to pick us up and take us the rest of the way to the church. It's a good thing, too, because the church is still a couple of miles beyond.

If I haven't learned anything else in my travels around Africa, I've learned that time and distance are concepts that the African mind just doesn't grasp. Also that African feet were never made for shoes. They are broad and flat and their soles are as hard and thick as any shoe sole. We try to get the kids to wear shoes to church, and they try; but after thirty minutes or so, you find most of them happily barefooted, carrying their shoes.

The church is a beautiful red brick, twelve-sided building. It doesn't have doors or windows, just large open arches in each wall, with a domed, red tile roof rising from each of the twelve walls, and at the peak of the roof, there is a white wooden cross about ten feet high.

As the service begins, the choir sings a couple of hymns; and the pastor welcomes guests to the Victoria Baptist Church. Jeanette looks at me, I look at her, and we both just shrug. *I thought we were at the Nile Baptist.* Oh, well, I guess we'll visit Nile Baptist another time.

I think the irony of it is funny. The Victoria Baptist Church overlooks the Nile River, and the Nile Baptist Church is on the shore of Lake Victoria. This is such a wonderful, strange, backward country. Our logical minds rebel at the contradiction, but it makes perfect sense to them.

As the service ends, a tall, silver haired lady introduces herself as Dorothy Ferris. She says she is another of the Global Outreach missionaries, like us, and the women's Sunday school teacher, and invites Jeanette to visit her class next week. We both like her immediately, so we tell her we'd love to.

Maybe we won't visit Nile Baptist any time soon, after all.

When we introduce ourselves and tell her that we're working out at Good Shepherd's Fold, she shakes her head. "Oh, I admire you so much. I could never do that. When I stop by for a visit, I can't stay more than a half hour or so. I just love the children, but thirty minutes is all I can take. "

She asks us what we're doing for lunch, and we tell her we don't really have plans, but that we have all day and don't really want to go back to the orphanage.

"Have you been out to Source of the Nile?" she asks.

We answer that we haven't been anywhere except Good Shepherd's Fold.

"I'm having a friend over for lunch today. Would you like to come, and then, maybe, we can drive down to the river and see the source."

Well, we tell her yes so fast she doesn't have time to rethink and change her mind.

After a wonderful lunch -- of course, any lunch besides beans and rice is wonderful -- we ride down to the river, to the place where it flows out of Lake Victoria. This is called Source of the Nile, and it is truly awesome. I think the awesome part is the history as much as the beauty, but it is beautiful.

I look in wonder at this longest river in the world, flowing between the green hills on each side. Then, I turn and look north, and try to imagine it traveling nearly 4000 miles through mountain gorges, desert, and the great swamp called the Sud, to Alexandria, Egypt.

I feel like I'm standing in the presence of someone great as I read the monument to John Hanning Speke, the first white man to see it. History says he's the man who discovered the source of the Nile. Of course, the Africans say he didn't discover it. They knew it was there all the time. Still, I'm impressed. I try to feel what he must have felt, and I think I come very close.

After I spend an hour or so with the ghosts of the past, Speke, Burton, Livingston, Stanley and Gordon, the others convince me that we need to return to the present, to Jinja, Wairaka and Good Shepherd's Fold. I'm reluctant, but I agree.

We ask Dorothy if she'll take us to the taxi park, but she won't hear of it. She says it'll be dark by the time we reach Wairaka and we'll have to walk through the shambas in the dark; she'll take us all the way out to GSF.

Heather has made some tortillas from scratch, added a burrito mix to our beans, and we are treated to a Mexican food supper. This has been the best day since we got here, and it doesn't end here. We are still on our day off, so we leave sing time and putting 115 hyper kids to bed to Kevin and Heather, and we retire to our room to read for a while. We even have electricity!

MONDAY, JUNE 30
Today we finished converting the goat shed into P7 classroom and plumbed another shower for the kids. I really felt useful for a change. We needed to drill some holes in the cement wall to hang the blackboard, but we haven't wired it yet, so we couldn't use the electric drill. I found a piece of quarter inch steel bar, and using a hand file I rounded the end and cut a star point in it. It was as good as any star drill you would buy in a hardware store.

The outside wall is open from shoulder high to the roof, but it doesn't let in enough sun light to read by, so again, I used my homemade star drill to drill a hole into Phillips room on the other side of the cement wall. Now we can tie into his electricity and run some electric wire for a light.

SATURDAY, JULY 5
Another busy week. Since I've not been faithful to record events daily anymore, many things go forgotten.

Today is field day. Before every school term, we treat the entire orphanage to a day of fun and games up at the Global Outreach field. Field day is kind of a combination school track meet and 4th of July picnic.

Luca and Philip are slaughtering two of the goats. When we went to the market the other day we bought a large supply of matoke and enough chipâtés and cokes for everyone to have one.

Jeanette, Heather and Kevin have walked the mile or so up there with the majority of the kids. I've stayed behind to load up all of the handicapped kids, their wheel chairs, crutches and whatever other paraphernalia is needed. It's a chore because most of them have to be lifted into the back of the lorry, but I have Luka, Philip, Moses and Ocham to help me. It takes us less than an hour to get everyone loaded, and off we go, clanking up the red dirt road, kids laughing and squealing, and the big white truck rolling a huge cloud of red dust behind us.

By the time we get parked and everyone unloaded, the games are in full swing. The teachers have roped off a running track around a good portion of the field, and some of the kids are making their third or fourth lap around. Even little Jeff, who is only five, is churning along, his little cheeks puffing in and out, and his arms and legs pumping. He has already done three laps, and I can tell he is just about spent. I run along beside him for a little ways, trying to cheer him on and encourage him. He goes on around another time, and as he nears the place where we are cheering, I can tell he's had it, but he just keeps on pushing, and then just before he gets to us, he collapses. I rush out onto the field, and scoop him up into my arms. He buries his face in my chest and just sobs. "Jeff, are you hurt?" I ask. He just shakes his head and continues to cry. "Talk to me," I say. "If you're not hurt, why are you crying?"

"I couldn't finish," he sobs.

Another one of the kids that has impressed me with her determination is Alisa. She's the one legged girl I have mentioned before. She has already won the sack race and the jump rope competition. I get tickled with her at home just playing. If any of the boys make her mad, she throws her crutch aside and goes after them on that one leg. She generally runs them down too. She has a prosthesis, but she doesn't like it because it slows her down. She can run faster without it.

It has been a long, exhausting day. It's good to come back and relax with a plate full of matoke, boiled goat, and a chipâté. The cooks have also cooked some dodo which is a green vegetable similar to collards, or maybe poke salad. For me, it's a great meal. I love the matoke, chipâté and dodo, and the goat is even good once you've picked the hairs out of it.

By the end of sing time, the smaller ones are pretty much ready for bed. It's my turn to put the boys down, so I make them all go to the kitchen to get their drink, then go to the bathroom, then line up so I can give each one of them a goodnight hug. I started this a couple of weeks ago, but night before last one of them came up with the idea of "and a kiss." So, I also have to give 50 boys from five years old to early teen a hug and a kiss on the forehead. You know what? I think I like it as much as they do.

We have learned each other's routines by now, so it's not quite as big of a chore as it was in the beginning. They know that once I put them in the beds, they don't get up again.

I have started reading them a story at nights about a pack of wolves living in snowy mountains. They are intrigued because they've never seen a wolf or snow. They are normally full of questions but tonight, by the time I've read one chapter, most of them are asleep, and the older ones who aren't asleep yet are ready for me to turn out the light.

By the time I get back to our room I'm more than ready to take my toothbrush and boiled water out in the yard, brush my teeth, and then hit the sack myself.

Jeanette says to me, "You know what tomorrow is?"

I think about it a minute, "No."

"Tomorrow is the seventh; we've been here a month now."

Hmmmmm, I think, *we've been here one whole month. It seems like a year.*

MONDAY, JULY 7

Today is the first day of school.

This morning, after the headmaster assembled all of the kids and teachers, he turned it over to me to make a first-day-of-school pep-talk, lead in the Uganda pledge of allegiance, and sing the Uganda national anthem. It's funny, I was in management for twenty years, but this really made me feel like somebody special.

After that, with the kids all in class, it's been as quiet as a hospital around here. About the only activity is Jjajja Mary washing the nappies in her wash tub. (I guess I'd better translate that sentence. Jjajja means Grandmother and the nappies are the baby diapers.)

The only other activity is Solomon, the crested crane, strutting around doing his mating dance when Jeanette comes into the yard. A few days ago, she made the mistake of dancing with him, and now he's in love with her. She had stepped out of the room while he was on the cement apron doing his little dance, which he does whenever the mood strikes him. Instead of just walking past him and going about her business, like the rest of us do, she stopped, bowed her neck, and started prancing around, flapping her arms by her side, and making a clucking sound in her throat. It was funny until he took it seriously and started chasing her around the yard.

I've spent most of the morning sitting in my "School Superintendent" office in the library, making sure the teachers and students have everything they need to get started.

Since I haven't been faithful to write down everything as it happens, I guess I failed to mention that a few days ago I enlisted the help of two of the ten year old boys, Eric and Louis, in straightening up the old two car garage, and turning it into a lending/research library. We put a small table and wooden chair in one corner, and created an office for me. Up to this time, the garage had been used to store a myriad of closed cardboard boxes. When I started going through the boxes, I found they were almost all filled with donated books and school supplies.

There were already a couple of bookcases with a few books on them, so Louis, Eric, and I lined one whole wall with more bookcases made with cinder blocks and mubule boards. Mubule is the toughest wood I've ever seen. You can't even drive a nail into it, so it will hold a weight of books without bowing.

Now we have a library with well over five hundred books in it. I've set up a system where the older kids can even check out books, and the younger ones can come in a few at a time to read.

I've finally gotten a handle on how to limit the number of kids I let in at a time. I've made Louis and Eric my librarians. They are in charge of who to let in and who can check out books. Now I can come in, write letters, work on my journal, or do school superintendent work, and leave the hassle of running things with the two boys. It works like a charm. They love the responsibility.

153

Speaking of books and reading, Jeanette has started a special reading get-together for a few of the teenage girls. They meet in one of the smaller classrooms twice a week, and Jeanette is reading them one of Janette Oak's books. They really get into the story because Jeanette is pretty good at changing her voice for the different characters and makes it very interesting. The girls really look forward to these times and the treats Jeanette always has with her for snacks.

TUESDAY, JULY 8

I think I'm finally beginning to understand Uganda English. I was sitting on the front steps this morning before school, drinking a cup of coffee and watching the children play, when Secunde, one of the twelve year old boys, came toward me crying.

"What's the matter now?" I asked.

"I beat my leg with a stone!" he wailed.

I studied on this for a minute and then asked, "You beat your leg with a stone? Now why would you beat your leg with a stone?"

"But for me, I was playing football," he said through gasps and hiccups. "I was passing from heah, while Ruben was disturbing me, and Kajuna abused me for Ruben. Then, when I kicked at the football, the stone beat my leg."

I looked down at a bloody big toe, and it all became clear. He was playing soccer with Kajuna, another of the twelve year olds.
He ran too close to Ruben, the donkey, who chased him, which he loves to do. Secunde tried to dodge Ruben at the same time he kicked at the soccer ball and stubbed his big toe on a rock. Then to add insult to injury, Kajuna laughed at him.

"Okay," I said, "let's go fix it."

Jeanette was busy giving out vitamins at the time, so I sat him on a stool in the kitchen, began to clean his wound with a piece of gauze soaked in peroxide and put a bandage on it. About that time she came in. "Where are your rubber gloves?" she scolded. "It'll be a miracle if you don't get AIDS before you leave here."

To change the subject and take some of the heat off of me, I related the story to her.

"I know what you mean," she laughed. "Yesterday one of the girls came up to me and said, 'can Nemutebe come off of the wall?' The third time I asked her what she was saying, she took me by the hand and led me to where Harriett, also called Nemutebe, was standing in the corner for punishment. I don't think I'll ever understand what they're saying."

WEDNESDAY, JULY 9

Wow! That was rather exciting! Kevin and I just had to confront a band of angry men armed with sharp pangas and spears at our front gate. We knew they were after Clinton, one of our dogs, but we didn't know why. He had just come home with deep cuts on his head and face. The one on his head was bleeding badly.

Heather and Jeanette had taken him up on the front steps and were trying to clean him up and stop the bleeding when the men showed up.

After listening to them all screaming at once and waving their weapons, we summoned Philip to ask them what the problem was. It seems that the men had seen, or were told, that Clinton, Shadrach, and a stray dog had attacked a herd of goats and killed three of them. This was hard for us to believe because we have goats out loose, and the dogs have never bothered them. We tried to explain this, but these men weren't having any of it. They wanted blood, and they didn't much care if it was the dog's or ours.

We were finally able to reason with them by telling them that we would take care of the dogs ourselves, and offered to pay the owner for the goats. He agreed on 15,000 shillings, or about fifteen dollars.

As they were getting ready to go, however, good old tightfisted Philip called the owner back and said, "But if we pay for the goats, we want them." The man stared at him for a minute and then nodded. I guess we'll be having goat again tonight with our beans and rice.

After Heather took Clinton into town to have him sewn up, we tied him to the axel of the lorry until we could decide what to do with him. We're certainly not going to kill him like they would have done. We'll have to try to find them a home away from livestock, maybe in the city somewhere.

We haven't seen Shadrach. They may have found him and finished him off already.

FRIDAY, JULY 11

I'm sitting here on the front steps watching the donkey mow the grass while the preschool class learns some tribal dance. They are as cute as can be, marching around in a circle to the typical African drum and chant. I have really come to love African singing and dancing, but then, you already knew that from our Rwanda trip.

It's a very serene morning. Looking out over the valley below the house, I can see over the tops of the mango and banana trees and little shambas, and there in the distance, is Lake Victoria, seeming to float above it all. It's a very strange optical illusion.

I was helping Philip move some dirt and gravel earlier this morning to cover the French drain, but Jeanette made me stop. We have an outbreak of mumps in the camp. I'm sure I've had them, but I do have a sore throat and swollen gland behind my ear. She says if an old man like me gets the mumps and works moving dirt, it could be serious. She's right, of course. I guess if it wasn't for her, I'd have the mumps fall on me, and get AIDS, and who knows what all. I seem to stay pretty healthy, though.

It has been a nice pleasant morning, almost like an early fall day in New Mexico. It rained a slow drizzle most of the night, and now there is a brisk breeze blowing off of the lake. All of the kids and most of the staff are bundled up like it's the middle of winter in Vermont. To me, it's a welcome relief from the humid heat.

Days like today make me wonder if I would be content to stay here for a long period of time. I don't think I would ever want to stay for ten or twenty years, the way some of the missionaries have. I'm still missing home too much to think like that. I had a bout of homesickness last night so bad I got out all of the pictures of kids, grandkids and my dog, Cisco, and had a good old pity party. I'm okay this morning, though. I think having the children in school and not having to deal with them every minute of every hour helps.

I don't know what God has planned for us after this. I guess I wouldn't mind if it was to just enjoy my retirement and write. I'd like to finish my book someday. We will, of course, do whatever God calls us to do and go wherever He leads us. I just hope it's not to run an orphanage. Been there! Done that! Not that it's been all bad; in fact, some of it's actually been fun. Well, maybe fun isn't quite the right word; maybe interesting is a better word.

FRIDAY, JULY 18

I see I've let another whole week slip by without making an entry here. The weeks seem to be going by pretty fast now.

Jeanette has had her hands full trying to reorganize the medicine cabinet and straighten out all of the medical records for everyone. Sometimes I think she has the hardest of the jobs around here, certainly the one which starts earliest in the day. She sent me out to the trash dump this morning with a big bag of outdated medicines. I have to bury everything. If we just throw things in the pit to burn, an hour later, we see some child playing with it out in the yard. This includes everything from old coffee tins to used syringes.

Just giving the babies their daily vitamins and medicines takes a good portion of her day. She had a bit of a time with that at first because when she took the vitamins upstairs to the baby veranda, they would all crowd around her with their hands raised up to the point she couldn't move, and at the time she couldn't tell one toddler from another. She realized she was probably giving some children vitamins more than once, and some weren't getting them at all. So she taught them to sit against the wall in a straight line, and they were to sit there until she was completely finished "serving" what they viewed as a treat. It wasn't long at all until there was complete order and quiet the moment she came through the door onto the veranda.

We all try to pitch in and take care of minor scrapes and cuts, but being responsible for everyone's health has to be a daunting task. Her medical bible is *When There Is No Doctor.* She spends a lot of time studying that.

As for me, my week included worrying about the drought stricken crops, (we haven't had a good rain in over a week), repairing one of the clothes line poles that fell under the load of laundry, handing out school supplies, and working with Ruben. Ocham, Moses and I are trying to train him to do something besides eat grass, like pull a plow or drag. We're hoping to use him to help clear the land. I'm sorry to say he's not enthusiastic about the whole process, though. We have to put him in a homemade squeeze chute to get the harness on him. He tolerates the three of us pretty good and doesn't try to do any real damage with his heels and teeth.

He does seem to delight in terrorizing the rest of the compound, though. Jeanette and the kids are certainly afraid of him. She calls him the donkey from hell. He stays tied to a long tether, but if they come within his range, he chases them with his ears back and his teeth bared.

I believe he's finally decided that we three are his buddies, maybe because we won't take his nonsense.

I noticed the other day that he stands out in the sun all day and never has any water. When I told Moses to fill a wash tub and take it out to him, Moses looked at me like I was crazy. "Give the donkey water?" he questioned. "Yes!" I said. "You like to have a drink of water sometimes, don't you?" He shrugged and did as he was told.

Now, I know that goats get enough liquid just from the vegetation they eat, but when Moses put that tub of water down in front of Ruben, he drank it dry.

Changing a people's mind set is a difficult chore, and not always in the best interest of the people, but from now on, I plan to make sure that someone keeps fresh water out for Ruben, the dogs, and the goats when they are put up for the night.

I've even taken to going out into the maize with a panga every few days and cutting Ruben a few green cornstalks. He loves that. I even pick him an ear or two occasionally.

Philip scolded me a day or two ago and told me that the maize was to make posho for the orphanage when the ears get ripe.

I always listen to Philip's advice, but this time, I told him that the little I give to Ruben won't make that much difference in the long run. What little posho we can make at harvest won't make a dent in our needs. We still have to buy one hundred kilos of posho every other week or so, anyway. I wish we were self-supporting. Maybe once we get moved out to the hundred acres at Buundo, we will be. For now, though, those are just dreams for the future.

I was sitting in my office a while ago when Nemutebe came up and asked what I was doing. When I told her I was writing a letter to my daughter, she wanted to see a picture. I went to the room and got out our photo album, and we sat down on my front step to look at it. Of course, what started out with two kids turned out to be twenty-five kids all trying to crowd in to look at once. They press their faces so close in, I can barely turn the pages and, of course, the only ones who can see are the ones whose face is pressed next to the book. I know I shouldn't let it bother me, but I get so frustrated with them. I tell them to sit in a circle in front of me, and I'll pass the book around. That works for about three seconds, and they are all hovering over me again.

They are intrigued with my daughter and my grandson's fiery red hair. They can't believe that it comes that way naturally. They are even fascinated with Jeanette's fine blond hair. Every time she sits on the front steps for a moment's rest she has at least four pairs of hands playing with her hair, twisting it and braiding it to make plaits and cornrows.

Charles, one of our five year olds, had the whole compound in stitches yesterday. He had gotten some yellow corn silk from the kitchen, draped it over his head, and went around telling everyone he was Auntie Jeanette.

SATURDAY, JULY 19

Today we loaded the lorry with me, Jeanette, the Van Pelts, Philip, big David, three of the teachers and the twenty-six kids from P5 through P7, and came down to the agricultural fair near Source of the Nile. Unlike our state fairs, they don't bring in the produce from their farms; they actually take out small plots of land on the grounds and grow the stuff here. It's really very interesting to us and educational for the kids. They even got to watch a cow give birth to a calf, and saw their first camel. Morris fell in love with the baby camel and pleaded with me to buy it. That's all we need, a baby camel. We already have a useless donkey, a crested crane that has amorous affections for my wife, and two dogs that kill goats. I'll have to admit, though, I was pretty smitten with the baby camel, myself.

Except for having a great day, our field trip was pretty uneventful. The Baptist missionary here can't say the same. While he was looking at an exhibit he was aware of several men crowding around him really tight. As I've mentioned before, this isn't too uncommon here in Africa. When he felt a hand reach into his pocket, however, he knew it was more than the normal crowding. He grabbed the arm, and twisted it back into a hammer lock. "If you struggle," he said, "I'll break it."

A Karamojong woman standing nearby saw the commotion and asked, "Thief?"

"Yes," Paul said. "Thief."

She reached over, picked up a spear from the corner, and with a smile, said, "Let him run."

The man sank to his knees pleading, "Oh no, I don't want to run." If he'd tried to run he wouldn't have made it twenty feet. "I see by your Bible that you're a Christian. In Jesus' name, forgive me." Paul, having spent several years in Uganda and knowing that "forgive me" doesn't necessarily mean forgive me and has no sense of remorse or repentance to it, it just means don't punish me, he said, "Oh, in Jesus' name I will forgive you, but you're still going to be arrested for trying to pick my pocket."

Lately, the town has had a rash of break-ins. A couple of the missionaries have been robbed in their homes at gun point. At one place, they poisoned the guard dog, captured the askari, and told the missionaries that they would kill him if they didn't let them in. They walked off with all of their money and most of their household goods after pistol-whipping the missionary. I hope this thief is part of that band of thugs, and his arrest will stop that activity. The problem is, if you report it to the police, they say, "Okay, send someone out in the morning to pick us up, and we'll investigate it." Police protection here is almost non-existent.

We're pretty safe out at Wairaka. To begin with, Wairaka is a quiet little village of shambas, and the people don't have anything of value to steal. Also, everyone knows that, even though we live in a big house, we're an orphanage, and all we have is a bunch of kids. I suppose they could take our posho and beans, but then they'd have to carry it to Jinja on their backs. I guess there are some advantages to being out in the bush.

MONDAY, JULY 21
As you can well imagine, mail day is an event we celebrate around here, and we struck gold today. It was one of those, "I have good news and bad news" things, though.

The good news is that we got a letter from Deb with pictures of Tyler, a care package from my folks, and a 9x12 manila envelope with close to a dozen letters from our church family. We have spent all evening laughing, crying, and sharing.

The bad news is it takes me all day to get the box from my folks. I have to catch a taxi from Wairaka to the taxi park and a boda-boda to the post office on the other end of town. I've explained how that goes.

When I check our mail box, there is a note that we have a package. I do what I think is the natural thing and take it in to the postal clerk. She reads the note over several times, the way they do when they don't have a clue, and then says, "You have to take this note to the customs agent."

I nod, "Okay, where is the customs agent?"

She makes a vague gesture with her arm, and says, "Theah."

"There, where?" I ask, not unreasonably.

"In the customs office." Her attitude says, "Where do you think you'd find the customs agent?"

"I've never been to the customs office," I explain. "Do you think you could give me directions?" Now the truth comes out. She doesn't know where the customs office is, either.

"Have a seat over theah," she says.

I wait for about thirty minutes before her supervisor comes back from lunch and tells me, "It's over by Starcom." *Of course, it's over by Starcom, back downtown,* I say to myself. How silly of me to think it might be near the post office where packages come in.

I am able to grab another boda-boda without too much trouble and am back downtown within fifteen minutes. I go into customs, show the agent there my note, and wait while he reads it three times. He gives me a blank look and says, "There is a woman theah." I argue with him for another fifteen minutes before he discovers that "the woman" who is supposed to be clearing custom's packages at the post office is, in fact, sitting in the back room taking her lunch break. He finally agrees, reluctantly, to go back to the post office with me and clear my package. "Wheah is your car?"

"I'm sorry, I don't have a car. I rode a taxi into town."

"How will we get to the post office?"

"I guess we'll have to get there the same way I got here, ride a boda-boda, or walk."

He looks at me like I'm kidding. When I return his incredulous gaze, he says, "Follow me, we'll have to take my motorcycle." He leads me around to the back of the building, and there sits a Vespa motor scooter with a spare tire where a passenger seat should be. I get myself perched on top of the spare tire and here we go, swerving through traffic and dodging potholes.

At the post office, he makes me open the box and goes through everything inside, laying each item out on a table.

My dad has included several packages of beef jerky and about fifty dollars worth of vegetable seeds for our garden. He doesn't know what the beef jerky is, so I have to open a package and give him a stick before he lets me keep them. He tells me he will have to send the seeds to Kampala to the Minister of Agriculture for an official stamp before he can release them to me.

I argue, in vain, that they are hermetically sealed in envelopes and couldn't possibly be contaminated. He just shakes his head. Rules is rules.

Here we are living in a country where there are no standards of sanitation. You buy meat that's been hanging out in the market for days, fly blown and sun blackened. You go to the clinic where the clinician doesn't wash before he treats you. You have to cook or peel everything you eat and boil your water for twenty minutes before you can drink it, and they are worried about a few packaged seeds that I want to stick in the ground so that some orphans can have fresh vegetables with their beans and rice.

I shake my head defeated. "Okay, how soon before they will be sent back to me?"

He just shrugs. I'll never see those seeds again. The Minister of Agriculture will have the finest vegetable garden in Uganda.

I gather up what's left and try to get it all back in the shredded box. As I go out through the gate, here is "the woman" back from lunch. She has a stool and a small table under a huge jacaranda tree. She waves me over and tells me I'll have to take everything out at her post. "But I just cleared customs inside," I try to explain, waving my customs declaration form at her.

"I'm not customs, I'm postal department," she says importantly. I lay everything out for her inspection. She barely looks at it, stamps my form, collects 2,000 shillings, and waves me on through. I'm not sure whether that was a postal service fee or bribe, but it doesn't matter. It was only two dollars.

I'm glad to finally be out on the street. I fully expect one of them to chase after me and tell me that they have to send me to Kampala for the Minister of Agriculture's stamp. Nothing is easy in Africa!

THURSDAY, JULY 23

One of the items that was in the care package from home was a solar shower. I take it out early in the morning filled with water, hang it on a fence post, and leave it in the sun all day. When I took it in the shower with me that first evening, I was treated to the most glorious hot shower. It holds enough hot water that Jeanette and I can both have a hot shower, but only if we soap up in the cold water, and then rinse off with hot, or the other way around. If we're really frugal with it, we have enough left to take into our room and fill our wash basin. Now that's a useful invention.

The first night, after I had taken my shower, I asked Philip if he'd like to try it. I noticed him later out in the new shower, taking an African bath with it. He would wet a rag with the hot water, and then wash his face, arms and legs, but he never just stood under the water.

It makes me wonder if they ever bathe all over. I guess that's something I'll never know.

We've been getting away a lot more, lately. We've spent almost every Sunday going into town to Victoria Baptist church. Sometimes, we go over to Dorothy's house to visit and relax, but sometimes we go to the Jinja Sailing club. Jeanette and I discovered it a couple of weeks ago. It's a very nice restaurant right down on Lake Victoria. They have matoke, posho, chicken and goat at their buffet, but they also have the most wonderful lake tilapia. Their tables are scattered around a large lawn under giant trees only a few yards away from the lake. We go there after church and spend all afternoon just watching fishermen out on the lake, read, or write letters.

The staff doesn't seem to mind. We get the buffet, and they bring us cokes, or my favorite, Stoney. I guess Stoney is a ginger beer. I love it. It's so gingery it makes your nose tingle. I get my fill of tilapia, matoke, and ginger beer for the week, and then I can go back to the orphanage and eat my beans and rice, washed down with boiled water until next week.

One day last week, we called Damali aside and told her to pick five other kids to go with us up to the YWAM prayer garden. It's only about a thirty minute walk up the hill. The garden is in a beautiful setting at the base of the mountain behind us. Below, you can see the green patchwork of shambas and sugarcane fields, and in the distance, the blue of the lake spreading forever into the haze of the horizon. There is a small park of evergreen and eucalyptus trees and in the garden, there are several bougainvillea-covered trellises with benches where you can sit and read, meditate, or just look out over an awe-inspiring landscape. It's a good place to come, be alone with God, and maybe find a part of yourself that you have overlooked because of the pressures of life.

It gives us and a few of the kids a chance to get away from the hubbub for a while. Kevin and Heather go for walks during their time off, but since we have to stay here and hold down the fort, I don't know where they go.

I took five or six of the kids on a long hike a couple of days ago.

We hiked up through Wanyange and then climbed Mwidi hill. Mwidi hill is actually a small mountain with pretty steep sides back behind Global Seminary. There is a narrow dirt road that goes up to Busoga College on top, but we went right up through the forest. I discovered that we have Vervets monkeys only a half mile from the orphanage.

Sometimes Jeanette and I put a rope around the necks of Clinton and Shadrach and take them for an outing right around the compound. They really look forward to those times, and, of course, when we do this we have ten or twelve youngsters shouting, "Can I go with you." "Even me, even me." It's never ending, and invariably we wind up taking as many as we can handle. We have begun to put our foot down though, and sometimes we just tell them. "No, Auntie Jeanette and I need to get away for a while. Maybe next time." For the most part, they go on about their playing now and don't pester us too much.

SATURDAY, JULY 25

The morning is overcast today. Out over the lake, about two miles away, there is a rain storm. We can see lightening playing through the magnificent thunderheads and can hear the distant grumbling of the thunder.

We have walked down the road to Mwidi primary school, next to the highway, bringing some of our kids to a traditional dance competition. None of our kids were prepared to participate, but we thought it would be fun to just come and watch. The competitors are dressed in costume, some the flowered gomas, and some grass. It's the same old wild, primitive, beautiful African sound that I've come to love so much.

Some of the dances and costumes are surprisingly like the Tahitian dancers you see in Hawaii. The only difference is when the dancing really starts to get wild, the women in the audience begin that high pitched trilling with their tongues that is, again, so typically African.

As we sit here watching the dances, I can hear the rain begin to patter on the tin roof. I don't mind walking home in the rain, but I'm not too keen on the thunder that's accompanying it. I haven't heard any lightening strikes close by, but I'm still concerned about the kids being out in an electrical storm.

Well, we made it back home, drenched, but safe. The competition was a lot of fun, and the kids really enjoyed it. I know it can't be helped, but it still bothers me that only a few of the kids can participate in events at one time. We try to work it where we alternate groups and the same kids don't always get to go, but there's always some who get left out. The babies hardly ever get to go anywhere, and the handicapped kids get left out a lot. Today, we loaded Joshua Tabingwa in his wheelchair and brought him and two of the other wheelchair kids.

You may remember my first day here I described a boy on the ground at my feet who was so crippled that he looked like a broken grasshopper. That was Joshua. I have come to love him so much. It puts a lump in my throat and brings tears to my eyes with shame at the revulsion I felt when I first saw him. If there was ever anyone who would be justified in being bitter and angry at what life had handed them, it would be him. Not our Joshua, though. I've never met anyone with a sweeter spirit. He always has a ready smile and doesn't have a problem with laughing at himself. Secunde, who is our fastest runner, challenged me to a race the other day. Needless to say, by the time I was getting my second wind, or getting winded for the second time, Secunde had crossed the finish line. All of the kids were howling in glee, but Joshua called down from the porch, "That's okay, Unca Rrah; you can probably beat me in a race."

Jeanette has started a physical therapy program on his bad arm. She massages his hand, and then gently stretches his fingers out. Then at night, she puts the hand in a brace and wraps it tightly with an ace bandage. I know it's uncomfortable for him, but he just looks at her with worshipful eyes, smiles and says thank you.

She has also been working with Rani, our Indian girl, and another of our wheelchair children. Rani is suffering from severe bed soars from being in her wheelchair so much of the time. Jeanette has taken on the chore of bathing them and keeping antibiotic cream on them. I really don't know how Jeanette does all that she does.

There are things that happen here that are almost beyond our naïve American comprehension. The other day when we had field day, I had loaded Rani up with the other handicapped kids and taken her to the Global field. When I unloaded her chair, something hung up in the folding mechanism. I removed the seat to try to fix it, and cockroaches scattered everywhere, from right inside her chair. I had the typical American reaction of disbelief and horror. When I finally got my rage under control, I turned to Philip, "I want you to go back to the orphanage right now and get the roach killer and spray this chair. Then tonight I want you to take everything out of her room and spray it good!!" Poor Philip, it certainly wasn't his fault, but right about then, I was angry at Africa, and he was African. At that moment, he was fearing me.

"Yes, Unca Rrah, I will stay home and do it now." I calmed down sufficiently to put my hand on his arm and give him a smile. "No, my friend, I want you to enjoy the games; but as soon as they are over I want you to take care of it."

Now if Philip is indispensable around here, Tall Mary is invaluable. Of all of us here, she's probably the most suited to be here. She is truly one of God's special people. You can see her jogging up the trail, from her home below Wairaka, about 7:45 in the morning. She begins her workday making sure all of the kids are washed, combed, and dressed for school. While they are in school, you may see her helping in the kitchen, helping Jeanette with the medicines, or doctoring. She cuts and braids hair, delouses their heads, and treats for ringworm, lances boils, and clips fingernails. During lunch break she serves, and then jogs back down the trail to fix lunch for her own family. By one 1:00 she's back at the compound to help the little guys get out of their school uniforms and into play clothes. Then you may see her playing jump rope with the girls or playing football with the boys. Sometimes she just sits on the front steps, surrounded by children, reading or telling them a story. She seems to always be smiling, even when she is chasing some kid or reprimanding them for some infraction. She stays through supper, again helping serve, and then helping the clean up crew with their chores. When she leaves around 6:30, it's always with a wave and a goodbye. Then she jogs down the trail to fix supper for her own family. She is "mother" to 115 children and never seems to tire of it. Tall Mary, you're one of a kind. Thank God for people like you.

MONDAY, JULY 27

One of the projects we've been working on here is to try to paint some of the more needy areas. Philip has already painted the front entry and it looks great, so now, we've decided to sand and paint the baby's veranda on the second floor. Since the kids love to be involved with any project, Kevin and I have enlisted some of the bigger boys, Moses, Godfrey, Ocham, Morris, Francis and Noel to do the sanding. I stayed up there with them for a while, supervising and doing a little of the sanding myself, but then I turned it over to them to finish, and went down to take care of something else. When I came back up to check on them, I found them happily dusting each other with the white chalk they have sanded off the walls, face, arms, hands, everything that's not covered.

"Look Unca Rrah, were wazungus, just like you."

I double over with laughter. "Do not move," I instruct them. Then I run down to get Jeanette, Kevin and Heather to come up and look while I run for the camera. This is truly a Kodak moment.

WEDNESDAY, JULY 29

This morning as I'm puttering around out in the yard, I notice that Solomon is drooping his left wing and there are blood stains on the white feathers. He won't let me approach him close enough to tell what the problem is, but I can tell the blood is dripping from under his wing. Kevin is in town, and Jeanette and Heather are at a missionary ladies Bible study and luncheon, so I call Philip out to try to help me catch him.

Catching a crested crane that doesn't want to be caught is a chore. To begin with, he stands about four feet tall and can swing a pretty mean uppercut with his wing. Not only that, but if he really decides that he doesn't want to be caught, he can easily sail up to the top of the roof.

He doesn't do that, though, and only runs away when we try to grab him. We finally get him trapped inside the screened porch. Once we get him surrounded, he calms down and I walk right up to him and lift his wing. I don't know how he got it, but he has a deep cut on his rib cage. I send Philip into the kitchen to get me cotton balls, peroxide, and bacterial ointment. After we doctor him, we walk him back outside. He cocks his head at me, sticks it under his wing to inspect our work, and then takes flight to the top of the roof. It's early in the afternoon, but I believe he's put himself to bed.

We have put a hasp and padlock on our shower door to keep the kids from washing their clothes, filling jerry cans, or who knows what else, in our shower.

Right after supper, I take my towel, soap and shampoo out for a nice cold shower. It's been overcast and rainy, so my solar shower never got hot. I unlock the padlock and hang it on the hasp outside the door. Just about the time I get my head all lathered up and my eyes squeezed shut, I hear this giggling on the outside and the lock rattling in the hasp. I get my head rinsed and my eye against the crack in the door just in time to see Nicolai, our six year old Romanian boy, running around the corner, laughing his head off. I unhook the latch on the inside of the door and give it a shove. It won't open. The little beast has locked me in.

Betty, one of our cooks, is in the outdoor kitchen so I call her over, fish the key out of my pocket, (for once I'm thankful that I have to take my clothes in with me when I shower), and hand it over the top of the door to her to unlock the lock. She is giggling, the other women in the kitchen are giggling, and now I start to laugh. If I'd thought about it, I'd have paid Nicolai 100 shillings to lock Jeanette in.

Nicolai is one of the Walkers adopted children. Being Romanian, he is, of course, white. Well, he's mostly white. I think his little hands and feet are permanently stained red from the dirt here. Either that or I have yet to see him clean. The other little boys may be stained red too, but being black, it doesn't show.

SATURDAY, AUGUST 1
As I've mentioned before, Jeanette has a certain way with the kids

and staff. She never misses an opportunity to witness to them. This morning, while she was dosing the kids for their mumps, colds, flu, tonsillitis, malaria, bad teeth, and eye infection, I heard her talking to one of them. She keeps a running medical sheet on each child in a loose-leaf notebook, but apparently she didn't have a sheet for this one child. "Oh, no!" she cried, "Your name isn't in my book. That means I can't treat you. Is your name in the book of life?" The little girl gave her a quizzical look and shrugged. "You know, Jesus has a book just like mine. You need to tell Jesus that you want Him to put your name in His book." And then, she proceeded to tell her how she could do that.

WEDNESDAY, AUGUST 5

There is a situation here which makes my own sense of homesickness more acute, if that's possible. We have three brothers: Louis 9, Paul 7, and Charles 5, whose father died of AIDS a few years ago. Their mother is still alive, but has the HIV virus and is afraid she is dying, as well. Even if she weren't sick, life is hard here for widows. The Uganda custom is that when a man dies, his family comes to the home and takes everything -- furniture, cooking pots, goats and chickens. All they leave is the hungry children.

Having heard of us, and knowing that her three boys would fare better here, she had them turned over to us.

At least once a week, Louis asks me for paper, pencil, and envelope so that he can write to his mommy. He writes the sweetest letters telling her how much he misses her, how school is going, and that he will be glad when school is over so that they can come home for a visit. She hasn't come to visit them that I'm aware of, but again, about once a week, I deliver a letter to them from her. When he gets them, Louis gathers his brothers under the big bougainvillea and reads the letters to them.

Yesterday, I was sitting on the porch when Charles crawled up in my lap, laid his head against my chest and said, "Unca Rrah, I don't want to be here anymore. I want to go home."

When my eyes cleared and my throat opened up enough to speak,

I said, "I know Charles, I'm praying about it." We sat there, holding each other and giving each other comfort for about thirty minutes before he jumped down to play with Ochaki, and I returned to work.

I know their mother thinks it's to their advantage for them to stay here, but I've come to realize that family is more important than advantage.

Their school term is over September 5. I'm praying that they can go home for the three week break-------and not come back. Oh, yes, I'll miss them. I've come to love them very much, but I'll know that they're happy

MONDAY, AUGUST 10

As I was sitting here in my office doing school superintendent work, (writing in my journal), it began to rain drops as big as gumdrops. I rushed out yelling for the boys in P7 to come help me move the maize from the parking pad into the wood shed. Everyone in the compound had spent all day Saturday harvesting it and laying it out on the pad to dry. When it is sufficiently dry, we will take it down to the mill to have it made into posho.

Heather has done a fabulous job of contacting the Tip Top Bakery, Kakira Sugar Works, and the Madhvani family to get donations of bread, matoke, papaya, posho and beans. We pick up a half a truck load of day old bread once a week from the bakery, and the other stuff is delivered to us once a month. It has really helped cut our food budget. That and the donation we get from Feed the Children will just about take care of our groceries.

We're hoping to get four or five hundred kilos of posho from our own maize. That'll help a great deal, too. We also harvested our beans, but we'll be lucky to get three meals out of them.

FRIDAY, AUGUST 14

About a week ago, I don't remember the day now, Headmaster Fred and I went to Kampala and spent all day trying to get our school certified under the Uganda curriculum. After battling city hall, showing our records and registering me as the school administrator, we were able to be certified as a boarding school.

Now I'm sitting here on the front steps anxiously waiting for the Department of Education inspector to come, look us over and give his approval for us to continue to operate. I feel like an expectant father. I know we have a good school. We have a very dedicated and diligent headmaster in Fred. We also have eight great teachers who provide our children with as good, if not better, education than they would get in the village school. Even though this is in no way due to my leadership, I am quite proud to be its leader.

In only a couple of months, we have gone from all classes meeting in the dining room to separate classrooms for seven out of nine classes. Of course, we had to convert a goat shed into two classrooms and a storage shed into the third one, but now we can boast preschool through Primary seven and a special education class for our handicapped students. We have organized a reference and lending library with over five hundred books, and I am trying to get a football team started.

Do I sound like I'm thumping my chest? Maybe I am, for what "my" teachers and students have accomplished. School Administrator, Good Shepherd's Christian Academy? You bet, and proud of it!

SUNDAY, AUGUST 17

I finally met Victor, the pastor of the Victoria United Pentecostal Apostolic Church. He came by the other day to ask for a bag of posho for his family and a loan of 5,000 shillings. We gave it to him even though we know we'll never see the 5,000 shillings again. I figure that's what we're here for, though, not just to take care of the orphanage, but to help whoever needs it, within our limits, of course.

After he got the money and posho, he turned to me. "I would like for you to come to my church, and preach on Sunday." This took me by surprise since I hadn't met him up until now, but I said, "Yes, I'd like that."

The church is what I'm used to. It's between Jari and Kyuga in size and style, mud brick walls, dirt floor, tin roof. He has a few wooden benches, but most of his congregation sits on mats on the floor. He has a small wooden table for me to lay my Bible on while I preach.

I have prepared a message about the apostle Paul, and I feel very confident. I spent three days putting it together. I preach for forty-five minutes, and if the shine in Jeanette's eyes is any indication, I did well. I got several amen's.

WEDNESDAY, AUGUST 20

We almost lost Ocham during the lunch break today. He was playing football while one of the girls was flying down pell-mell on the rope swing. They collided, hitting him full force in the chest. The impact lifted him off of his feet, flipping him backward. He hit his head on a root, knocking himself out cold. When we got out to him, he had stopped breathing, and we couldn't find a pulse. Jeanette was afraid that the jolt had stopped his heart, so she and Kevin began giving him CPR. They finally got him breathing again, but it took a good twenty minutes before his eyes fluttered, and he regained consciousness enough for us to get him on his feet and into the lorry to take him into town. When Kevin took him in the clinic, the nurse wanted to give him a malaria shot. "He doesn't have malaria," he told her. "He was knocked unconscious. He may have a concussion." The nurse looked at him with a blank expression and said, "Well, he could get malaria."

THURSDAY, AUGUST 21

Ocham and I have come to Jinja this morning to get him a follow-up PPF shot. After giving him a pain relief shot, the nurse replaces the needle and starts to give him a second shot. "Excuse me, ma'am," Ocham says, "You forgot to put in the medicine." She looks at the empty syringe and says, "Oh, sorry."

I plan to tell Jeanette, "If I ever get sick here, just take me to the nearest airport and ship me home. Don't let them treat me here."

SUNDAY, AUGUST 24

What a nice birthday!! Jeanette cooked it up with Dorothy for us to come into town yesterday and spend the weekend in peace and quiet at her house. She fixed a fabulous supper last night. I had a *hot* shower before bed. (I'm afraid I stayed in there for at least a half an hour.) And she made us a breakfast of fried eggs, bacon and sausage this morning. This is almost like civilization. We will go to church in a few minutes, eat lunch at the Jinja Sailing club, and then spend all afternoon watching old John Wayne movies.

This Dorothy is my kind of lady. When her husband died after many years of illness, she decided to see the world. She spent several months living on a kibbutz in Israel, (she was already in her sixties by then), climbed Mt.Tabor and worked on the Jericho archeological dig. Now she's a missionary in Uganda. Contrary to the country western song, she cried when Ol' Yeller died, she's washed in the blood of the Lamb, and she's a John Wayne fan. And, if that isn't enough, she loves old books. She has a first addition of *African Game Trails* by Theodore Roosevelt that I would cut off the little finger on my left hand for.

MONDAY, AUGUST 25
Jeanette has a new vocation, or maybe it's an avocation. She is now a master goat wrestler. As we were going up the road for our walk yesterday, we noticed that one of the goats had gotten its rope tangled to the point that he was wedged under the fence and could hardly move. When I tried to free him, he kicked and squirmed so hard I couldn't even get a grip on him or the rope. I told Jeanette, "See if you can hold him still long enough for me to untangle his rope." She grabbed his front legs and threw her body across his to hold him down while I tried to un-wrap his hind legs. I've seen goats not tied up this secure during a goat-roping at the 4H rodeo. When it was all over and the goat was free, Jeanette's hair looked like a hay stack all over her head, her shirt tail was out and she had red dirt all over her, including a big smudge on her face, but you know what? She was quite beautiful at that moment.

TUESDAY, AUGUST 26
We celebrate birthdays once a month for everyone who has a birthday in that month, and this month I happen to be included in the festivities. The staff bakes seven to ten cakes and decorates them with the names of those turning a year older. Sometimes we have as many as 12-14 kids at a time. We light candles and sing *Happy Birthday* to each one individually.

It takes a while to do that, but we want each one to feel special. After that, each kid gets a cavera filled with goodies, a new shirt, and a toy. Tonight, I'm wearing a party hat along with five or six of the children. My cake is not quite big enough for 59 candles, but there are still enough to light up the whole room! Hey! If the power goes off tonight, we're in good shape! I'm reminded again how much I love these kids as some of them bring me their homemade birthday cards and letters, so many I think we can cover the walls in our little room with them.

WEDNESDAY, AUGUST 27
I just heard a blood curdling scream coming from right outside my office. Naturally, I ran right out to investigate.

It seems Jjajja Mary came out of the indoor kitchen and found Solomon bathing in her nappy-wash tub. Right now, she's chasing him around the yard with a posho paddle and giving him what for in Lugandan.

When they heard the scream, all of the kids and teachers came pouring out of their respective classrooms and are now standing out in the yard laughing and pointing.

I don't know where Jeanette, Heather and Kevin came from, but they have joined in the revelry now, as well.

Of course, when Jjajja Mary discovered that she had an audience to entertain, she and Solomon both really started to put on a show. She will chase after him, brandishing her paddle; he will flap away from her, squawking, and then turn, droop his wings and do his little dance. They both seem to be enjoying their little game immensely.

I don't know how old Mary is, probably not much older than me, but she's very grandmotherly. She's big and wide, the way a grandmother should be, but she's surprisingly spry for her age and bulk. On field day, the kids had a dance competition and Mary joined in. She must have been quite a dancer in her prime.

FRIDAY, AUGUST 29
Francis Okulo and I have walked down to the highway, caught a

RALPH AND JEANETTE REAVES

taxi, and then walked to the dentist office in the center of town. He has had an abscessed tooth for a couple of days now, and aspirin doesn't seem to touch the pain. I am finally impressed with a medical facility here. It's relatively clean. The dentist even has his instruments bathing in a steamer. As Francis sits down in the dentist chair, the doctor opens his mouth and examines his tooth. "Nnnn, it is an old filling. I can drill it out, clean out the abscess and refill it." He smiles at me.

Alright, finally someone who seems to know his business.

The dentist walks over to his steaming tools, picks up one in his fingers, and then drops it back onto the tray. "Ahhh, that's hot!" he says. With that, he picks up the tray with towels, takes it over to his sink and proceeds to run regular tap water over the tools to cool them. Now tap water in Jinja comes right out of Lake Victoria and is more dangerous than muddy water out of an irrigation ditch at home.

"There," he smiles, "that's much better."

So much for sanitation.

SUNDAY NIGHT / MONDAY MORNING, SEPTEMBER 1

What a night!! It's about two AM. About midnight, one of the dogs began yelping and crying. I could tell that he was in distress rather than just barking, so I got up and walked out into the yard where they were tied under the lorry. Shadrach had wrapped himself around a rear tire so bad he only had about six inches of slack in his chain. (Didn't I just tell a story similar to this about goats?)

I crawled under the lorry to try to extricate him, but it was so dark, I couldn't see how to get him loose. Just about the time I was ready to give up, I saw a light and Jeanette's legs. "Anything I can do?"

"Yeah," I said, "shine that light under here." She shined the flashlight under the truck, and after fifteen minutes or so, I was able to get him free. I took him and Clinton out and tied them to a pair of spare truck wheels lying in the yard. I figured they couldn't get tangled up with these, and the wheels are too heavy for them to drag far.

Since we're up anyway, we decide to go on around back and make a potty stop before we go back to bed.

"Oh, no," Jeanette says, "Ruben is loose." I look up on Florence's front porch, and sure enough, there's that naughty jackass with his head down in her bag of maize, just chomping away. When he hears me come up on the porch, he lifts his head out of the gunny sack and backs his ears. I know he's too strong to lead with the rope around his neck, if he tries to run, so quickly I whip a couple of loops in the trailing end of the rope, and before he knows what's happening, I have a snaffle bit around his nose and take him back out into the yard. I can't find the stake he was tied to in the dark, so I just tie him to the swing set for the night. Moses will have to move him in the morning.

Finally, after more than an hour since I went out to check on Shadrach, we are climbing back into bed. I don't have the light off five minutes when there is a terrible racket in our room. In my drowsiness, I wonder if, somehow, Ruben has followed me into the room and is crashing around in the dark. Jeanette sits bolt upright in bed thinking the same thing, I guess. Then on listening more closely, I realize that we have disturbed the rats in the ceiling, and they are scurrying around up there. As I lie here staring into the dark, I hear Jeanette say, "And black rat takes the lead around the far turn, coming up on the inside rail." We both start to laugh so hard we can't go back to sleep. As we lie here in the dark listening to the pack thunder above our bed, we crack up again and again.

Now, who said living in an orphanage in the middle of Africa is all work and no fun?

TUESDAY, SEPTEMBER 2

Being isolated out here in the boonies, and not having a radio or television, we don't always get current news. Therefore, it was late yesterday before we heard the tragic news of Princess Dianna's auto accident and her death. She was very special to the Ugandans. She was very special to the entire world, I guess, but the Ugandans had a special affinity for her. Our compound is in deep grief for her today.

I have declared a holiday from school so that we can have a special day to commemorate her life and death. Jeanette read a really nice eulogy that she prepared. I am going to read a scripture, and then we will break up into small groups to pray for her and the royal family. I feel sorry for Florence and Rita both. They have spent their day in their rooms crying. You would think they had lost a member of their family, and maybe they have.

SUNDAY, SEPTEMBER 7
I want to be home so bad today!! We talked to Bryan, our son-in-law, last night, and he told us that he had taken Deb to the hospital to give birth to our newest granddaughter. He said he would call us back as soon as she was delivered. I'm afraid I left Jeanette to take care of most of the nightly chores while I sat by the phone. Kevin and Heather have gone on a camping trip to celebrate his twenty-ninth birthday, so we have the duty this weekend.

I waited in the office until eleven, when Jeanette came down and said she was ready to go to bed. It's now about ten in the morning, and I've been sitting here waiting for the phone to ring since six o'clock.

Jeanette just came in concerned that something has gone wrong with the delivery. We made the decision to turn the orphanage over to Rita and Florence and go into town to call them from Starcom.

SUNDAY EVENING, SEPTEMBER 7
What a bonehead Bryan is.

Naturally, it took us the normal hour and a half to get to Starcom using a taxi and boda-boda. (The van is still out, and Kevin and Heather have the lorry.)

We bought a calling card and called Bryan, even though it was one AM in Phoenix. He answered in a sleepy voice and said, "Oh, yeah, I must have forgotten to call you back."

Here we are, sitting in darkest Africa, waiting for our only daughter to have a baby and wanting to be home to the point of depression, and he forgot to call us back. When I get home, after I give him a hug, I think I'll kill him.

Amber Jeanette was born at 11:48 AM, Mountain Standard Time (8:48 PM our time), and Deb had a very easy delivery. In fact, she said she actually enjoyed it.

On our way back to the taxi park, we decided to go to Biashara, the little Indian grocery and pick up some cheese for cheese sandwiches and a couple of apples. When we walked up the path from the highway, the kids saw us coming and ran out to the gate to greet us, yelling "Unca Rrah, Auntie Ja-nette, welcome home. Can I catch your cavera?" In Uganda English, that means can I carry your package?

I know I've done nothing but complain about being here and have repeatedly said I want to go home, but when fifteen or twenty kids of all ages try to hug me, hold my hand, and catch my cavera, I can't help but feel an overwhelming love for them and this place.

This evening, after sing time, I instruct all of the kids to find a place to sit, and be quiet for a moment. "Before we take the little kids to bed tonight, Auntie Jeanette and I have an announcement. As you know, our daughter in America is going to have a baby. Well, last night, she gave us a little red headed granddaughter named Amber Jeanette, and our daughter wants you to celebrate her birth with us, so she sent everyone a sweetie." With this, Jeanette and Heather begin to hand out pink "it's a girl" suckers to each child. "Now, I want you to wait until tomorrow to open them," I say. "I don't want to come upstairs in a few minutes and find sticky suckers in your beds or in you hair.

"You don't really think…" Jeanette starts to say.

"No, but I thought it was worth a try."

After I went up and tucked the thirty or so little boys in, got them all watered and bathroomed, and read to, I came back down to the main dining room where Kevin and Heather had already started "big kids prayer group." I slipped in so as not to disturb them and sat on a bench along the wall. I had only been sitting there for a second when Morris came over and sat down beside me.

"Unca Rrah, would you send this letter to your daughter for me?" He said, slipping a folded piece of paper into my hand.

"You wrote a letter to my daughter?" I asked

"Yes, while you and Auntie were in town. Will you mail it for me?"

I gave him a hug around the shoulders. "Of course, I will." I said

What joy!! What blissful joy! You can't even imagine how wonderful it is to sit here in our room at the end of the day and enjoy a nice crisp apple and a wedge of cheese. The apples are very expensive because they have to be shipped up from South Africa, but they are such a refreshing change from beans and rice. We will have to indulge in this luxury more often. Not only that but we bought a Hershey with almonds. We both only take one section so that we can do this again tomorrow. Who would have ever thought that we would be hording a Hershey bar and savoring an apple like it was some gourmet dinner. Ah, the joys of living in the bush in darkest Africa.

As I start to get ready for bed, I come across a folded piece of paper in my pocket. I read it, hand it to Jeanette with misty eyes. She reads it, hands it back to me and a tear spills over and runs down her cheek.

To our baby amber

I think your enjoying the life I thank your people for helping us may the Lord help you so that you may grow up as me

I know that God wanted you to be on the world I just want you to know that Jesus is your personal Saviour and know that God is the one
who created you to stay in the world I have neve seen your pictures but I think you can send me one of your pictures

I want to pray that God may help you so that you may grow and study
well I know God will help you and you will grow up well

My name is Morris I live in Uganda Uganda is were God wanted me to
be I think I can give you my address So that you can write back

God Bless you so much and he may keep you well

WEDNESDAY, SEPTEMBER 10

I just looked out beyond the fence and there are four or five boys up in the mango tree. Kajuna and Secunde came to me a while ago and asked if they could go out there and pick the ripe mangos. I told them, "Not right now. I don't have time to go with you, and you won't stop with the ripe ones."

They have no sense at all. Once they begin picking, they pick the green ones as well as the ripe ones. They are supposed to pick them and bring them to the cooks to prepare for supper, but they eat as many as they bring in. I did the same with scuppernongs as a kid. The only problem is they eat them peeling and all; consequently, they will all have a bellyache tonight.

When I get out there to take names and paddle behinds, I'm surprised and shocked to find Fred Kagje among them. Normally Kagje is a model kid and is never in trouble. He is one of the ones who had polio as an infant and has to use crutches to walk.

I send the rest back to the house to await their punishment, and I walk with Kagje while he hobbles along. I think waiting and thinking about a paddling is better punishment than the actual swat I'll give them.

Kagje won't look up at me. Finally I break the silence, "Didn't you hear me when I said you couldn't pick the mangos?" I ask.

"Yes," he mumbles.

I shake my head. "I'm really disappointed in you, Fred."

"I know. I'm sorry."

As we walk along, a light comes on in my head. As I said before, I'm beginning to learn that sometimes their English doesn't always mean what I think it means. I remember, now, that if you ask them a question in the negative, they will answer in the positive. When I asked, "Didn't you hear me?" his answer was, "Yes, I didn't hear you." I should have known that Fred would never deliberately disobey me.

So I rephrase my question. "Kagje, were you with the other boys when I said you couldn't pick the mangos?"

"No, sir."

"So, you didn't hear me."

"Yes, sir."

The spoken word is not the only source of misunderstanding here. You have to watch their facial expressions as well. I was asking one of the teachers if she understood something the other day, and her response was a soft nasal "Nnnnn" with uplifted eyebrows. After asking her the same thing a few times and getting the same response, I realized that that's the same as us nodding our head and saying, "Uh huh."

I pride myself on picking up foreign languages fairly easy, but I'm not sure I'll ever learn to speak English, their brand of English, anyway.

FRIDAY, SEPTEMBER 12

We have spent all day in Jinja today, going from one official office to another, trying to get our visas and work permits straightened out. When we first arrived in Uganda, we asked for a one year work permit. For some reason, the official at the airport stamped it for three years. Now the official at the Immigration Office here in Jinja is telling us that our visas are only valid until the 26th of September, but that our work permit is for three years, so we'll have to pay $500.00 each for the other two years on our work permit since the airport official only charged us for one year. We have tried to explain to him that we were planning to leave in November anyway, so we don't need the extra two years. Talk about your catch 22s. We have to be out of the country by September the 26th, but we have to pay $500.00 each to extend our work permit for another two years, and I can't seem to get it across to him that we don't want to stay another two years.

After visiting three other official offices, the last one tells us that they can't straighten out the problem in Jinja. We will have to go to the Immigration Commissioners office in Kampala on Monday.

They don't seem to realize that we don't have transportation to zip into Kampala on Monday. If it takes an hour and a half to go eight miles from Wairaka to Jinja, what's it going to take to go eighty kilometers to Kampala?

When we get back home, I find that the coach of the National Soccer team has been waiting for me to return. He has heard that I have been trying to get some of my boys organized into a soccer team so that they can compete with the Moslem boy's school in Bugembe and the teams at Wanyange and Iganga. He wants to volunteer his time to coach my boys on Saturday afternoons. This will mean that he will have to take a taxi from Kampala to Jinja, change to a taxi coming to Wairaka, and walk up the shamba path to the orphanage, just like we do. All of a sudden I feel ashamed that I complain about what they take for granted.

The boys on the team are overjoyed that they have a real coach now, and not just Unca Rrah, who doesn't even know how to play soccer. By the end of the afternoon, however, they are having second thoughts. They thought they would just come to Global and mess around with the ball, like they do with me, but he has really put them through a workout. A few of the younger ones who were not really serious in the first place, have decided to drop out of the team. I tell them okay, but if they do, they'll have to go on back home. They are not allowed to stay and get in the way. I'm not a very popular guy with them right now.

To add to my frustrating day, I just broke a tooth. If you think I'm going to get it fixed here you'd better think again. They would probably want to give me a shot for malaria before they yanked it out with a pair of pliers.

SUNDAY, SEPTEMBER 14

It's been a very pleasant day. We did our normal Sunday routine of going into town to church, but today, Dorothy asked us if we'd like to take her car out to Bujigali Falls, just the two of us. Bujigali Falls is a place north of the city where the Nile tumbles over seven low cataracts. The river is very fast right here and there is quite a bit of white water. We watched some traditional native dances, watched a man go over the falls clinging to a sealed, plastic jerry can, and just enjoyed each other's company without 115 kiddos to help us.

Now tonight, as we are getting ready for bed, our door flies open with a bang, and there stands Nicolai with his arms outstretched. "Auntie Ja-net, I need a hug." It's hard right at this moment to think what a brat he normally is. We both burst out laughing and, of course, give him the biggest goodnight hug he's had in a long time.

MONDAY, SEPTEMBER 15

90 degrees, 90 percent humidity, twenty-three people in a taxi, and eighty kilometers to Kampala, it's no wonder my back is killing me this morning.

At the stop in Bugembe, they filled the taxi with eighteen people, and then stopped on the highway for five more. People were sitting on top of people. I had to sit leaning forward the entire trip while Jeanette had to lean back in an uncomfortable position. They didn't even have room for one passenger's goat. They had to tie him to the luggage rack on top of the van.

There is a bell that bongs whenever the car goes faster than the approved speed, and it was going off constantly. The driver drove on the wrong side of the road most of the time, trying to pass other traffic. He narrowly missed a headon collision twice, and once, he had to hit the barrow-ditch when he tried to pass a car that was passing a car. I think it's quite appropriate that their road signs read "no parallel driving," rather than "no passing."

It's not surprising that traffic accidents are the number two killer in Uganda, AIDS being number one.

We learned a long time ago, however, that to just survive here, we have to give our lives over to God on a daily basis, and trust Him to keep us safe. Believe it or not, during this trip, neither of us was particularly afraid.

We didn't want to go all the way across Kampala to the taxi park, so when we got to the center of Kampala we had the driver stop to let us and our luggage off. When we got on top to get our luggage, the little goat was standing up there on stiffened legs, with tears running from his eyes, but I'll swear on a Bible, he was grinning.

Carrying our suitcase, we walked the four or five blocks up to the Speke Hotel and checked in. People looked at me curiously as we passed, not because I was walking and carrying a suitcase, but because I wasn't carrying it on my head the way a sensible person would.

The Speke is one of the older hotels in Kampala, very quaint, but nice. We have really enjoyed our stay here. It is wonderful to take a hot shower right in the room, and not have to walk outside and around to the back to go to the bathroom in the middle of the night. Not only that, but we treated ourselves to tilapia for dinner last night. It's kind of funny how taken-for-granted things can thrill you when you've had to do without them for a while.

Our business with immigrations started a little rocky. Naturally we got the man whose job it is to figure out why you can't do what you need to do, and then work toward that end. I got the same run around the official in Jinja gave me. "You can't extend your visa past the twenty-sixth of September, but neither can you shorten your work permit." After arguing the absurdity of this for a good half hour, he decided that if I got a letter from Global Outreach explaining the problem, that his superior might be able to do something. Fortunately I had foreseen this possibility, had written a letter of explanation on Global Outreach stationery and signed it myself. When I presented it to him, he looked at it, and then at me, and said, "You must leave the letter, your work permit and your passport. The Immigration Board will review it tomorrow afternoon."

We very reluctantly left everything that proved who we were and why we were there, and left the building. Over lunch, we decided this just wouldn't do. We returned to the Immigration office, and this time got a woman who seemed to be all business. We explained to her that we lived up country eighty kilometers, couldn't possibly return tomorrow, and couldn't afford a hotel and meals for another day since we are volunteer missionaries and have no money, and that's the truth of it.

She looked briefly at our paperwork, walked into an office that was marked Immigration Commissioner, and returned a short time later with our papers and a smile. "You will have to pay seventy-five thousand shillings each, but the commissioner will extend your visa and change your work permit to one year."

A hundred and fifty thousand shillings, around $150.00, is a lot to us because we aren't drawing any salary, but it is better than the $500.00

we were told we'd have to pay.

The taxi ride back to Jinja wasn't too bad. They stopped loading at only fifteen passengers. Getting out of the taxi park was a chuckle though. The taxis all around us were not moving because they didn't have full loads, so our driver tried to go between two other taxis. The only problem was there wasn't enough room for a van to go between them. This poses little concern for an African taxi driver, though. He maneuvered his vehicle between the other two, and with about enough space on either side to pass a piece of paper, he drove on through. We waited with clenched teeth to hear the rending of metal or at the least, the scraping of paint. He was a veteran taxi driver, however, and no people, or vehicles were damaged.

If the trip from Kampala to Jinja was easy enough, the speed bell only went off two or three times, the ride from Jinja was a nightmare. The taxi we were in was a piece of junk. The seats were torn, springs were sticking through, and the only way they could keep the door closed was for the fare collector to hold it closed as we drove. We had to wait in the taxi park for more than an hour for a full load, and then we made no less than ten stops.

I guess it was a successful trip, though. We arrived home tired and hungry, but safe, and no worse for the wear. We accomplished what we went for, although at this point, I think we'd have been just as happy with having to leave on the twenty-sixth. Again, twenty children met us at the gate, yelling "Welcome home! Can I catch your cavera?" They're always so glad to see us. It makes us live on a see-saw. One minute we're ready to throw up our hands and run screaming down the shamba path, and the next, we're ready to knuckle down and give our all to these wonderful, loving kids.

WEDNESDAY, SEPTEMBER 17

Again, as we are going up the dirt road for an evening walk, we notice that Alisa, who is helping put the goats in the shed for the night, is having trouble with one that has circled the bush that it's tied to until it's rope is strangling it to death. It has stopped breathing, its tongue is purple and hanging out, and when the poor thing tries to bleat, it just makes a gurgling sound. I try to untie the knot, but it is so tight I can't get my fingers in it. Frantically I gasp to Jeanette, "I need a sharp knife." At this point, Jeanette strikes out running to the house to get one. As she goes through the gate, a group of boys look up. "Quick, Ocham, Uncle Ralph needs a sharp knife." Ocham immediately runs into the kitchen, comes out at full speed, and sprints into the field where I'm trying desperately to loosen the rope around the goat's neck.

"Ocham, hold the knife away from your body!" Jeanette screams as she tries to catch him, "All we need is for you to fall and stab yourself."

When Ocham reaches me and hands me the knife, Alisa looks at me with huge liquid eyes, "Unca Rrah, you're not going to kill her are you?"

"No, dear," I reply, "I'm not going to kill her. I'm trying to save her." The rope is biting into the goat's neck so tight I can't even get the blade between its neck and the rope, so I just start sawing on the rope and hope I don't cut its throat in the process.

I finally cut through it, and miraculously don't stab the goat. I'm afraid we're going to have goat for supper tomorrow, anyway though, because she just lies there with her tongue hanging out and her eyes bulging. I massage her throat for a minute, and finally, I see some life come back into her eyes. In another minute, she struggles to her feet and meekly follows Alisa back to the goat shed.

SATURDAY, SEPTEMBER 20

Jeanette has been sick for two days now. She first began to feel bad Thursday night, and then all day yesterday she has been throwing up. She has become so weak from the vomiting and diarrhea she can no longer go around back to the bathroom. I had to fix her up with a bucket next to the bed. At first, we thought it was malaria, but we've had dysentery in the camp, so now I'm sure she's got that. It's crazy, she's the one who always wears rubber gloves when she treats the kids and staff, and yet now she's gotten sick. I'm never careful, but I'm as healthy as a horse.

I had to fire one of the teachers yesterday. Teacher Fred, our headmaster, brought it to my attention that her records had been altered with white out. Before I confronted her with it, I walked up to the teacher's college at Wanyange, where she had attended. The headmaster there was very cooperative and dug her records out of the cardboard box that is his file cabinet. Come to find out, she didn't have the wonderful grades her records showed. In fact, she didn't graduate. She had been expelled for poor grades. When I confronted her with it, she didn't try to deny it, so I had no recourse but to let her go. I didn't fire her for having bad grades, or for not graduating, although if we want to retain our certification as a school under the Uganda curriculum, she has to have a valid teaching certificate. I let her go for falsifying her records and lying to us. Still, I felt bad having to do it. She was actually a pretty good teacher and the kids all liked her.

MONDAY, SEPTEMBER 22

I'm really getting worried about Jeanette. She is no better. In fact, she is worse. She can barely lift her head off of the pillow now. Her strength is completely gone. I called Beverly Cathey to come pick her up and take her into Jinja to the clinic. They diagnosed her with malaria, of course, amebic dysentery, and an E. coli infection. They gave her a shot for the malaria; it can't hurt her, and they put her on Flagil for the dysentery. We've been giving the kids Flagil for a few days now. Jeanette says she knows now why they run from her when she tries to give it to them, and then spit it out as soon as she turns her back. It must be some nasty stuff.

TUESDAY, SEPTEMBER 23

Jeanette just called me into the room and said, "Please don't let me die here." I've been worried, but now I'm terrified. We're losing her.

I went out and found Damali and asked her to get the praise team together to pray for Jeanette. My plan was to join them in the office and pray with them, but when I was right outside the office door, I could hear Damali inside praying. "Satan, I command you in the name of Jesus to leave Auntie Jeanette! I bind you in the name of Jesus! I bind you and you have no power!" Her prayer was so powerful, and touched me so much I began sobbing right there in the hall. I couldn't go in, but it didn't matter, they didn't need me. I stood there and listened as each one prayed. These are such wonderful kids. I've never known any like them and probably will never meet any others quite like them.

This evening just before bedtime, Kevin and Heather came over and asked if they could pray with us. They laid their hands on her head and also prayed some pretty powerful prayers. When it was over, I told Kevin that I was taking the van into Kampala tomorrow morning. I have to get Jeanette to a real doctor. We have been told about an Irish doctor there and I've got to take her to him. The clinic in Jinja just isn't helping her. I can't take her home. Even if we had tickets and reservations, she's too weak to make the trip. I'm really afraid for her now. I'm not even sure she can make the trip into Kampala.

WEDNESDAY, SEPTEMBER 24

Since we don't have an appointment, we have to wait for about thirty minutes to see the doctor. I think the receptionist can see how bad a shape Jeanette is in, though, because she has finally slipped her in between two people who do have appointments.

After examining her, the doctor tells her she does, in fact, have malaria and E. coli, but she doesn't have amebic dysentery. She has bacterial dysentery. Not only is Flagil not helping her, it is killing her. He gave her another shot and put her on what we hope is the correct medicine this time.

This has scared us both, so we have made a firm decision to leave as soon as we can get our affairs in order.

We stayed through the hard time of the adjustment, the birth of our granddaughter, the problems with our visa and work permit and Jeanette's illness. Now it's time to go, and now that we have made the decision to leave, I'm anxious to do it and get it over with. I guess I felt the same way when I made the decision to leave TWA, but I don't remember this feeling of urgency. I think I was too afraid of not having a steady salary anymore. I should be afraid now of not having a job or any prospect of a job when I get home. Somehow, though, I just haven't thought it out that far.

SATURDAY, SEPTEMBER 27

Another field day! Heather has made up some gold, blue and red ribbons for the winners of the various events, and she and Kevin feel that as school administrator, I should present them during the little ceremony we have planned. I agreed to do it if they would assist me.

Jeanette was not up to going to Global for the events, but she is attending the awards ceremony. She's also not up to greasy goat meat and matoke. The only thing she's been able to keep down for the last week has been oatmeal that Tall Mary has made for her daily. Frankly, I don't know if it's the new medicine she's been taking, Tall Mary's oatmeal or Damali's prayers that have strengthened her, but the day after I brought her home from Kampala, she started to get better. She's still very pale and weak, and she's lost about eight pounds, but I believe she's going to live now.

I've been so preoccupied with Jeanette being sick that I've neglected to say that at the same time, Moses has been just as sick with dysentery. Jeanette had spent a good bit of one night with him out on the back varanda, just staying with him and giving him his medicine. We took him off the Flagil, put him on the same medicine as Jeanette, and now he's also on the mend. Sometimes I wonder how many people here die from the treatment as much as from the disease. Whereas Jeanette lost about eight pounds, Moses lost twice that much and he was a skinny kid to begin with. Bless his heart; he's nothing but a skeleton now. He's so weak he was unable to participate in field day, so I let him help me and Heather with the ceremony.

Kevin and Heather took our decision to leave pretty well. I think they about half expected it after all that's happened. Their only request is that we stay until they have a chance to take a short break and do a camping trip up at Murchison Falls. We agreed, but I'm quite worried for them to do it. There's been some rebel activity in that area lately.

The staff and kids are sad that we're going, though. They've always known that we were temporary, and we're only leaving four weeks earlier than planned, but they are all moping around with long faces. Teacher Florence came by the room yesterday to tell us how sad she is that we are leaving. She says Jeanette is the only mzungu who has ever treated her as an equal. She's been a good friend. We will miss her very much. We will miss them all very much.

MONDAY, SEPTEMBER 29

Jeanette called Rebecca and Betty, the two kitchen supervisors, in this morning and told them that she'd like to give them her little portable tape player, some tapes and some sheet music. She's been helping them with special music for their little church choir for the past few weeks now. Giving them a tape player and tapes is like giving them a piano or an organ for their church. As you know by now, musical instruments in an African church is a goatskin drum and a cooking-oil can filled with pebbles.

I've decided to give Philip my Panama shirt. The one he has is patched where the rats have chewed it. I also intend to give a couple of my better golf shirts to Ocham and Moses. Godfrey likes my old TWA uniform shoes, so I'll leave them with him. I told Florence I'd leave her my solar shower. She was thrilled. I know she won't use it as a shower, but at least it'll give her hot water to take her African baths.

THURSDAY, OCTOBER 9

Today is Uganda's Independence Day, so to celebrate it the government has declared it a school holiday and the school district is sponsoring a football (soccer) day up at the teacher's college at Wanyange this afternoon. Teams from Bugembe, Wairaka, Wanyange and Iganga will be playing. We, the four wazungus, have promised to take the team up to play and everyone else to watch and cheer as soon as they get all of their chores done. It's one of the few times that the entire home will participate in an event. It will mean that many will have to walk, and we will take the van and the lorry with the little kids and the handicapped. It's going to be a chore but it'll be worth it, I think. We've been on the kids all morning to get finished so we can leave right after lunch, but they are more interested in fooling around and dodging work than going, it seems.

THURSDAY NIGHT

Well, just like most parents, we took the kids up for the football match, even though some of them didn't deserve it.

The work that the boys have been doing with the coach is very evident, and I can't help swelling with pride when they beat the Iganga team, and then the Wanyange team, but then I have to encourage them, and tell them that they played their best when they were beaten by Bugembe. I can't help but believe that they would have won if Moses had been up to playing, but I made him sit this one out. It nearly broke his heart, especially when they got beaten, but I thought it was best.

We had a pretty good cheering section too with Damali, big Susan, Betty and Alisa as the cheerleaders. We all had fun, but now everyone is worn out.

FRIDAY, OCTOBER 10

Every Friday one of the staff says which age group gets to stay up late to watch a video. Normally it will be ages twelve thru seventeen or ten through seventeen or something like that, so the ten to twelve year olds pester you all day to see who gets to stay up until eleven and who has to go to bed at nine. I blew the lid off this evening by announcing that the twelve to seventeen year olds had to go to bed at nine and the five to twelve year olds got to stay up until eleven. Of course, the twelve to seventeen year olds were furious with me. Then the whole thing backfired on me when most of the five to twelve year olds fell asleep watching the video, and I had to go upstairs no less than four times to put down a riot with the older group.

Poor little Faithie was acting up so bad during the first part of the movie, I put her on the wall out on the porch, and then got busy and forgot her. When I found her, around midnight, she was crumpled up, sound asleep on the floor, right where I'd left her. I picked her up in my arms and carried her up to bed, and tucked her in. When I laid her down, she sleepily opened her eyes and said, "Unca Rrah, can I come off of the wall now?" I felt so bad it brought tears to my eyes.

SATURDAY, OCTOBER 11

Kevin and Heather left for Murchison Falls this morning, and things have gone down hill ever since. The Volkswagen is down again so they had to take the lorry. I'm glad they're getting to go before we leave, but I'm uncomfortable being left without transportation. Satan seems to be throwing everything he can at me. Not that it's anything I can put my finger on, just little things. The kids have been running amuck. "She's abusing me!" That could mean anything from, "She called me a name," to, "She got in my way while I was trying to jump rope." "He beat me," meaning, "he pushed, bumped," or possibly, "hit me."

Like any parent with unruly kids, I'm up to my eyebrows with it. I've got five kids on the wall right now. I'm going to run out of wall space, and it's not even lunch time yet. Thankfully, no one has really been hurt, and there have not even been any infractions bad enough to break out the posho paddle.

Sometimes, I feel like I've neglected to include Kevin and Heather in many of my stories, but to do more than I have, I'd have to be able to get inside their heads and feel their feelings. I guess what I'm trying to say is, I've taken their presence and their involvement for granted to a certain degree, and when they're not present, we feel it. This is a difficult job at best. I can't even imagine doing it without them, and I don't envy them doing it alone until the Walkers get back in five weeks.

Right after I wrote that, I decided that I needed to leave the compound for a few minutes, even though that meant leaving Jeanette completely alone for a while, so I took the panga and went out in the field to cut some cornstalks for Rubin. I was in sight of everything that was going on so I wasn't really neglecting my duties.

When I took them to him, he backed his ears and turned his heels to me like he was threatening to kick, well that tore the rag off the bush for me, and the old sinful nature that I had as a rough cowboy came back. In a blind rage, I picked up a dead tree-limb about six feet long and as big around as my wrist and let him have it right across the haunches. He bolted, hit the end of his rope and went to his knees, trembling.

I was so angry with him and myself, I went over and sat down under the mango tree and bowed my head. "Oh, God, please forgive me. I don't know what's come over me today. Please take this anger and frustration from me." I looked up to see that Ruben had come close to me and was stretching out his neck toward me. I reached out my hand and scratched him between the ears, then handed him a green cornstalk. "I'm sorry old fellow," I said, "Will you forgive me?"

Did I say that Satan was throwing everything he had at me today? In the afternoon, a tremendous thunderstorm blew in from the lake with high wind, torrents of rain, and hail stones as big as mothballs. The huge tree, that has been leaning dangerously over the drive since the last storm, went down, taking out our telephone line and falling directly across the drive, blocking the gate. I called Moses, Godfrey, Ocham and a few of the other big boys to help me try to cut through it with a panga and a dull ax. Kevin and Heather took the good ax from the outdoor kitchen camping with them. It seemed like a good idea at the time for them to take it.

It took us a couple of hours, working in the pouring rain and growing darkness, but we finally got it chopped in two. I attached the cable to the top half, and pulled it out of the drive with the lorry. You should have heard the boys when I finally had it clear of the gate. "Yeah, ha-ha, we did it." They spent the rest of the evening congratulating themselves, and excitedly talking about their great adventure to anyone who would stand still long enough to listen.

The bottom half of the tree, which is the smaller half, is still attached to the stump. The termites have eaten out the center of the tree up to about three feet above the ground and the storm just buckled it, bent it over like a drinking straw. At least it's not blocking the drive now.

Philip is off visiting relatives somewhere. I'll let him and some of the boys finish cutting it off at the stump and chopping up the rest of the top section tomorrow when it's not raining.

I'm thankful that it was raining cats and dogs when the tree went down. Everyone was inside watching *Dances with Wolves*. If there had been any kids playing in the yard, someone, or several would no doubt have been injured or possibly killed. I had even put Ruben in the backyard today so that he would have some shelter from the big jack-fruit tree back there. God was certainly watching over us.

Since it is already dark by the time I can get into some dry clothes and eat a bite of supper, I have to take my shower by lantern light again. When I come out, the entire compound is dark -- the house, my room, everything. The UEB has chosen tonight to turn off the power. I guess taking a shower by lantern has its advantages. When the power goes off, you don't know it.

SUNDAY, OCTOBER 12

Why is it that things seem to go to pot around here while we're here alone? I got up this morning to the news that there has been a break in the water line, and we have no water, oh, maybe a couple of jerry cans left from yesterday, but certainly not enough to get us past breakfast. I can't even call the water commission to report it. The tree took out our phone line yesterday, remember?

Now, life in Africa being life in Africa I can't even go to the neighbors to make a call. Our neighbor lives in a mud hut with a thatch roof and a dirt floor. The nearest phone is either up at Global or, maybe YWAM. Both are only a fifteen minute walk, but finding someone there this time of day on a Sunday morning may be a problem. Not only that, but reporting it won't get us any water until it's fixed, and this being Sunday, that ain't likely to happen.

After conferring with Rebecca and Betty in the kitchen, I realize that there is nothing to do but haul water in jerry cans from the bore-hole in Wairaka, and the sooner I get started the better.

We have a huge old two-wheeled wagon, so I call Moses and Ocham to see if we can hook Ruben up to it. They look at me with that dubious, questioning look that I've come to expect from Africans when you ask them to do something that they've never done before. They think it's too big and he's too little.

"Hey!" I tell them. "I've seen donkeys smaller than him pulling a wagon easily that big filled with fifty gallon drums." I wish we had some right now.

"But Unca Rrah, Ruben disturbed the harness and now i'tis

finished."

"Ah, why didn't you just say that Ruben broke the harness in the first place?"

From somewhere they come up with an old wooden wheelbarrow that has an iron wheel, but it seems sturdy enough. I figure we can get four jerry cans in it. I'm hesitant, though. I'm not sure I can push a wheelbarrow with four 20-liter jerry cans filled with water, uphill, on a dirt path for a mile or better. Oh well, nothing to do but cowboy-up and give it a try. I guess if I can't make it, I can always unload as many as I have to and then go back for them. It'll just mean more trips. I figure we'll have to make at least a half a dozen trips as it is.

Ocham, being African and used to this kind of thing, comes up with the brilliant idea of strapping two jerry cans to the bicycle. Africans haul water that way all of the time. In fact, it's not uncommon to see them haul a double bed, mattress and all, or a chest of drawers on a bicycle. I've already talked about seeing hundreds of pounds of matoke being carried on a bicycle.

I choose Moses, Ocham, Godfrey, Francis and Noel to come along to help push. Of course, I have to tell another twenty-five that they can't come. Jeanette is up now, but is still weak. I don't like leaving her by herself to hold the fort, but there's nothing that can be done. She reminds me that she has Rita, Florence, Rebecca and Betty to help her. She's worried about me, so I remind her that I have five big strapping boys to help me.

"Humph, five big strapping boys indeed," she says. "Ocham probably only weighs a hundred and fifteen pounds, and Moses is still weak from his illness and is less than a hundred. Don't let him do too much, and don't you." I nod as I head off down the path.

I was right, coming back up that path with a full load is a chore, but we each push for a short distance and then turn it over to someone fresh. We make the first round-trip in just under an hour. We might have made it quicker, but it seems that half of Wairaka has the same idea and there is a long line at the bore-hole. After the second trip, one of the boys suggests that we try the bore-hole over by Kakira. It's a little further and we will have to pump the water by hand, but at least we can use the hard packed road most of the way.

On the way back, we see Dorothy on the road and she tells us that she has called the water commission from Global. That's good news. As I am standing there talking to her, I hear a noise that sounds like a metal shed collapsing. I look up at the bend in the road just in time to see one of the huge sugarcane lorries barreling around the corner going about seventy miles an hour. We look on in horror as he plummets toward us, almost out of control. Three men sitting on top of the mountain of sugarcane are all white eyes in black faces. Obviously, the driver will not be able to stop before he reaches us. He hits the ditch on our left and runs up the embankment, tipping his load dangerously over us. He misses me, standing by Dorothy's door, by inches. He is so close, some of the sugarcane that falls off of the stack strikes my shoulder. Then without ever breaking his speed, he continues on down the road to the Kakira Sugar Works.

Dorothy is livid. "Is it any wonder that road accidents are the number two killer in Uganda!" she almost screams. I just breathe a sigh of relief and a short prayer of thanks that we are not splattered all over that red dirt road.

Lunch is a welcome break, but I'm crestfallen when I discover that the kitchen help has already used most of the water we hauled from Wairaka to boil the beans and rice for lunch. At this rate, we're just staying ahead of the need. We'll have to make at least one more trip to Kakira just to make supper.

On our second trip from Kakira, as we start down the long driveway from the road, several kids run up the drive to greet us with the news. "Unca Rrah, the water has returned. I'tis no longer finished." We made that last trip for nothing, but I'm just happy we didn't have to get up tomorrow and do it all over again.

Somehow, my shower is quite refreshing tonight. Even though it's cold, I'm grateful for running water. Again, it shames me a little that I'm always so concerned about my own comforts. Yes, I have to shower in an outdoor shed with cold water, but how many of my neighbors have to haul water from the bore-hole or even the lake every day of their lives.

MONDAY, OCTOBER 13

Tonight after supper, Snettles, Jeanette's five year old clowning personality, finally got out of the trunk. With the good help of some of the children, Snettles showed in a pantomimed skit how one cannot out give God. The skit was effective, and all the kids were so excited to have a clown sprinkling "happy dust" on everyone and everything. Snettles was sad she had not come around more often.

TUESDAY, OCTOBER 14

Today was bittersweet. The kids and staff put on a going away party for Jeanette and me that was splendid. The staff presented us with matching goma and African shirt. Tall Mary gave us a beautiful grass sleeping mat that she wove herself. The little kids performed the dance that I've been watching them practice for so long, and then the older kids presented a play that they worked up themselves with the help of Rita and teacher Florence. It was a crack up. Moses was dressed as me with a jacket, tie and briefcase, although I've never worn a jacket or tie, and never carried a briefcase since I've been here. Francis, Ocham's brother, was dressed as a woman. They even found a woman's wig for him to wear. He, of course, was Jeanette. Then they went through the pantomime of Moses (me) being school administrator and Francis (Jeanette) handing out medicines to a few of the smaller children from an old red, white, and blue Café Francais coffee tin that the kids were always vying for as soon as Jeanette emptied one. We laughed until our sides ached. Then we cried at the love and dedication that went into what they had done. We are ready – no, anxious - to leave now that we have made the decision to do so, but my heart aches at the thought of leaving them.

WEDNESDAY, OCTOBER 15

Today is the day! Most of the kids have come by for one last hug and goodbye. Even Kajuna has come to say goodbye and shake my hand. Secunde has been standing on the front porch with tears filling his eyes for the last thirty minutes as we load Beverly's car. She and Dorothy have asked if they may take us into Entebbe. We are relieved that Kevin and Heather won't have to leave the place unattended to take us.

Fred Kagje has been conspicuous by his absence. I've glanced around for him while I pack the car, but I don't see him with the other children.

"Godfrey, do you know where Kagje is?" I ask.

Godfrey hangs his head, "Yes, Unca Rrah, he's out under the bougainvillea. He's very angry and doesn't want to see you."

I nod and head out to the bougainvillea. When I approach, he turns his back on me.

"Weren't you going to tell me goodbye?" I ask.

He doesn't answer so I take his shoulder and turn him around. There are tears running down his cheeks. "Why are you leaving us?"

"Fred, you knew we'd have to leave someday." He just shakes his head.

I put my arm around his shoulder and point out toward the path. "Do you see that path?" I ask.

He nods.

"Do you remember how, whenever Auntie Jeanette and I would go to town, you would watch the path so that you could see us when we returned and come out to greet us?"

He nods again.

"Well, you just keep watching the path and one day, you will see me walking back up it, coming home."

He turns, throws his arms around me and begins to sob, "But Unca Rrah, I love you, and I will miss you."

"I love you, too, Fred, and I will miss you, oh, so much." I choke through my own sobs.

When I get into the car and we begin to pull away, most of the kids have lined both sides of the driveway. Some are crying and some are just solemn. I see Secunde still standing on the porch, tears running down his cheeks. Joshua is on the ground at the foot of the steps, his withered hand raised in a wave.

Timothy is standing by the gate at attention, with that impish grin of his, his white, lense-less sunglasses on, and his hand raised in a military salute. Nicolai is running along beside the car yelling, "Goodbye, Unca Rrah, goodbye, Auntie Jeanette."

I return Timothy's salute as we pass through the gate and then slump back into the seat. I'm afraid I'm not very good company until we pass through Jinja.

I've hated this place, and I've loved it. I've been frustrated with the people. I've gotten sick of beans and rice. I'm tired of taking cold showers in a mud shed, and I hate the overcrowded conditions.

They say that when Livingston died, when the Africa that he loved killed him, his followers removed his heart and buried it at his compound, then shipped his body back to Scotland. I guess my heart is still back there, buried in that compound, buried in 115 wonderful children, buried in a cantankerous donkey and an over proud crested-crane.

I hope my promise to Kagje wasn't empty. I hope to return someday, but for now it's time to go home. I want to go home. I need to go home.

12:30AM, THURSDAY, OCTOBER 16

We are sitting here in the lobby of the Entebbe airport waiting for the Egypt Air representative to show up. I'm a little apprehensive. There is no Egypt Air ticket counter, or office, and we seem to be the only ones waiting to check in. Our flight leaves in about an hour. I know they fly into here because we flew in on them five months ago. Unless, of course, they have suspended service since we came in.

We made our reservations and got our tickets through Seagull Travel in Jinja, and you know what I think about officials in Jinja. Dorothy assures me that Purvi, the owner of Seagull, is very reliable, but right now, I have my doubts.

Our trip from Wairaka to Kampala with Beverly and Dorothy was enjoyable. We finished some of the shopping that we were never quite able to do and had a great lunch at the Belgian Butcher Shop on Goba Road. We even treated ourselves to real ice cream.

On the way back, Dorothy pointed out a house on the side of the road and said, "Now, there's a good example of what we call African

Engineering." On one wall, there was a hand painted sign that read, *sign pai*. Around the corner on the adjacent wall, it continued, *nter*. Now, how would you like for him to do your business signs?

Beverly and Dorothy helped us get settled in at the Victoria Inn, a nice little bed and breakfast type place, although they serve supper as well. We had arranged for a day room there so that we'd have a place to rest and freshen up before our flight. We left word with Hakim at the desk that we'd like to have supper around seven, after we'd had a nap. When we woke up, it was dark. I mean it was really dark. Uganda had given us a last parting shot by turning off the electricity. Somehow, Hakim prepared us a delicious chicken supper in spite of the dark, and we had a romantic candlelight dinner.

When it came time to leave for the airport Hakim called a taxi for us and then helped us load our luggage.

Now, I have talked a great deal about the taxis in Africa, how they are these nine passenger vans, however many they try to cram into them. Tonight, however, the taxi that showed up was a tiny little Honda to transport us, four big suitcases, one Rubbermaid Rough-Tote, two carry-ons and a very large wicker basket. When we had all of it crammed into the back seat and some in the small trunk, there was just enough room for me to get in the front passenger seat with Jeanette sitting in my lap. She was right up against the top of the car, even with her bending her neck forward. As we were getting ready to pull out, Hakim shouted, "Wait, I'm going along to help you carry your luggage into the airport." I tried to tell him that there wasn't room and that I could handle it, but he wouldn't have any part of it. He was going. Somehow, he opened the back door without all our luggage spilling out onto the ground, and then wedged himself between the wicker basket and the door, which he couldn't close. "That's okay," he grinned, "I'll just hold it shut." So, off we rattled like the Joads headed for California in *Grapes of Wrath.*

Now, here we sit, in a dark lobby, by ourselves, hoping that soon someone who looks like an Egypt Air ticket agent will show up.

SATURDAY, OCTOBER 18

I'm sitting in JFK airport watching the sun rise. Actually, it's raining and overcast, so I can't really see the sun rise, just watch the sky turn to lighter shades of gray as the sun tries to burn through.

Obviously an Egypt Air employee did show up in Entebbe along with twenty or thirty other passengers. Our check-in was uneventful. We didn't even have to pay excess baggage. The Egypt Air employee said since I was a retired airline employee, he would put us in first class if there was room. He didn't, so I guess there wasn't.

Again we caught a Cairo taxi to take us out to GR's house. You guessed it, he got lost. After about an hour of wandering around the dark streets of Cairo, we finally found the building and had a wonderful dinner with GR and his family. When it was time to check-in for our flight, GR took us to the airport and helped us get checked in first class. Funny how well things go when the station manager is a friend of yours.

The tour we booked during our one-day stay in Cairo was full, but enjoyable. We saw and toured the pyramids and sphinx.

Now, Jeanette suffers from claustrophobia, so when we began our descent down the narrow little path into the depths of the Pyramid of Cheops, she started to hyperventilate. I know it's not funny, certainly not for anyone who has claustrophobia, but try as I might, I couldn't convince her that the pyramids have stood for over four thousand years and they were not going to fall on her today.

She did much better with the canal cruise around the Pharoanic village. This was a unique tour that showed us how life was four thousand years ago in Egypt.

In the evening, we took a dinner cruise on the upper Nile. The dinner was good, and the entertainment was great. The Egyptian music, belly dancers and whirling dervishes were very interesting, and Cairo by night from the river is something to behold.

THURSDAY, NOVEMBER 13

Almost a month has gone by since we left Uganda. We had only been home two days when we were advised by Global Outreach that their annual missionary meeting and banquet was being held in Tupelo, Mississippi that week, and as G.O. missionaries, we were invited. So, it was back on the airplane to Nashville and a rent-a-car down the Natchez Trace Parkway to Tupelo.

Since we had spent almost a half year living in their shoes, it was nice to finally meet the Walkers. We had many things to discuss, laugh and cry together over, including why we felt the need to leave before they returned. We'll never really know, of course, but I hope they can understand.

I don't know what God has planned for our future, whether we will ever do any type of missionary work again. I have been given a job on the island of Kwajalein in the Marshall Islands out in the middle of the Pacific Ocean. It's not as a missionary per say, but I'm sure that if God is sending me out there, He has something for me to do. I do know this, as long as I have tried to stay in His will, He has taken care of all of my needs and most of my wants. I don't see any reason to change that arrangement now.

CHAPTER 8
YOU CAN GO HOME AGAIN

OCTOBER 10, 2000

Three years ago this month, almost to the day, I wrote in this journal how ready I was to leave Uganda. I said how hard it was to say goodbye to the kids and our friends. With tears in our eyes and a lump in my throat we pulled out of the gate at Good Shepherd's Fold; in my mind, probably for the last time.

Now, here I sit making plans to leave here on November the 9th to return to Jinja, and I'm as excited about going back as I was to leave.

A few weeks ago, we received a call from Dorothy Ferris asking Jeanette if there was any way she could come back over for a month to help her with the annual meeting of her students. Jeanette asked me what I thought about it. I responded with an enthusiastic, "You bet."

At the time we left, I knew we had to leave, but I didn't really know why. Oh, I believed that it was because Jeanette had been so sick. I also knew it had a lot to do with being homesick and needing to see family and that new little granddaughter we hadn't seen yet.

Now, with three years behind me, I'm convinced that it was because that's when God wanted me on Kwajalein. Even though it doesn't always fit our schedules, He always does things in His perfect time.

Since this is a story about Africa, and not about Kwajalein, I'll leave those details for another story. I will say this much, though; God sent me to Kwajalein just as surely as He sent us to Africa, but I jokingly tell people that Kwaj was God's reward to me for living at

Good Shepherd's Fold. Now He is rewarding me again by letting us go back to Uganda.

As I look back in my journal to the first few weeks we were there, all I see is frustration, hopelessness, and longing to go home. At one point, I even told Jeanette, "It's too bad this will be an experience we will not remember fondly." How wrong could I have been? I don't think there has been a day in the last three years that we haven't thought about the orphanage, the kids, the work there, and how close it made us to each other, and to God. We believed that we were going in order to give something to God and to the children of GSF; little did we know at the time that He was sending us in order to give a precious gift to us.

I laugh now, and sometimes cry, when I recall the memories, all good ones; even the hard times, the cold showers, the never ending beans and rice, the rats in the ceiling, even carrying the jerry cans full of water from the bore-hole. I guess they wouldn't be memories if they hadn't been hard.

WEDNESDAY, NOVEMBER 1

We are finally on our way after two false starts. The first hesitation we had was when the situation in Israel worsened, and then the USS Cole was blown up in Yemen. Since we have to fly through Egypt and Sudan, both hotbeds of Muslim hatred for Christians now days, we were uncomfortable, to say the least.

Then when there was an outbreak of Ebola right in Uganda, we decided we shouldn't go at this time. I don't know what it was that finally decided us to go, except that we couldn't reach Dorothy to tell her we weren't coming. When we did finally reach her, we had changed our minds again and had decided to cowboy-up and go anyway. I had reasoned with Jeanette that every time there was an outbreak of hanta virus on the Indian reservation near Gallup we didn't try to run away from Albuquerque. After all, the reservation is only ninety miles away. Gulu, where the Ebola is, is a good hundred and twenty miles from Jinja.

We had a few days to think it over while we visited our son Eric in Tampa, and I stayed in touch with the World Health Organization right up until the day we left to make sure it was contained in the Gulu district.

As for the fighting in Israel and the possibility of terrorist retaliation --- oh, well, we're trusting God to keep us safe. We have to trust Him the whole time we're in Africa anyway, every time we get in a taxi, or drink the water. For that matter, we trust Him in everything we do at home, every time we drive to church, and for sure every time I get on my motorcycle. It's just that at home it's not quite as hostile an environment. Hostile or not, though, I love Uganda, and I love working with missionaries.

MONDAY, NOVEMBER 6

Well, once again we're faced with the decision whether to continue or not. As we are sitting in the gate area at JFK awaiting our departure for Africa, Jeanette sees the headlines of a newspaper in the seat beside her. There on the front page, in bold type, it proclaims, "Hundreds die as Ebola breaks out of the Gulu district of Uganda and spreads to Mbarrare, southwest of Kampala." That's still fifty miles from Victoria Inn at Entebbe, but now we know that it's on the move and can be anywhere.

I suppose a sane person would call it quits at this point, and I'm sure Jeanette would if it weren't for me. She won't come right out and say that she doesn't want to go now, but I know that's her inclination. I guess mine is to go on. I've prayed about it, and I don't have a strong feeling that we shouldn't. I don't know what is compelling me to go on, even in the face of danger, but something is. This aside though, I've told Jeanette that I'll abide by her wishes. If she feels strongly that we shouldn't go, we'll see New York tomorrow, and then turn around and go home. She says she'll leave the decision up to me. I guess we'll go on.

WEDNESDAY, NOVEMBER 8

It's about two o'clock in the morning. We're sitting on the airplane at the Khartoum airport. So far, the trip couldn't have gone better. We took a dayroom in Cairo to rest and clean up during our seven hour layover. We didn't really want to spend over a hundred dollars there, but I wasn't about to sit in that filthy Cairo airport for seven hours after an all night trans-Atlantic flight.

The cleaning crew is going through the airplane picking up old newspapers, plastic cups, and other flotsam that passengers always leave on airplanes. The little, turbaned, Sudanese, who leans across me to pick up a soiled pillow and blanket, nods and smiles at me. I haven't seen any sign of Muslim discontent from anyone, in either Cairo or here. It seems that our worrying was for nothing.

I'm quite impressed with Kenya Airlines. Our plane is a new Boeing 737, and the crew is very "smart," in their crisp clean uniforms. In my own opinion, they outshine both Egypt Air or Olympic.

What a thrill!! I'm looking out of the aircraft window at the most beautiful African sunrise I've ever seen. The rift valley is below us with a covering of mist running its length, and Kerinyaga (Mt. Kenya) is sliding into view. The Aberdare Mountains are visible between the valley and old Kerinyaga, and now below, I can see Lake Nakuru.

My voice trembles with emotion as I turn to Jeanette and say, "It feels like coming home."

As we deplane and start for the terminal in Nairobi, a Kenya Air representative meets us at the gate, "Mr. and Mrs. Reaves?"

I'm apprehensive as I say, "Yes?"

"If you will give me your tickets and passports, I'll take them to immigrations and get you cleared and checked in for your Entebbe flight."

I turn and give Jeanette a puzzled look. I've never had a representative from any airline, including my own, meet me at the gate to speed me through immigrations. If I was impressed with Kenya Air before, now I think they're unbeatable.

All good things must eventually come to an end. As we are sitting on the plane waiting to depart, I look out the window and notice that they have parked the airplane next to us too close. I can see that when they parked it, it was empty and hadn't been fueled yet, and the wing tip was probably a good three feet above our wing. Still too close, but understandable; I've parked airplanes very close in the past myself. Now, however, as they are putting on fuel, the wing of the other has come down until it is only inches above and behind our wing. I shake my head and point out to Jeanette that there's no way they are going to move our airplane with that one there. It baffles me how Africans get themselves into situations like this. We sit there for a good thirty minutes past departure while several men in mechanic's overalls stand around underneath looking and scratching their heads. Finally, a pickup truck pulls under the wing of the other plane; the driver stands on the roof, and with his hands, pushes up on the now fuel-filled wing, while a tug driver backs us out under their wing. By some miracle, we clear with inches to spare. When we are clear, I turn to Jeanette, "I don't know why they didn't just take a tug, back him out of the way and then back us out."

"They only had one tug," she says.

African engineering?

It reminds me of the time in the Kampala market when the taxi tried to force his way between two other taxis. I remember we made it that time, too. There's an old saying, "God watches out for fools and little children." I'd have to add, and Africans.

LATER IN THE DAY, VICTORIA INN, ENTEBBE

Boy, if I thought flying over Kenya felt like coming home, stepping off of the airplane at Entebbe airport and returning to Victoria Inn really was coming home. The smells of Africa even bring back memories. In her book, *Poisonwood Bible*, Barbara Kingsolver says that when her character returned to the U.S. after many years in Africa, the thing that struck her was the absence of odor. There was nothing to smell. That is absolutely the truth. The other thing that strikes you is that American English is flat. African English, even though difficult to understand, is very musical.

We walked down to the lake a while ago and passed a primary school with the little children inside reciting their lessons in unison. That really did it for me. I can't tell you how good it is to be back. I'm so glad we didn't back out in New York.

FRIDAY, NOVEMBER 11

Last night was a no-sleeper. I don't know if it was just jetlag catching up with me or the excitement of going up to Jinja today and the possibility of going to Buundo to see the kids.

Anyway, I'm sitting at a picnic table on the lawn at Victoria Inn listening to the birds wake up. I can hear the signature sound of Africa in the morning, the coocoo-coo-coocoo of an African morning dove, a hornbill laughing his head off somewhere out there, an owl, and hundreds of weaver birds. Now the Marabou storks have started clacking their huge beaks down by the lake. For some reason, they like to hang out with the pelicans, which is strange. The Marabous are carrion eaters, and the pelicans only eat fish.

The Marabous are funny the way they perch on the top branches of a tree. I guess their bodies are too big to get into the inside branches, and when you see them congregate, there may be twenty or more standing right on top of the tree.

The grey dawn is just breaking out over the lake, revealing some thunderheads, and in the distance I can hear the faint rumble of thunder. It is the beginning of the rainy season, so it'll probably rain later in the day.

Getting up this early and writing brings back memories of Rwanda, when I used to get up at four in the morning to work on my sermons.

SUNDAY, NOVEMBER 12

Another sleepless night! I think I must have dozed off and on through the night, but I doubt that I got three hours real sleep. I'll be glad when my brain catches up with my body. It seems like whenever we make this trip, Jeanette gets sick, and it takes me at least three days to get over the jetlag.

She spent most of yesterday in bed with cold symptoms and dizzy spells. I, on the other hand, had a great day. I took Dorothy's friend Anita and a visiting Sudanese pastor to show them beautiful downtown Jinja. It was so good to walk the main street again, see old friends in the shops and practice the little bit of Lugandan that I knew.

After we walked both sides of the street, I took them down to the open market. I remember my first visit here, when I could barely hold down my lunch for the smell. This time when the old man who cooks the chipâtés on the scrap of oil drum offered me one, I ate it with gusto while I washed it down with a warm ginger beer.

On several occasions, as we passed the different stalls, someone would call, "Hey mzungu!! Have you returned?"

"For one month only," I would explain. "But don't worry, I'll be back on Tuesday with the lorry to do the marketing for Dorothy Ferris."

"You come to my stall. I'll give you the best prices."

I probably told a half dozen people that I would come to their stall on Tuesday, and I will. If there's one thing I learned from Philip, it's how to bargain at the market.

I will miss him this trip. My marketing day will be bittersweet. You see, we learned about a year ago that he had died of AIDS. We knew, of course, that he was very thin, and Jeanette was treating him for a boil that just wouldn't heal, but we had no idea that he had AIDS. It was a shock.

TUESDAY, NOVEMBER 14

Boy, it just gets better and better. After spending most of the morning haggling with my friends at the market, we came out to Global to deliver the food and sleeping mats for Dorothy's visiting ladies. I think she's expecting about one hundred. There are bunk beds for about fifty. The remainder will have to sleep on mats on the floor. They won't care. Most of them are from outlying villages and are used to sleeping on dirt floors.

When we get the lorry unloaded, Jeanette, Anita and I decide to walk down the road to YWAM. Now we are on the trail that goes down through the forest and little shambas to GSF. YWAM being a couple of hundred feet above GSF, I can look over the trees, and get my first glimpse of the red tile roof that was the orphanage. The memories just come flooding over me like a tidal wave.

The home is vacant now, and the gates are locked. The orphanage moved lock, stock and barrel out to "the land" about two weeks ago. I've never seen it empty of children, and it's a little eerie.

The askari sees us at the gate and comes to see what we want. I explain to him that we used to live here and would like to show our friend where we stayed. He opens the gate for us and then leaves us alone to wander around. As I pass through the gate, I see the stump where the boys and I chopped down the fallen tree. It's not hard for my imagination to picture the yard filled with laughing, happy children playing football and swinging from the rope that still hangs from the high limb, and my emotions threaten to overwhelm me.

When we walk around to our room, it's padlocked, so we can't look in. It's just as well, I guess. The cold water shower shed is still there, but there's no evidence that the high-roofed pole barn was ever an outdoor kitchen.

As we get ready to leave, I look back at it all, the big vacant house, the empty yard, the outdoor kitchen with no activity. It's depressing. It's almost like looking at something that has died and left a lifeless carcass behind. I thank the askari and hand him a thousand shilling note. He seems to realize that we have just visited a dead friend.

I had wanted to walk on down the path to Wairaka, but Dorothy is waiting for us at the road and is anxious to get back. Oh well, maybe another time.

THURSDAY, NOVEMBER 16

Every time I think I've reached an emotional peak, something else happens that's even more sensational. We have come out to "the land," to the Good Shepherd Children's Village at Buundo, to see our kids for the first time in three years.

Today is the day they've chosen for the grand opening and dedication ceremony of the children's village. I'm so glad it just happened to coincide with our trip here. This will be a celebration that will make our field day look like a backyard barbeque. There will be dignitaries from the Jinja government offices, Global Outreach and Samaritan's Purse, plus some other old friends like Victor from Victor's church and others from Wairaka.

As Jeanette and I arrive at the outer gate to the village, we just cannot believe our eyes! We can see at least five beautiful red brick buildings, all laid out neat and orderly. There are two other large open structures and a huge water tower up on the hill above the housing units. (We find out later that they have a very deep well with pure water, and they no longer have to boil it before using it.) It is just incredible what Samaritan's Purse has accomplished here. This is the Walker's vision come true! We can only praise God as we begin the drive up to the village. We see Ruben in a field to the left of the road, and Jeanette wonders if Solomon is here, as well.

The first of our kids to see us is the praise team. They are in the open auditorium practicing the songs they are to perform for the ceremony. Needless to say, we have disrupted that. The director finally throws up his hands and releases them, and they come pouring out yelling, "Unca Rrah, Auntie Ja-net."

We had determined that, because of the Ebola, we would try to avoid as much physical contact as possible. You can kiss that idea goodbye. We have kids all over us, touching, hugging, climbing. I don't even try to hold back. I'm openly sobbing as I try to hug and kiss each of them, and Jeanette is doing the same. Nicolai has her hand in both of his and is holding on like he's afraid she will disappear if he turns loose.

Then, as if that wasn't an emotional mountain, we look down the road about a hundred yards and see teacher Florence coming with the rest of the kids. When she sees why the praise team is jumping up and down and screaming, her mouth drops open and she breaks into a run towards us, and we towards her. When we meet, the hugging and crying starts all over again.

The next person we see is Jjajja Mary. She and Rose are in the kitchen stirring the lunch posho and beans. When she sees Jeanette, she drops her paddle, rushes over and pulls Jeanette to her ample bosom. Then she holds her out and looks at her with big tears making blacker rivulets on her already coal black face. She envelopes her in another embrace and then holds her out to look at her again. She does this three or four times without either of them saying anything, but both of them crying silently.

While this is going on, I hug Rose and say, "Rose it's so good to see you again."

"The same to me," she says shyly.

Alisa has latched onto me like Nicolai did with Jeanette. She is the one-legged girl who used to refer to herself as my "lovely daughter." I'm sure she meant my loving daughter, but she was always my lovely daughter to me. She has grown into a young woman now, no longer the little girl who used to throw her crutch aside to chase the boys, and always won the jump rope competition.

While we are standing in front of one of the dormitories, we see a bus coming up the road. This is the road that we chopped through with the pangas, and where I backed off into the swamp. It is a wide well-graded road now.

When the bus gets to where we are, we see that it is filled with the older children who are staying in Kampala now while they go to secondary school. They see us, and all try to lean out of the windows to greet us with big grins on their faces.

Moses and Ocham are the first to rush to us, and then I see a beautiful young woman coming toward us. Damali always had a quiet grace about her. Now she's tall, slender, and elegant. She seems to radiate an inner beauty that was always just beneath her little girl appearance. Now, I do a Jjajja Mary. I hug her and then hold her out to look at her. She's gorgeous!

As we are hugging and trying to talk to Damali, Moses, Ocham, Francis, Noel and Big Susan, we hear a voice behind us calling, "Unca Rrah, Auntie Ja-net!" I see Jeanette look out to the road and throw her hand up to her mouth, tears filling her eyes. I turn and see Fred Kagje running up the road. Yes!!! Fred, running. No crutches, no braces on his legs. I lose it and start blubbering like a baby - again.

He is overjoyed and is talking so fast that I have to stop crying to understand what he's saying. "Unca Rrah, you told me to keep watching the path, that some day I'd see you coming up it. I watched it and watched it, and now you're here." Needless to say, I can't speak for a good long time. I can't remember a day that I've wept so hard for so long, so many different times. Through it all, he is holding Jeanette's hand with both of his own.

The ceremony is over now, and the hugging and crying has abated somewhat. Finally, I find a minute to get away from the crowd and walk out into one of the fields where Ruben is tied.

"Hello, old pal," I call. His head snaps up from his grazing, and his ears pivot at the sound of my voice. He stretches out his neck and lets out a long, loud bray that I'm sure can be heard a mile away. When I stretch out my hand to him, he snuffles at it. "Sorry, I don't have any green corn for you today." I scratch between his ears for a minute and then rejoin my wife and the kids who are still pressing around her, vying for her attention.

When I see Wayne Walker I ask, "Where is Solomon? I haven't seen him around anywhere."

He chuckles, and says, "Oh, he took off one day, following a Mrs. Solomon and we haven't seen him since."

As we drive down the road to leave, I ask Dallas Abendroth, the GO missionary who has chauffeured us out here today, if he'll stop at the gate and let me take a picture. This is almost the exact spot where I backed off into the swamp.

Taking a picture is only a ruse, of course. I've taken dozens of pictures today. I just want a chance to live in the past for a moment. I look around at the swamp on both sides of the road, give Ruben one last goodbye wave and then pan around with my video camera. I wish I'd had it when we lived here. Can you believe we went through what we went through and didn't have a video camera to record any of it?

I look at what is here now, and remember what was here when we used to come out to work, and I'm again very impressed with what the Walkers have done with the help of Samaritan's Purse. Now that we've walked through the village and seen all the buildings up close, it's more than what we thought we were seeing on the way in this morning. There are now four small dormitory houses, each with its own bathing and toilet facilities, and a small kitchen in each house. They have a large barn/warehouse where they make their own furniture, an outdoor kitchen, the open-sided auditorium and a guest house where we can stay next time we come for a visit. They also have an optimistic farming program and a good portion of the one hundred acres cleared.

It's not the same Good Shepherd's Fold where we came and served, but then I guess there have to be pioneers in every new venture. I'm just glad that God allowed us to be a couple of the pioneers here.

I hope we can come back in another three, four or five years. It will truly be a children's village by then, one with a secondary school and church for the entire district, a self-sustaining one with cash crops, and maybe even a shop that will market the furniture that they make. I'm gratified and humbled that Jeanette and I got to be in on the ground floor of this amazing ministry.

Macoma jeba zibwe!!! (Praise God!!!)

SUNDAY, NOVEMBER 19

After church this morning we went to the Nile Resort Hotel for lunch. It's new since we were here in '97. The meal was good but more expensive than we are used to at the sailing club, and I couldn't get any matoke. Who ever heard of a restaurant in Uganda where you can't get matoke? It is a nice hotel for Jinja. I hope it boosts tourism. This area needs something to get it back on its feet.

We are at Bujigali Falls now, which is right down the river from the hotel about five or six miles. It's hot! We're pretty much into the rainy season, and not only is it hot, but it's so humid the sweat is just pouring off of us.

There is talk of putting a dam below the falls. I will hate to see that happen. They are so beautiful, and if they build a dam, the backwater will cover the falls, and they will be no more.

You know, if my grandchildren ever get a chance to visit Africa, it may be a whole different Africa, an Africa where the wild animals are only in zoos, and all of the beautiful falls on the Nile are covered up by hydroelectric dams. I hope it never gets to that, but I'm glad I saw it now. No, I wish I'd seen it in the fifties, before Amin, when Jinja and Kampala were beautiful cities and Uganda was, in fact, the pearl of Africa. Well, I guess you can't stop progress.

MONDAY, NOVEMBER 20

AWA – Africa wins again! That is a common slogan among the

missionaries.

We haven't had any water since yesterday. We can't bathe, can't wash dishes and can't flush the toilet. I went downtown this morning and bought a case of bottled water to drink, make coffee, etc. and then I put buckets out under the eves of the house to try to catch enough rainwater to bathe with and flush the toilets. I guess if it doesn't come back on by morning, one of us, me, will have to go to the bore hole down by the market and fill up some jerry cans. Where have I heard that story before? At least, this time, we're only talking about enough water to serve four of us, not a hundred and twenty, and I have a vehicle to haul it in, too. What am I complaining about? I've got it easy, almost like a town dweller.

TUESDAY, NOVEMBER 21

It's rained all day today, and it's down right cold. We've been sitting around all morning, reading, writing postcards, and getting on each other's nerves in general. It doesn't take long for cabin fever to set in. Jeanette has finally just gone to bed to try to get warm and beat the boredom. Dorothy suggested that she and Anita go downtown to Seagull Travel to reconfirm their safari reservations. I wish there was some way that Jeanette and I could go on safari with them, but there's not. We were thinking maybe we would at least try to go to the Outspan outside of Nairobi for a night, but that seems a long shot at this point. We'll probably just sit around the Nairobi airport for several hours until time for our connection.

I finally got bored enough to go out in the rain to empty my buckets into the jerry cans. I think we have enough to last us another day.

WEDNESDAY, NOVEMBER 22

Hurray!!!! The water is on. Maybe we can take a shower today. Four days without water is a time that tries men's souls. It came on for about an hour yesterday afternoon, but there wasn't enough pressure to fill the roof tank, so we couldn't shower. We've all been taking African baths, but after four days, we are getting a little ripe.

We ran the filter all day yesterday, but only got one quart to drink.

We boiled about two gallons, so we can survive if it doesn't stay on. I'm down to a couple of jerry cans of unfiltered, un-boiled water, so if it goes back off, I guess I'll have to make another trip to the bore hole. Tomorrow is Thanksgiving.

Dorothy and Anita are planning to drive out to one of the villages to bring some of her ladies in for the graduation. It's a village way out in the bush. We worry about her going out like that by herself, but she's been doing it now for so many years, it doesn't bother her.

Jeanette and I have decided to walk down to Biashara to see what we can scrape up for a surprise Thanksgiving dinner. I know Jeanette is feeling homesick during this holiday time. So am I, a little. It's normally a time of family-get-together for us. When you boil it all down, though, I'm glad we're here.

Friday, we will go back out to Global for Dorothy's graduation ceremony for her ladies. There are a couple of them who came in from the Gulu area, so we have taken the precaution to isolate them from the others. They understand. As they say here, "Everyone is fearing the Ebola." I saw in the newspaper yesterday that the doctor from Mkerere, who selflessly went to Gulu to try to curb it, came down with it and died. I guess if it has a good side, it's that you don't suffer long. You're generally dead within twenty-four hours after contracting it. You suffer mightily, though, for those twenty-four hours, bleeding from every orifice, even sweat glands.

THURSDAY, NOVEMBER 23

Today was a great Thanksgiving! Jeanette and I cooked chicken breasts, baked some white sweet potatoes, made stuffing, and I made my famous squash, cabbage, carrot and cheese casserole. I could write out the recipe, but then I'd have to kill you and scalp you. It's a secret recipe handed down from my Cherokee great-grandmother, you see. The tribe gets very hostile when it's divulged. Actually, it's one I came up with from my own garden for a church social one night, but I'm still not going to give you the recipe.

We've just finished having leftovers for our supper, and we still have enough for one more heaping plateful. I don't want to save it, so

I take it down to see if our night askari wants it. I see that he has a small fire going out by the gate, and is roasting a single ear of corn.

"David, have you eaten yet?"

He indicates his roasting ear with a smile. "I'm going to eat now."

"We cooked too much. Do you think you would want this?" I lift the cover off of the plate. His eyes nearly bug out at the amount of food on the plate.

"Happy Thanksgiving," I say as I turn to go back upstairs.

FRIDAY, 24 NOVEMBER

Back out to Global this morning for the graduation. As we drive up, the ladies are in the meeting hall, waiting. When Dorothy gets out of the car, she is greeted with a hundred voices trilling their high pitched welcome, and every now and then, someone will throw up their hand and yell, "Heh!" This is their way of showing great respect, and they do respect Dorothy; more than respect, they love her. Lillian, one of the ladies who works at Widows Mite, told us out at the Nile Resort the other day, "You know, this is my real mother."

After the graduation ceremony, Dorothy gathers everyone together for a group photo and then the fun starts. We have a regular old Ngoma. How do I explain an Ngoma? Well, it's dancing, chanting, drum beating, tongue trilling, and a good-time-was-had-by-all occasion. It sounds like Rwandan church, but there's no preaching.

In their chant, I hear the phrase, "Webele, Yesu," which means "thank you, Jesus." They are dancing around a small bush and at a certain point in their song; they mimic wrestling with someone, kicking them, and then everyone shouts "webele Yesu," and they all trill, throw up a hand and shout, "heh!" The pantomime is Jesus wrestling with Satan and kicking him out of heaven.

Dorothy just joined in, swaying her body in time to the music and shouting, "heh." Sometimes, I think she's more African than West Virginia mountain woman.

Would I be redundant if I said I love and miss Africa? I'm still not sure that I'm cut out to be a full time missionary, and I know I'm not cut out to run an orphanage full time, but I do love these people.

SATURDAY, NOVEMBER 25

We've come out to Buundo for one last goodbye to the children and the Walkers. There is no sulking or tears this time. The kids are happy to see us and, of course, we are happy to see them. I think now that we have made a trip back, they realize that we can and will return whenever possible.

Bonnie Sue takes us on a tour of the entire place and shows us the bungalows. They are so nice. Each bungalow has two bedrooms that sleep six to eight kids per room, a room for a houseparent, and a large living/eating/classroom area with a sink where they can wash their own dishes.

Right behind each bungalow, there is a bathhouse with showers and a regular toilet, not just a hole in the ground with two rocks on either side. The bathhouses also have large sinks where the children can wash their clothes, and at least one of the bungalows has bathing and toilet facilities for the handicapped kids.

When Bonnie takes us out to show us the guesthouse, which is still under construction, she says, "And when you come back next time, this will be your house."

Jeanette and I look at each other and say, almost in unison, "When we come back, how about if we come as houseparents and stay with the kids?"

"That's even better," Bonnie says with a grin.

As we finish up and get ready to leave, I call big Susan over and give her a big hug. "Are you still my girl?" I ask. She is another one who has turned into a beautiful young woman.

"Yes, I am," she affirms with a loving smile. "Always."

Before we leave, we make a last trip down to the big kitchen where Jjajja Mary is working. She and Jeanette hug goodbye, and here there are more than a couple of tears shed.

As we drive through the gate, Ruben lifts his head, points his ears at the car and brays as if to say, "Goodbye old friend, bring me some green maize stalks next time you come."

DECEMBER, 2002

I'm sitting here in my recliner chair listening to *Phantom of the Opera* on our CD player, sipping a cup of coffee, warming my socked feet at the wood-burning stove, and reading a letter from big Susan. She has written a couple of times now, as have Joshua and Godfrey. Susan is telling me about how well she is doing in school, about the great things the Praise Team is doing around Buundo, and that her friend Betty Babirye had to go back to the village because she failed her grade in secondary school.

Joshua is worried that he will turn eighteen this year and not be allowed to stay at the children's home because he is not eligible to go to secondary school. Schools in Uganda are just not equipped to handle severely handicapped kids.

Godfrey's news is that Ruben died. I already knew that. The Walkers spent a couple of days with us when they came home on leave last time. Wayne thinks someone poisoned him. I can't imagine why, although Jeanette says the thought crossed her mind a couple of times. It's more likely that he was bitten by a cobra or black mamba, being tied down by the swamp the way he was. It's sad, but he was pretty worthless. I've come to accept death in Africa as just part of life there. We've lost so many of our African friends. I console myself with what a glorious reunion it'll be when we all meet in heaven. Imana ishemwe!!!

Someone asked me the other day, "So, Ralph, what do you want to be when you grow up, a cowboy, a missionary, or a writer of books?"

In case you're interested, the answer was, "Yes."

Printed in the United States
43270LVS00003B/73-132